The Dog Days of Murder

M.K. Dean

Redclaw Publishing

Published by REDCLAW PUBLISHING

Cover art by Melody Simmons, Bookcoverscre8tive.com

Edited by N.N. Light Editing Services

To all the dogs I've known and loved in my life. You make every day better in every possible way.

Contents

Chapter One

Lucy was a charming beagle puppy with soft black ears and liquid brown eyes. Unfortunately, she was also incredibly itchy. Even as I examined her, she dug at her collar with a hind foot, spinning it around her neck in a circle. Her skin was inflamed and crusty and bore the distinctive odor of infection.

"We're going to have to trim her nails to minimize the damage she's doing to herself," I told her owners as I continued to look for a primary cause for her scratching. Surprisingly, there were no signs of fleas. The worst of her dermatitis was centered around her face and ears, not typical locations for flea reactions.

The Andrews family were gathered in a cluster around me as I checked out their new puppy on their front porch. Even though the heat and humidity had skyrocketed in our little neck of the woods, I tried to perform my examinations outdoors whenever possible. The lighting was better as a rule. Jody Andrews had brought out a pitcher of sweet tea, which I'd declined on the grounds that I liked my pancreas in working order, though as the sweat dripped down the side of my face, I was tempted to cave in and accept a glass. The twins, Billy and Bobby, had stopped chasing each other around the yard on my arrival and now stood beside their father as I did my examination. Even Granny Andrews was in on the action, sitting in a nearby rocker. A serious Sudoku fan, she scribbled away at a puzzle while I worked.

Lucy's lesions, combined with the ferocity with which she scratched, made me highly suspicious that she had a contagious form of mange known as scabies. Absently, while I explored her coat with gloved hands, I asked, "Is anyone else in the family itching?"

As one, the Andrews family began peeling out of their clothing.

"Stop!" I didn't *quite* shriek, but it was pretty close. I threw up an arm to block my vision. "I don't do people! Just *tell* me."

Thankfully, when I peeked under my arm, my clients had stopped undressing and were arranging their clothing back into place. The weirdest thing is they weren't in the slightest fazed by the notion that their veterinarian might have wanted them to strip, nor by my appalled reaction when I made it clear I did *not*.

Fortunately, no one in the family was itching themselves.

"Okay," I said rapidly, afraid they would change their mind and start undressing again, "I think little Lucy here has mange. There are two kinds of mange. One is contagious and the other is not. I'm going to get some more gloves so someone can hold her while I do a skin scraping and we can try to figure out what's going on."

The twins immediately began fighting over who would get to hold the puppy.

I nipped that notion in the bud. "I'm going to have your dad hold Lucy for me, but I'll need the two of you to assist as well." I pulled out a spoon from one back pocket and a can of squeeze cheese from the other. "Billy, you're going to keep Lucy distracted with the spoon of cheese."

Before Bobby could protest being left out, I demonstrated how to load the spoon and handed him the can. "Bobby, your job is to make sure Lucy doesn't run out of cheese. Think you two can handle this?"

Nodding hard, the two boys focused on the task with great solemnity.

"Okay, now wait until I say to give her the cheese, okay?" I left them to go to my car where it was parked in the shade. The back was open, and my German Shepherd, Remington, peered through the metal grill separating the passenger area from the cargo hold at my approach. Normally, I wouldn't have left him in the car in this heat during my appointment, but one look at the itchy puppy, and I'd put him back in the car with a sun shield covering the car and all the windows rolled down.

"Sorry, Remy." I held up my gloved hands. "No petting until I get rid of these."

He gave a long-suffering sigh, and I smiled as I pulled out a scalpel blade and several glass slides. I placed the dropper bottle of oil in my front pocket and set up my microscope on the open ledge of the Subaru. It was a cheap unit, something I used for field work, but it would get the job done today. If I needed a more precise instrument, I could go into town to old Doc Amos's clinic.

When I returned to the Andrews' porch, I handed a pair of disposable exam gloves to Hugh Andrews and watched as he forced his meaty fingers into the tight-fitting vinyl gloves. After dribbling a drop of oil on my slide and removing the cover on the blade, I explained what I needed to do.

"Mange mites live on the skin and inside the hair follicles. I'm going to do several scrapings to try to figure out if we're dealing with mange, and if so, what kind. I have to be a little mean to Lucy while I get my samples. That's where the cheese comes in. Give her the cheese, Billy. And Bobby, you stand by in case we need a reload."

Lucy happily attacked the spoon when Billy shoved it under her nose, and Bobby hovered nearby ready to squirt more if it was needed. In the meantime, Hugh held the squirming puppy while I pinched her skin and took scrapings from along her ear margins and some of the bald patches on her head. When I thought I'd gotten sufficient material, I carefully swiped the blade on the oil covered slide until I spread the sample in a thin layer. Taking my supplies back to the car, I disposed of the blade in my sharps container and examined the slide under the microscope.

The boys followed me to the car and peppered me with questions as I scanned the slide. Did Lucy have mange? If she did, could we treat it?

"Because Grandad said when his dog had the mange, they poured motor oil on it and he died."

I closed my eyes and counted to five before looking through the lens. "Well, times have changed since then, Bobby. First of all, motor oil is deadly to animals. Back when your grandad was a kid, there weren't a lot of good options for treating mange, so people tried all kinds of things. But now we have much better choices. So, if Lucy has mange, we can definitely treat it."

The collective sigh of relief behind me practically ruffled my hair.

To my delight, I spied the culprit behind Lucy's scratching crawling through oil and hair on the slide. Of the various mites that cause mange, *Sarcotpes* was hard to find, so identifying it under the microscope felt a little like winning a scratch-off ticket. I offered the boys a peek through the lens, and they were in turns amazed and horrified. Billy thought it was the coolest thing ever, and I suspected there was a budding scientist in him somewhere.

Remy whined, begging to be let out of the car, but I wasn't keen on having him possibly pick up skin mites while we were here, so I told him he'd have to wait and took the kids back to their parents to explain the diagnosis and treatment.

"Right," I said briskly. "Lucy has scabies, which can be contagious to people as well as dogs. The good news is some of the new flea and tick medications are effective at treating scabies, too. But the bad news is this is something you can pick up from her, so we're going to have to limit contact with her until she starts getting better."

"Should we dip her?" Hugh spoke for the first time during the whole procedure.

I shook my head. "No, you're lucky there. The new meds don't require smelly dips." The old lime sulfur dips reeked like rotten eggs and stained everything yellow. "She'll need antibiotics for the secondary skin infection and something to help with the itching, but she'll be right as rain in a few weeks. Just make sure everyone washes their hands after handling her, and no sleeping in the bed right now. She needs to stay in a crate."

Collective protests from the twins were cut off by Jody. "It's not forever. You don't want the mange, do you?"

"That reminds me. If any of you do start itching, you're not the natural host, so any infection is self-limiting. But if you need to see Dr. Briggs, be sure to tell him that Lucy has scabies so he'll know what he's dealing with. He can prescribe an ointment if you need it."

Because human doctors rarely dealt with parasitic diseases in the U.S. these days, it wouldn't be unusual for a G.P. to miss scabies in one of their patients. Still, I might mention Lucy's infection the next time I ran into Chris Briggs, on the off-chance Jody forgot to do so.

After I vaccinated Lucy, I peeled off the sweaty vinyl gloves and dropped them in my waste container. I finished filling out Lucy's vaccination booklet, got up her medication, and scheduled her for her boosters in three weeks. Then I told the Andrews what to watch for, and not to hesitate to call if they had any issues before her next exam.

"She's not going to be fully protected against these diseases until she finishes her series of shots, and some of these viruses you can track home. So, don't take her to any ball games or parks until she's further along in her series."

The twins set up a wail. Apparently, they had a softball game that weekend and they wanted to show Lucy off.

"You can't let your friends play with her until she's over the mange anyway," Jody said with practical finality.

"That's right." I handed the boys a couple of brochures. "But there are things you can teach Lucy right now. See this website here? It lists all the things you should teach your puppy as she is growing up. It has videos and training tips and everything."

"I'm guessing no puppy class, either," Jody said with a sigh. "I was going to sign the boys up for a class in Clearwater at the pet store."

"Not until we clear her mange." Which gave me an opening to steer Jody away from a generic one-size-fits-all class from a chain store. "But you could do individual training with Deb Hartford. Then, once the mange is resolved and Lucy has a few more vaccines under her belt, she could join in Deb's basic puppy class. You should give her a call."

My friend Deb trained horses for a living but had decided to start offering obedience classes after rescuing a high-intensity Border Collie who'd needed an outlet for her energy and management of her many phobias. Sky was smart as a whip and would have had several titles after her name by now, if only she wasn't afraid of her own shadow. The Andrews couldn't ask for anyone better suited than Deb to train *them* to train their puppy.

"Deb's teaching dog classes now?" Jody looked relieved. "Oh, good. That's much better than going all the way to Clearwater."

Not to mention, the Andrews would receive personalized assistance in training Lucy for less than they would have spent at the store.

I removed the sun shield and ruffled Remy's ears as I got in the car, waving at the Andrews as we drove away. A quick glance at my phone revealed I'd received a call from Doc Amos, so I pulled over at the end of the drive to play the message.

The voice mail was a short, terse, "Call me when you get the chance."

Typical Doc.

Since I'd inherited a significant sum of money three months earlier, I'd been in negotiations to buy Amos Smith's veterinary practice. It made the most sense: Amos was in his seventies and was looking for an excuse to retire. He'd been unable to find a buyer for his small-town folksy clinic that lacked many of the bells and whistles of larger, more modern vet hospitals. I was tired of being on the road all the time with my house-call practice, and as I often filled in when Amos wanted to take a trip or spend an afternoon on the lake, I was familiar with the strengths and weaknesses of his business.

Running my own vet hospital had been nothing but a pipe dream until my friend, Amanda Kelly, had left me her estate. Owing to the fact she'd been murdered, and the substantial size of the inheritance, it was taking longer than I'd hoped to probate the will, even without anyone to contest it. However, Amanda's lawyer, Mr. Lindsay Carter, assured me that things were progressing in a timely fashion, and that I could expect final probate to be resolved by Halloween. Christmas, at the latest.

The prospect of financial independence had been enough to allow me to make some changes in my life. I'd cut back on my hours, now that I no longer had to work seven days a week to make ends meet. Once Amanda's cranky old Siamese, which I'd also inherited, had been successfully treated with radiation therapy for his thyroid condition, I'd taken my first vacation in years. I'd rented a lake cabin in the mountains and spent the week hiking with Remy. The time off had been so enjoyable, I found myself making longer, more ambitious travel itineraries. But the biggest change was making Doc an offer on his practice. I had big plans for what I'd do with his clinic.

I pulled out onto the road. There was no point in calling him back now. If he wasn't in the office, then he was either at home in his woodworking shop or out fishing. I'd go through town and stop by the clinic first.

Going through town had the advantage of taking us past the Dairy Delight, and I had a craving for a Polar Vortex, which is what they called their soft-serve ice cream combined with candy bar pieces.

"If you play your cards right, Remy, I'll get you a cup of vanilla ice cream."

Remy tilted his head to one side at the magic words, making me laugh.

Calling a Polar Vortex an early dinner wasn't exactly the healthiest choice, but we were in the middle of an unprecedented heat wave for the beginning of June. We were still weeks away from the dog days of summer, but the thermometer was already hitting 90 degrees with nearly 75% humidity. I'd go back to eating fruit and salads when the temperatures returned to normal. Though to be fair, these heat waves came more and more often these days. Summer seemed to start sooner and last longer each year.

And I just really wanted a Polar Vortex.

Remy and I consumed our ice cream sitting under one of the red-and-white striped umbrellas at the tables outside the Dairy Delight. Remy finished his little cup of soft serve in about ten seconds flat, and then looked at me hopefully as I spooned ice cream and candy into my mouth.

"Sorry, old man," I told him, wincing at the brain freeze the cold treat had triggered. "Mine's got chocolate in it."

He laid his head in my lap and blew air out so hard his lips fluttered, making me snort. "You're such a drama queen."

I wasn't the only one who'd decided ice cream was an excellent way to cool down on a hot summer afternoon. The line for the drive-in window snaked around the parking lot, and I frequently lifted my hand to wave at clients and neighbors as they drove past toward the exit.

Greenbrier was a small, rural community on the Virginia-Carolina border. It qualified as a town solely because it had been in existence since the mid-eighteenth century, when Scotch-Irish and German immigrants had settled in the area. John Linkous had built a sawmill, and the community had sprung up around it, with the Linkous family running things ever since. With less than a thousand inhabitants, most days it felt like I knew them all. I'd left the area to go to vet school, and then returned to help take care of my dad when he developed cancer. Up until recently, I'd resented having to come back, but a lot had changed these past few months. When my house burned down a few months ago, my neighbors rallied to my support, and I realized just how wonderful a small town could be.

Sitting in the shade outside the Dairy Delight with my dog, eating ice cream and smiling at my neighbors, my life seemed peaceful, uncomplicated, and fulfilled.

That should have been a red flag.

Chapter Two

AFTER WE LEFT THE Dairy Delight, I parked in the library lot and dropped off some books in the return bin. In my mind, this justified my leaving the car in the lot while Remy and I walked the few blocks to Doc's clinic.

Greenbrier Veterinary Clinic was located in a small, elderly strip mall. The building itself had lived through several incarnations, the latest being a video store before Doc relocated there. One of the challenges facing me when I took over was whether to operate out of the same building or start over from scratch. The mall had the advantage of being a town fixture for decades, as well as being in an ideal location, but there was something to be said for designing and building a clinic exactly the way you wanted from the ground up. Thanks to Amanda's estate, I would soon have the resources to do just that.

Out of deference for the possible patients in the waiting area when we entered, I had Remy on leash. His training was coming along nicely, especially since recent events had convinced me to take it more seriously, but he was still likely to upset any cats we might encounter, intentionally or not.

The first thing I noticed on opening the door to the clinic was that a pleasant doorbell had been added since the last time I was there. It was a nice touch, alerting Wendy Grisham, Doc's indispensable receptionist/technician, that someone had entered the building. The second "improvement" hit me a second later, as the pungent odor of cinnamon practically made my eyes water.

I stood in the empty waiting area, pressing a finger under my lip to prevent me from sneezing. Remy had no such recourse, and then gave a resounding sneeze himself. Looking around, I spied a white dispensing unit attached to the wall over the door leading out of the waiting area.

As I stared, the unit dispensed a visible puff into the air, and the scent of Christmas strengthened.

I frowned. It wasn't like Doc to rely on perfume to cover up odors. He was a big believer in bleach, which was just as irritating, but at least had the benefit of being a disinfectant.

It wasn't surprising that the waiting area was empty. Doc's schedule was sporadic these days. Truthfully, I'd been using his clinic as a back-up to my house-call practice for some time now. He allowed me to drop off lab samples to go out with his own and use his x-ray machine when needed. In return, I filled in for him when he wanted to take a few days off. When I took over, I'd revamp the surgery suite and hire someone who enjoyed such procedures to take over that part of the practice, as it had been years since I'd done any surgery myself, and I found it stressful. Buying Doc out only made sense for both of us, now that I had the resources coming to me.

Wendy came through the door to the treatment area and stopped dead in her tracks, as though I'd entered the building with a giant, hairy tarantula instead of Remy. Her chin-length gray bob was scraped back off her face with a tight hair band, which I assumed was the cause of her pinched look of dismay until she spoke.

"Dr. Reese." She shot a glance over her shoulder at the treatment room door and began walking toward me with one arm outstretched, as though she were planning to escort me out of the building. She was wearing purple scrub pants and a tiger-print top that was very out of character from her usual jeans and T-shirt.

Remy, happy to see an old friend, bounced off his front feet a few times and danced in place at her approach. He knew better than to jump on anyone, but unless I nailed his paws to the ground, I couldn't seem to control his enthusiasm.

"Hey, Wendy. Doc around? I got a message from him, but I was already in town, so I thought I'd stop by."

"Oh, Ginny." Wendy's face fell now, and my apprehension rose, my Spidey senses tingling.

"What is it? Doc's okay, isn't he?"

Remy, sensing something was wrong, abruptly sat by my side, his ears drooping to half-mast.

"Yes, Doc's fine, but—" She looked over her shoulder once more and moved closer. "You really should talk with him. He's probably down at the lake. Why don't you—"

The door to the treatment area opened, and a tall, thin brunette walked out. Waves of mahogany hair sat piled on her head. Her makeup was subtly applied, but to good effect, highlighting full lips and dramatic, amber eyes. She wore tiger stripes as well, this time in the form of a short skort, which emphasized her long, lean legs that, unlike mine, had nary a dimple. Instead of nursing clogs or running shoes, like most medical professionals I knew, she wore shiny black pumps. Her fitted scrub top was black, and almost as tight as a sheath dress for a fancy event. She topped off her ensemble with a white lab coat that came down to the end of her skort and bore a name tag that read *Dr. Burnham*.

"I'm sorry, we're not quite open for business yet. If you'll leave your name with Wendy, I'm sure she can schedule an appointment with you next week." Even her voice was sultry and smooth. She flicked a glance at Remy that was without warmth. It felt as though her primary concern at seeing him was that he was properly leashed.

He'd been wagging his tail on her entrance into the room but stopped when she looked at him.

The tiger stripes seemed to be a theme. Like an office uniform. Rachel Burnham's proprietary air, combined with the look of sick apology on Wendy's face, triggered a warning bell of alarm.

"Excuse me?" I said, feeling foolish at being left out of whatever turn of events had taken place. "Wendy, what's going on?"

My seeking answers from Wendy instead of her seemed to annoy Dr. Burnham, for she stepped in front of Wendy, as if to block any further communication with her.

"What's going on," Dr. Burnham said briskly, "is that Greenbrier Vet Clinic is under new management. As I said, we're not open for business yet, but if you'd like to call next week, I'm sure we can accommodate you."

I raised both eyebrows at Wendy, even as my mouth fell open. Remy whined and pressed into my side.

"I'm sorry, Ginny." Wendy's expression melted in misery, only to be wiped clean when Dr. Burnham shot a glance at her. "You really should go talk to Doc."

Dr. Burnham transferred her glare to me. "Ginny? As in Ginny Reese?"

As much as I wanted to rail at this Veterinarian Barbie, I swallowed my shock and anger. At least until I got this sorted out. If nothing else, Dr. Burnham was a colleague, and potentially someone I had to work with. I forced a smile through stiff lips. "That's me, Dr. Ginny Reese. I sometimes fill in for Doc here."

"Ah, yes." Her simple statement spoke volumes as she cast a glance up and down at my appearance.

I became suddenly conscious of how my damp T-shirt, the one proclaiming me as a German Shepherd mom, stuck to my skin, and of the grass stains on my jeans. It felt as though I'd been assessed as veterinarian material and come up wanting.

Be nice. Don't burn any bridges ... yet.

But while I was reminding myself to play nice with the new vet in town—the one who'd stolen my practice out from under me—Rachel Burnham apparently had come to a decision.

Her gaze became somewhat steely as she asked, "Aren't you the person who was videoed assaulting a man in a bar recently?"

Inwardly, I groaned. I was never going to live that down, was I? Outwardly, I pasted on another smile and said through gritted teeth, "Technically, he assaulted me first."

And he had. Derek Ellis had accosted me in the bar that night and threatened both me and my dog. I may have lost my temper a bit as a result. Apparently, the sight of a woman hauling a man around by his privates was viral-worthy. Especially since some wit had set the scene to a catchy pop tune before uploading it.

"I see." Dr. Burnham's tone carried the weight of disapproval, and as someone intimately familiar with such disapproval, I knew what was coming before she finished saying it. "I'm afraid Greenbrier Vet Clinic will no longer be needing your services."

Still smiling, I said, "I understand."

Which was a patent lie because I didn't understand any of it. How could she possibly be the new owner of GVC when I had been in negotiations with Doc? What the heck had happened?

We stood facing each other in an uncomfortable stand-off, with Wendy as a mortified witness, when the door to the back swung open. A swarthy man in an expensive suit came into the waiting area, already speaking as he entered.

"Rachel, what's taking so—"

He broke off to give me a stunning smile, showing off teeth so white they couldn't possibly be natural.

"Hello! I'm Dennis Montanaro. Welcome to Greenbrier Vet Clinic. My, what a handsome dog you have."

He beamed at Remy even while I pictured him as the wolf dressed in Grandmother's clothes as he interacted with Little Red Riding hood, if a young Antonio Banderas was playing the part of the Wolf.

"Dennis, this is Ginny Reese."

Dr. Burnham's introduction had a dampening effect on Dennis's smile. It snuffed out like a candle that had been capped.

"I see." His voice went cool, even as he gave me his own assessing once-over.

Part of me wanted to stamp my foot and insist they call me by my title.

"I was just explaining to her that we would no longer be needing her services as a relief vet here."

Was it my imagination or did they lean in toward each other, closing ranks against me?

"Well, if you change your mind, I'm easy to find. I can imagine that you might want some time off now and again." I was determined to be an adult here, even though I wanted to rage and cry. How dare these *strangers* come into my town and take over the practice I was planning to buy?

A flicker of uncertainty crossed Burnham's face, but she quickly quashed it. "I appreciate the offer, but I assure you, that will not be necessary."

"I'll be off then." I couldn't help glancing at Wendy, who seemed about to burst into tears. Instead of meeting my gaze, she focused on her clenched hands. I met Burnham's stare with some steel of my own. "Nice meeting you. Let's go, Remy."

We'd almost made it to the door when Montanaro called out. "Dr. Reese."

Finally. Someone was addressing me with the respect I deserved.

I turned around with a pleasant smile. "Yes?"

Montanaro's smile wasn't so pleasant. It had a kind of oily self-satisfaction that raised the hair on the back of my neck.

"My understanding is that you had an agreement with the previous owner to allow you to send out lab samples or perform such procedures as x-rays on your patients, is that true?"

I didn't like where this was going.

"Yes. I had a mutually beneficial arrangement with Doc Amos. This clinic served as a back-up support to my practice, and I filled in when he needed some time off." Though truthfully, I worked at the clinic at least two days a week on a regular basis, despite not being named as an employee on the payroll.

Montanaro nodded as if he'd known my answer in advance.

"That arrangement ends as of today."

"Wait, what?" I sputtered. "I don't know if you realize this, but regulations for house-call veterinarians require I have a working relationship with a clinic to handle such cases that can't be seen on an outpatient basis."

"I'm perfectly aware of the regulations." Montanaro practically smirked. "And as such, if we hear that you are practicing without such an arrangement, we'll be contacting the Board of Veterinary Medicine."

"You'll put me out of business!" The words burst from me. I was incapable of playing nice any longer.

"That's not our problem," Montanaro picked an imaginary piece of lint from the sleeve of his tailored suit and flicked it aside.

There had been times when I had wished Remy wasn't such a good-natured dog. This was one of them. The temptation to order Remy to "sic 'em" was strong, but the reality was that unless Montanaro was a squeaky toy, he was pretty safe from my dog.

My face on fire as though I'd spent the afternoon on the lake without sunscreen, I turned on my heel and marched for the exit, Remy at my side.

Montanaro couldn't resist a parting shot.

"Remember, if we hear of a single incident of you practicing without a formal arrangement with another clinic, we'll have your license."

His reminder was delivered with the cheer of someone wishing me a good day.

It took all my willpower not to flip him the bird.

Once out on the street, I took a deep breath. Remy thrust his head under my hand, and I stroked his silky ears. I had to find Doc and figure out what the heck had just happened.

Chapter Three

ANGRY AND UPSET, I drove out of town at a speed well above the limit and had to force myself to slow down before I got pulled over. The lake road was unmarked, barely wide enough for two cars to pass in the opposite direction, and hugged mountain curves. Speeding wasn't smart, no matter how disturbed I was.

Originally owned by Edward Bishop back in the 1930s, the lake and surrounding land had been deeded to the Jefferson National Forest by his heirs sometime while I was away at school. A thirty-minute drive out of Greenbrier, the locals still referred to it as Bishop's Lake, and it was a popular destination for hiking, biking, trail riding on horseback, and fishing. The timeworn paths cut by us as teenagers playing hooky from school were now well-groomed trails, and the state had stocked the pond with trout and put in a small landing dock for non-motorized boats. The odds were high I would find Doc out there. Though there were miles of trails surrounding the pond, there was only one that looped the water itself. If Doc was out there, we'd run across him at one of the fishing stations.

Despite the heat, a large number of cars were in the parking lot when I pulled in. No horse trailers, but many SUVs with bike racks. By the time Remy and I reached the main path to the pond, I regretted not wearing shorts. We'd make the circuit of the pond, I promised myself, and if Doc wasn't there, we'd head home. My t-shirt already clung damply to my back, and my jeans threatened to chafe. Remy, at least, could cool off by wading into the water. A luxury not afforded to me.

It was a lovely afternoon if you didn't mind the sweltering temperatures. On the far side of the pond, a couple walked their dog. Various fishermen were parked at other docks, and a photographer was taking pictures of the beaver lodge with a telephoto lens. I thought I saw a sleek brown head break the surface of the lake in that general region, even as a great blue heron flew slowly just above the water's surface to the far side where rushes poked up out of the mud. A redwing blackbird trilled somewhere nearby, and I was struck at how much this lake had been a part of my life all these years. When the land had been sold to the state, I'd feared it would ruin the place I'd loved so much as a teenager, but the truth is, incorporating the property into the National Forest had been the saving of it. Had the lake not been bought by the state, developers would have snapped it up long ago. Developers like the ones that had bought my old property and had been sniffing around the estate I'd inherited from Amanda.

Fortunately, as we'd parked at the end of the pond where most of the fishermen gathered, we came across Doc almost at once. He was sitting by himself on one of the small docks that jutted out over the water, a sun hat shielding his bald head and a cooler at his feet.

He didn't acknowledge our presence as Remy and I joined him on the dock, casting his line as though unaware we were there. I couldn't tell if he was ignoring us or if he simply hadn't heard us approach. He sat on a small folding stool with only the fishing hat for shade. How could he bear being in the broiling heat like that? Remy and I wouldn't be able to stay on the dock long. I kept forgetting that my recent pixie haircut meant I needed to put sunscreen on the back of my neck.

Remy was impossible to ignore, and when he shoved his nose under Doc's arm, he greeted the dog like the old friend he was. Remy's entire body curled with delight as he wriggled and wagged under Doc's attention.

"Mind the fishhooks," he warned, even as he stroked Remy's head. It seemed to me he was deliberately avoiding making eye contact.

He wasn't the only one. I found myself concentrating on his hands instead of his face, noting the nicks and cuts of a life lived hard, and fingers that bore the brunt of the nature of both his work and hobbies. After he'd nearly cut the tip of one finger off with a circular saw, his wife had insisted fishing was the safer of his pastimes and had booted him out of the workshop. The dirt under his nails testified to a day of baiting fishhooks and handling his catches.

I closed the open cooler, where a nice, fat trout lay on ice, knowing it would prove too tempting for Remy to leave alone. Doc had a little tub of nightcrawlers by his feet, and I trusted him to keep Remy's nose out of the container. His tackle box lay open beside the foot of the stool, and I flipped the lid shut. Then, not having a seat of my own, I leaned my elbows on the rickety rail of the dock and waited.

Doc must have found my silence unnerving because he abruptly stood up.

Perhaps abruptly was an exaggeration. More like he stood up in jerky stages, levering himself up from his low stool a bit at a time, much like a marionette being controlled by an amateur puppeteer. Without a word, he packed up his stuff. I picked up his cooler and followed with Remy as Doc led the way to the shade.

"Too hot out there," Doc said, pausing under a large oak tree to mop his brow with a faded, red bandana. "Not good for the dog."

"I appreciate you thinking of him. Didn't mean to break up your fishing."

"I was done for the day. Caught my supper." His grin faded as he finally looked me in the face. "I guess you heard about the sale."

I nodded, trying to keep the hurt out of my voice when I spoke. "I just came from the clinic."

"I tried to call you." He sighed and began trudging up the trail toward the parking lot.

I moderated my usual brisk stride to match his pace. Remy fell in at my side. "I tried calling you back. Got your voice mail."

He nodded without speaking, and as I watched him puff his way along in the heat, I realized talking would have to wait until we got to his truck.

I'm not used to walking slowly or holding my tongue, so by the time we reached the lot, I was brimming over with the need to speak. But I waited, hoping that my impatience didn't show, until we'd stored Doc's belongings in his little red pickup truck. Remy laid down in the shade provided by the vehicle and panted. Doc opened another, smaller cooler and pulled out a couple of bottles of cold ginger ale, offering me one.

I took it with thanks, and swallowed a fizzy mouthful while Doc did the same and gathered his thoughts. Finally, he spoke.

"Rachel Burnham made me an offer on the practice a few weeks ago. I turned her down. Told her I had a sale in the works. Thought that would be the end of it." He took another sip of soda. "Then she came back. Offered me more money. A lot more."

"But you *did* have a sale in the works. You were negotiating with me. You should have told me you were considering another offer."

"Aw, honey." Doc's face, red with the heat, seemed to melt. "You'd just gone on your first vacation in years. What was I supposed to do—interrupt your time off? We all know how hard you've worked since you've come back to town. And then there were the murders, and the fire on top of it. You deserved your break."

"What I deserved was a chance to make a counteroffer." I couldn't help it. My voice broke then. "Did I do something to upset you? So you didn't want me to buy your practice?"

He looked shocked. "No. Nothing like that. My dear, I should have retired years ago. Long before you moved back home. But there was no one else in Greenbrier to take care of the animals. Then you came, and bless you, it was easier because you picked up the slack and allowed me to have some time off myself. I kept meaning to retire, but I didn't have to, so..."

He shrugged. "But then you made me an offer, and I have to say, I realized how much I wanted to retire. To let go of the responsibility. To travel whenever I wanted to see the grandkids. Oh sure, by filling in whenever I wanted time off, you made it possible for me to have the best of both worlds, but it's not the same. You know what I mean. How you lie awake at three a.m. worrying about a case that's gone wrong. Or the headaches of running a business when the costs of doing so keep going up but none of your clients have any money."

I *did* know what he meant, but I didn't want to break his train of thought.

"Anyway, along comes Dr. Burnham with a ridiculous offer. More money than I'd ever thought I'd get for the business. Hazel kept pointing out we had to think of the kids, and what kind of legacy we could leave them, and she wouldn't let up on the fact neither one of us were getting any younger."

Poor Hazel. She'd been the vet's wife for nearly fifty years, with very little to show for it other than the utter devotion of the townspeople. But devotion didn't see you out comfortably in your golden years. Still, I couldn't let Doc's statement slide. "But you knew I wanted to buy the practice. That I had the money. It was just a matter of time."

He shook his head in a slow, measured manner that somehow conveyed both regret and remorse.

"That's just it, Ginny. She had an offer in hand, ready to go. She wanted an answer right away. While I knew you were good for it, last thing you told me was that it would still be another four to six months before your inheritance went through. I'll be seventy-six next week. Six months—even four—is a long time when you're my age."

Shock stuffed a gag in my throat.

You couldn't wait four more months?

I wanted to rail at him, to point out that I *had* worked for him for the last five years like a modern-day Jacob laboring for Rachel's hand in marriage. Didn't Doc owe me some kind of loyalty for that? Didn't that count for anything? Didn't the fact I was born and raised in Greenbrier, and that his clients were also my clients count for anything?

But then I heard my mother's voice in my head asking me what did I expect?

You're not good enough anyway.

Doc's face was spattered with age spots, and uneven patches of tanned skin spoke of too much time outdoors without sunscreen. Beneath his hat, his cheeks were pink with heat. He'd aged in the years since I'd returned to Greenbrier, no longer the hale and hearty man who'd been my inspiration for becoming a veterinarian. As arguments went, the one about time running out was hard to beat.

Not to mention, the sale was already a done deal and there was nothing I could do about it. I'd learned a lot about disappointment over the years. I swallowed my pride, along with my anger and defeat, and said, "I understand."

Relief lightened his features.

"Give it some time. I think you'll see this can work out to both your advantages. She's going to need someone to cover for her on her days off, and you'll still be able to refer your cases into the clinic. And now that you've got someone younger with better eyesight, you won't have to send your patients to Clearwater for surgeries. Who knows? You might be able to buy into the business someday."

No doubt this was the scenario he—or Hazel—had written to persuade him that selling to Burnham was the right thing to do.

"Uh, not going to happen. Dr. Burnham's partner—or maybe business manager—Dennis Montanaro made it pretty clear my arrangement with the clinic was over."

"What?" A thunderous expression crossed Doc's brow. "But that's not what we agreed on. I'll have a word with her—"

I held up my hand. "Hold that thought. I don't want to force anyone to work with me who doesn't want to."

"But your business!"

He knew as well as I did that I couldn't run a house-call practice without some sort of agreement with a full-service facility to take the kinds of cases that needed hospitalization when they arose.

"I'll ask Jamie Shively. Lord knows I send enough business toward Clearwater Animal Hospital as it is." I'd had to, as Doc had stopped doing anything that required anesthesia years ago. "I plan to drive out there tomorrow with a food basket to butter him up, but I feel confident he'll agree to serve as my back-up facility."

Doc was still frowning. "And if he says no?"

"Then I'll talk to the managers at the emergency clinic in Birchwood Springs. It will be fine. You'll see."

I didn't miss the irony of reassuring Doc when I wasn't certain of the outcome myself. I planned to bring Jamie one heckuva offering. This might call for an early morning run to Brenda's Bakery, for a dozen of the world's best doughnuts. If he turned me down, the odds of the Birchwood ER agreeing to the arrangement were slim at best. In the meantime, I'd have to call clients and cancel appointments until I got things sorted.

I was still a little shell-shocked at the turn of events. The last thing I wanted, however, was Doc intervening on my behalf. Even if he persuaded Dr. Burnham to change her mind—and there was no reason why she would—I refused to work anywhere on sufferance. No one had to tell me twice when I wasn't wanted.

I took my leave of Doc, but instead of going back to the lake, I returned to my car. I offered Remy cool water from my thermos, which he lapped eagerly from a nifty collapsible bowl I'd bought from some hiking catalog. Remy wasn't the only one looking for a way to cool down. With nothing else on my immediate plate this afternoon, I couldn't think of a better way to spend a few hours than swimming with the dog in my own pool.

Okay, technically, not my pool yet. Or maybe it was? Amanda's legacy to me included a huge estate home, complete with a swimming pool, as well as a ridiculous amount of money. But as the will hadn't undergone probate yet, I couldn't access the funds or move into the house. Only there was no one left to object to the terms of Amanda Kelly's will. Her lawyer, Mr. Carter, assured me that in due time, I would be able to do whatever I wanted with my inheritance.

I'd also been given to understand that no one would be particularly upset if I wanted to move in right away, given that I was currently homeless.

"Homeless" might be a stretch. My house had been burned down, and I had been lucky to get out with the clothes on my back and the animals. Everything else was a total loss. But I did have a place to stay, with my mother.

If you've ever met my mother, you'd know why I wanted to be in a place of my own as soon as possible.

Yet I found myself dragging my heels on making Amanda's house my home.

It certainly wasn't because of the house itself.

As I drove up the winding drive onto the property, I was struck anew by my fortune once more. The house was situated on a ridge with a stunning view of the valley and mountains beyond. Today, the Appalachians would be nothing more than a hazy blue smudge, but I'd take it. Besides the extensive, manicured grounds with the swimming pool, there was also a good deal of acreage, including fields for horses and growing hay, as well as a small barn and a riding arena.

It was the arena that caught my attention as I pulled in, and I stopped the car to watch. A rider on a sturdy blue roan turned circles on the fine graveled surface, kicking up little wheels of dust. After only a moment's hesitation, I turned the car toward the barn instead of continuing up to the house.

No sooner did I pull to a stop by the barn, then the rider dismounted and led the horse over to the gate. I watched as he removed his cowboy hat and wiped his brow, only to replace the hat and bring the sweating horse through the gate to the barn.

When I let Remy out of the car, a little blue heeler pup began barking with excitement where she was tied in the shade under the overhang. Remy ran over to greet her, wagging his entire body from side to side. I called him back, at least until she was no longer tied. The risk of one of them getting tangled was too great.

I nodded to the rider, who had stripped the saddle and bridle from the horse and was in the process of putting a halter on the roan. The thin, blue-checked cotton shirt the rider wore clung to his torso, and with the jeans beneath the leather chaps, he had to be roasting. I can tell you, when you grow up around cowboys, you don't tend to romanticize them the way some people do. When it comes to the kind of men I find attractive, I'll take a soccer player over a rodeo champion any day. But the sight of Joe Donegan in cowboy boots and leather chaps could change my mind. Yes, indeedy.

"Looking good."

No sooner had I spoken, I could have slapped myself. My statement was open to interpretation as to whether I was referring to man or horse.

Joe Donegan, the rider—as well as the local sheriff and my ex—nodded in return as he patted the horse's damp neck. "I'm glad I bought him. Too good a deal to turn down. Though once you moved the horses off my property, I had no choice but to move him too. Can't leave a horse by himself out there."

"Doesn't hurt there's a riding ring here as well. Not to mention plenty of trails in the mountains."

Joe had done me a big favor agreeing to board Amanda's old rescues and my own horse during the murder investigation. It was only fair to let him bring his new horse here until he found a companion or two for him. Horses are social creatures. You can't have just one horse.

I didn't mind the company, either.

Joe, however, only had eyes for his horse at the moment. "Dustin here has got a nice turn of speed. Makes me think I might take up barrel racing again."

"In your copious free time."

He laughed at that. "Probably why you haven't taken your own horse to any shows lately. Or do you call them events instead?"

"Depends on if I'm doing straight dressage or combined training. Dressage only is a show. With CT, it varies. Sometimes it's an event. Sometimes they're horse trials. Truthfully, most of the facilities around here aren't set up to hold dressage, cross-country, and stadium jumping all at the same place. Not enough land."

"I'm guessing there's a time issue with you as well," he said, as he led the gelding into the barn.

I followed. Inside, Joe walked the horse into the wash rack, attached cross-ties to the halter, and began to hose Dustin down.

"That, and the fact I'm not fond of wearing a wool jacket in 90-degree weather. Sometimes I think I should have taken up ice skating instead of eventing." I handed Joe the rubber-backed sweat scraper before he asked for it, admiring the brisk manner in which he flicked both sweat and water from Dustin's slick sides.

Joe chuckled at my comment. "You'd have to drive a long way for rink time to skate around here."

Dustin pinned his ears and tossed his head when Joe turned the water down to a trickle and tried to hose the horse's face. He set aside the scraper to take hold of one of the cross-ties to steady Dustin's head. "Oh, come on, you big baby. You'll be itchy if I leave sweat marks on your head."

The horse gave in with poor grace, standing in place, but trying to evade the water until Joe was done.

"You planning to ride?" Joe asked as he recoiled the hose.

I shook my head. "Nope. Too hot for me. I'm heading up to the house with the dog for a swim."

"Oh?"

Darn it, he didn't have to look so hopeful.

I spied both the trap and the way out at the same time. Smiling, I made the offer knowing full well he'd have to turn me down. "I'd invite you to join us, but I don't imagine you've got a swimsuit with you."

"I need a suit?" He waggled his eyebrows in a hokey, suggestive manner, making me laugh.

"I don't intend to scandalize my neighbors before I even move in." Not that anyone was close enough to see the swimming pool. It was one of the advantages of Amanda's enormous estate.

"Well, it so happens I do have a suit with me." Joe's lazy drawl sent a little frisson of response up my spine. "It's about time I taught Toad to swim. So, if the offer is still open..."

The trap I thought I'd avoided sprang shut around me without warning. "Uh. Sure. I'm just going to go up and—" I made vague motions in the direction of the house.

"You do that. Take Toad with you. I still have to cool Dustin out and put the tack away, but then I'll join you."

His sly smile suggested he knew exactly how much the notion of swimming with him rattled my composure and he was looking forward to more of the same.

Perhaps he'd think my face was red from too much sun. "Sure. No problem."

I wouldn't give him the satisfaction of being right.

Chapter Four

I LEFT THE CAR by the barn and walked up the hill with the dogs. Toad happily frisked alongside Remy, and the two play-growled and chased each other as we hiked up the slope. Remy ran out of steam before the five-month-old heeler did, and his tongue hung out of his mouth like a huge roll of salami by the time we reached the pool. Without hesitation, he galloped toward the edge of the pool and threw himself in with a huge splash. Toad's mouth fell open in the most incredulous expression of shock at his actions, and then she raced around the lip barking furiously at him. Remy made a lap around the pool, avoiding the far end where the water spilled off the edge into a waterfall, and came out the stairs, only to shake a heavy sheet of water as Toad ran up to him.

"Don't worry, little one," I reassured the puppy. "Last year he was just as afraid of the water as you are."

I'd spent quite a few evenings in Amanda's pool last summer, teaching Remy to swim, and then tossing balls for him while Amanda and I sipped wine coolers. After I'd found her drowned in the pool this past spring, it had been hard for me to find the same enjoyment at being there, but Remy's delight in swimming chipped away at my reluctance to use the pool. Besides, there weren't that many safe ways to exercise a big, energetic dog in the summer.

The first few times we'd come, I could barely look at the pool, let alone dip a toe into the water. Every time I thought about it, I recalled that bitter, brutally cold day when I tried and failed to pull Amanda's body out of the deep end. I had to get over my aversion to the pool or sell the house.

I was in a gray zone concerning access to the property. As Amanda's sole heir, a situation that had surprised me as much as it had her brother, all of her resources came to me. Even though the probate hadn't been finalized,

I'd been given the keys because there were animals needing care in residence. I'd refused to abuse that privilege by moving in before the probate went through, but there was no harm in taking advantage of the long evenings to hang out by the pool with the dog before heading back to my mother's place for the night.

As such, I'd taken to leaving a swimsuit at the house. After making sure the dogs were not doing anything dangerous, I let myself into the lower level of the house and hurriedly changed into my bathing suit. I avoided glancing into the mirror as I peeled off my clothes. The best thing that could be said about my suit was that it was new, and the flared skirting tried its best to look decorative and not like camouflage.

As an afterthought, I checked the small fridge behind the wet bar, and discovered there were still a couple of beers present from last summer. Grabbing the bottle opener, I took them with me back to the pool.

Remy was in the water again, cruising around the surface like a sable crocodile. Toad barked hysterically, and dashed back and forth to the edge, threatening to bite at the water. No sign of Joe, which was a relief.

I left the beer on the poolside table and stood at the stairs leading into the water. Despite the sun baking my shoulders, a shudder went through me, as though I were once again looking down in the pool as sleet fell around me. Involuntarily, I glanced at the deep end of the pool, where the cement formed a basin. For a split second, I imagined a dark form there at the bottom, but when I blinked, it was gone.

I can do this.

I'd been working my way up to this for weeks now. First rolling up my jeans and dipping my toes in the water while Remy swam and played. Then changing into my suit and dangling my legs over the edge. The day before, I'd gotten as far as sitting on the stairs. There, I'd replayed memories of laughing last summer with Amanda while we coaxed Remy into the pool. How she surprised us with a bin full of floating dog toys. I recalled how blissful the cool water felt on my skin and the pleasant shock of being splashed when Remy shook water off his coat. The unrelenting heat had helped overcome my reluctance to enter the pool as well. But there was a difference between kicking my heels in the water and swimming.

The last time I'd swum was the day I'd attempted to pull Amanda's body from this pool.

I eased myself down the steps into deliciously cool water. Remy swam enthusiastically toward me, and I snatched up one of his canvas dog toys and chucked it. He turned like a shark and powered after it, with Toad racing along the ledge trying to get there first. She stretched out over the edge as far as she could to grab for the toy, only to tumble in.

Oh no!

She burst through the surface paddling for dear life, splashing so hard she almost went vertical. Remy was on a collision course for the toy, and I was afraid he'd mow her under, or that she would bite him in her panic. Without thinking, I dove under the water and struck out for the two of them.

I needn't have worried.

Remy ignored Toad in favor of his toy, and having snatched it, made for the stairs. Toad, seeing her hero swimming away, followed. Together they climbed out of the pool, dripping at least a third of its contents with them. Toad stood at the edge with her sides heaving, only to shake and dash off after Remy, who was playing keep-away with the toy.

And I paddled in place, shocked by my instinctive reaction.

I struck out for the edge so I could grab onto the lip and catch my breath. I wiped the water from my face to see Joe staring down at me.

He was nearly as wet as I was, having rinsed himself with the hose. His bare chest was distinctly hairier than I'd remembered as a teen. Would a little chest hair have improved Michelangelo's David? Having the evidence in front of my eyes, I would have to say yes.

"Aw, you put her in the pool without me." Joe put his fists on his hips, and his mouth twisted with annoyance. "You could have waited until I got up here."

Both dogs ran up to him, slinging water. He bent to pet them, but they scooted off again, chasing each other.

"Not on purpose. She fell in." I pointed to the table. "There's cold beer if you want it."

"Maybe in a bit." He crossed over to the stairs and entered the pool, a blissed-out expression on his face as he did so. "That's more like it."

I moved away from him in search of another one of Remy's toys. I had to scrabble at the side of the pool to reach it, tossing it over my shoulder once I did. Remy saw the movement and threw himself into the air like a champion dock-diving dog. He hit the water with a splash and struck out for the toy with sure strokes.

Toad yodeled her frustration from the side.

"Should I lift her in?" Joe's brow furrowed as he looked at his dog.

"Not yet. See if she gets in on her own."

We watched the dogs play for a while, and eventually Toad couldn't stand it any longer. She crouched on the edge of the stairs, pawing at the water as Remy went in and out, and finally she pushed herself off after him when he swam past. We cheered, and Joe swam over to guide Toad out when she seemed to lose her way.

"The hardest part is for them to find the stairs when they can't see them," I said after it seemed clear that Toad was growing more comfortable with the water.

By this point, Joe had fetched his beer and leaned back with his elbows on the edge of the pool as he took a swig. I'd accepted the other bottle from him but kept my distance.

"Aren't you worried about how the water runs off over the ledge like that?"

Joe indicated the end of the pool, which was of an infinity design. Water spilled off over the edge to recycle back into the pool from below. From a certain angle, it appeared as though you were swimming into the horizon.

"Yeah, I'm not too keen on that myself," I said. "I plan to talk to someone about altering the design, but that would probably cost a bloody fortune."

"Which you now have."

He lifted his beer in a mock salute.

I grimaced at him. "Not if I spend it on expensive things like re-designing the pool. Or landscaping. Did you know the maintenance for the lawns and flower beds comes to five thousand a year?"

Joe choked on his sip of beer. "You've got to be kidding."

"Yeah, my reaction too. I can't afford the upkeep, not without more income coming in. There's only so much I can expect off the proceeds of Amanda's existing work, no matter what Laney says about her thriving Etsy store."

Laney Driver had been Amanda's agent, and was still in charge of her catalog of artwork and merchandise.

"Yeah, but it's not just art, right? There's investments and other property, too," Joe said, setting his bottle aside to ruffle Toad's wet head as she ran up to him.

I took a moment to enjoy his obvious pleasure in his young dog's excitement before answering. "To a certain extent. Her brother Brad had indeed run the family company into the ground, so her stock in it isn't worth much. With new management, the company could turn around. I don't know. She had other investments, though. But what am I saying? We're still talking about more money than I ever expected to see in my entire life."

"I almost forgot." Joe lifted his beer in another toast, this one sincere. "I hear congratulations are in order. So, you bought Doc's practice after all this time."

"You heard wrong."

Just like that, the easy-going man was replaced by the detective, as he stiffened into alertness. It reminded me of when Remy spotted a bunny from across the yard. Dog to wolf in the blink of an eye.

"What happened?"

Well, that was to the point.

I shrugged, pretending it didn't bother me. "Someone made him a better offer."

"Someone ... You're saying another vet moved into town and bought him out? Like that?" He snapped his fingers with a frown.

Put like that, it did seem odd. It's not that Greenbrier was a teeming metropolis or anything.

"Yep, just like that. I guess Hazel pressured Doc to sell sooner rather than later."

My show of indifference didn't fool Joe.

"It's not like you wouldn't have the money eventually." Clearly, he couldn't give it up. "What about the sale of your old place to the developers? Or the insurance money from your house?"

"Calling a forty-year-old mobile home a house is being generous, and you know it. The insurance company felt the same. The payout on it was a pittance." While nothing I had owned had been valuable in monetary terms, the very fact I couldn't produce receipts or serial numbers made the insurance company offer a lump sum that hadn't begun to replace what I'd lost in the fire. "As for the property itself, Riverside Development low-balled it. They had their reasons. Flat land, too close to the flood plane and without any structure standing? By the time they were done with me, I felt lucky to get them to take it off my hands."

"What happened to the fighter who took down Amanda's killer?"

He meant it as a joke, but I gave him a wan smile in return. Put me in front of a snarling Rottweiler, and I knew what to do. I was the one you called when you wanted to deworm a snake, retrieve a vicious Chihuahua from inside a wall, or test drive a new horse you knew nothing about. I'd been the kid who'd rappelled down a rope inside a cavern with friends the first time I ever went spelunking. But when it came to the personal stuff, to standing up for myself, I tended to roll over and show my belly at the first hint of confrontation. Unless, of course, you threatened someone I loved.

Tell me you no longer loved me, and I'd be out the door so fast it would make your head spin.

"So, who bought the clinic?" Joe asked.

The chlorine from the pool must have started to burn my eyes because I felt the sting of tears. Remy brought me his toy, a long cylindrical bumper that floated in water, and dropped it with a splat in front of me. I chucked it over my shoulder and then ducked at the resulting splash when he leapt in after it. That gave me an excuse to wipe my face before speaking. "A woman named Rachel Burnham. She's very ... fashionable."

Joe frowned for a split-second before lifting eyebrow. "You say that like it's a bad thing."

What could I say that wouldn't sound catty? "She was wearing heels and a tiger-print skort. Not exactly the sort of clothing that lets you roll around on the ground trying to trim dog toenails, and certainly not something you'd want sprayed with anal glands or any other noxious fluid."

This time, both eyebrows went up. "What the heck is a skort?"

"It's a set of *very* short shorts with a panel over the front and back so it looks like a skirt. Think mini skirt. In an animal print."

Remy made for the stairs and ran back toward me with the toy in his mouth, trailing at least a gallon of water. Toad ran alongside him, bumping his shoulder as she tried to snatch the toy from him.

"Okay, I'm getting a visual." Joe grinned, but something in my expression made his smile fade. "What does this mean for you?"

Remy ran up to me again, but with Toad on his heels, he refused to drop the toy. I tugged at it a moment, and then almost fell backward when he suddenly let go. Tossing it once more, I paddled my way back to the side of the pool and gripped the ledge as Remy plunged in.

"Good question." I explained the requirements of a house-call practice before continuing. "I plan to talk to the vet in Clearwater tomorrow. I suspect Jamie will say yes. I refer all my surgeries to him now as it is."

"Why don't you open your own practice here in Greenbrier? You already have a devoted client base, and you have the resources now. If it's not enough money to build from the ground up, surely the bank will extend a loan based on your available collateral. That would also solve your income issue over time."

"I could do that. Though I'm not sure there's enough local business for two full-service clinics. My house-call business fills a different niche." I sighed as I thought about all the work starting a clinic from scratch would entail. "Or I could quit altogether. As you said, I have resources now. I don't *have* to work if I don't want to for a while. I could travel, think about what I want to do next."

"You could," Joe agreed thoughtfully. "But it doesn't sound like the Ginny Reese I know."

What do you know about me anymore? You left twenty years ago.

That wasn't fair. We'd both left town when we graduated from high school. I'd just had a hard time getting over the fact that Joe had left first, and his plans hadn't included me.

"Maybe not. But it sure sounds tempting," I said. Sometimes I dreamed about what I would do with unlimited free time. I could get my mare, Scotty, to more than one local horse show a year. Get some decent hiking in: Dragon's Tooth, Rock Castle Gorge, Molly's Knob. Train Remy for search and rescue, the way I'd always said I would. Heck, I could even take up painting. For all I knew, I could be another Amanda Kelly.

"Perhaps for a month or two," Joe drawled. "But you'd be bored out of your mind in no time."

"Maybe," I said with a shrug. "It would be nice to find out."

I picked up my watch from where I'd left it on the edge of the pool. It was getting late. I still had horses and cats to feed here at Amanda's, and Ming was waiting at my mother's house. Perhaps Joe would take a hint from my actions? I didn't want to get out of the water in front of him.

As my luck would have it, not only had he picked up on the fact I'd checked the time, but he'd also noticed my reluctance to leave the pool.

"You haven't been out of the water since I got here." Joe punctuated his own statement by getting out of the pool and reaching for one of the towels I'd left sitting on the table under the sunshade. I could only hope he'd grabbed the less furry of the two beach towels that had been in my car. Judging by his reaction when he mopped his face, my hope was in vain.

German Shepherds shed a *lot*.

"It's hot out. The water is nice and cool." I sank to my chin in the water and avoided making eye contact with him.

He plucked a few errant Shepherd hairs off his face and slung the towel around his shoulders. "You sure that's the only reason?"

I hadn't intended to snap, but that's exactly what I did. "What other reason could there be?"

"I dunno. Maybe you're avoiding me?"

"That's ridiculous."

His feet appeared at eye level in front of me. If I sank any lower, I'd be blowing bubbles, so I held my figurative ground.

"How much longer will you be staying at your mom's?"

The sigh I released rippled the pool's surface. It was easier staring at the water than meeting his gaze. "I dunno. Until the will is finally probated, I guess. Truth be told, even though I love this place, I feel a little weird about the idea of living here. I think of it as belonging to Amanda, not me."

"So sell it. Or make new memories. But the sooner you get out of your mother's house, the better. It's like you're a teenager again." Joe dropped down until his thighs rested on his heels, and his hands on his knees. "I'm saying this as a friend, Ginny. You need to get your mother's voice out of your head."

"What's *that* supposed to mean?" No concerns about sounding peevish now. His statement irritated me, and I wanted him to know. I flashed a glare up at him.

"Just what I said. You're a competent, successful adult. Don't waste your life trying to live up to someone else's standards. And don't let her diminish what you've achieved."

I was about to retort that a lot had changed in the last twenty years, especially the fact I no longer had a teenager's body, but my gaze was caught by a long, ugly mark that creased the inside of Joe's thigh like a burn.

"What the heck is that?" I squeaked, nearly submerging when I let go of the lip of the pool to point.

Joe stood up with effortless economy and stepped back as though we were partners in a dance. "Nothing."

"You call that nothing? That's a score from a bullet! Joe, you were *shot*." I floundered toward the edge of the pool and gripped the smooth tiled lip so hard my fingers blanched.

His trademark self-deprecating smirk twitched over his lips. "Yeah, I know. I was there."

The scar was at least as wide as my index finger and tracked in a straight line across the inside of his right leg.

"That's right next to your femoral artery!"

"That wasn't the only thing it was next to." He brushed his nose with the back of his hand in amusement as my glance tracked to the next most important thing a man could possess in that general region. Some men might say *the* most important thing in the general region.

Though heat rushed into my face, I didn't allow myself to become distracted. "You could have bled out."

He knelt again when Toad came running up to him sideways, wiggling in her delight. His smile as he took her damp face in his hands was easy and relaxed. Man and dog gazed at each other in uncomplicated affection.

For the first time, I noticed the fine lines around his eyes from time spent in the sun, and the afternoon light glinted off one or two silver threads in his sideburns. Though he'd undoubtedly shaved that morning, the shadow of stubble darkened his jawline, giving him the air of a disreputable pirate. Time had not stopped for him any more than it had for the rest of us, but it had made some sort of deal with the devil on his behalf. He'd been handsome as a high school youth, but he was heartbreaker material now.

He seemed unaware of my frank perusal.

With a final swipe of his hand over Toad's head, he said, "Yep. Kind of puts things in perspective, you know?"

He had no idea.

Chapter Five

By mid-August, eight weeks later, my mother still couldn't let it go.

"I can't believe you just rolled over and let Doc sell his practice out from under you."

We were sitting at a booth in Sue's diner, and my mother's voice, used to projecting over a classroom of children, was especially carrying. Wincing and hunkering down behind my menu wasn't really an option. Instead, I ignored her.

Sue's sister, Kim, smirked in my direction as she flipped open her notepad. "What'll it be?"

I sighed and pushed the menu aside. I might want a burger with fries, but green things were a bit thin in my diet, and Sue made them the way my granny used to: mushy and cooked within an inch of their lives, in the true, Southern style. "I'll take the vegetable plate."

I gave Kim my choices, mightily resisting the urge to choose both mashed potatoes and mac and cheese as my sides, and she jotted them down before adding, "We got hush puppies today. Want them instead of a biscuit?"

I brightened at the thought. "Yes, please."

Kim turned to my mother. "Just coffee for you, Mrs. Reese?"

My mother was known for scarcely eating enough to keep a bird alive. Most of the wait staff in town knew better than to press any kind of food on her, or woe be unto them.

"What kind of pie do you have?" My mother fixed her schoolteacher's glare on Kim, as though she might provide the wrong answer on a math test.

Kim lifted her eyebrows at the unusual request but rattled off the choices. "Pecan, chocolate, and blackberry cobbler."

My mother studied Kim for a long moment with narrowed eyes before asking, "Do you have any rice pudding?"

Kim's expression took on that of a deer caught in headlights. Actually, deer looked less blindsided. "I believe so."

"I'll have that then. Just a small dish, mind you."

And with that, Kim was dismissed. I released my breath slowly. The food ordering was complete. One hurdle down. My mother might have made a disapproving grimace at my choosing hush puppies, but I'd gotten points for going with the vegetable plate.

"I said," my mother repeated, more loudly this time, "I can't believe you let Doc sell his practice to someone other than you."

"I heard you the first time, Mother." And so had the rest of the diner, no doubt. "There's nothing I can do about it now."

My mother leaned back against the backrest of the booth; her eyebrows elevated in exaggerated disbelief. "I don't see why not."

Talking about clients or colleagues in public made me uncomfortable. The last thing I wanted was for someone repeat something they'd overheard me say. I glanced around and lowered my voice. "Because, as I've said before, there's nothing I can do about it. The practice has been open under new management for nearly two months now, and Dr. Burnham was very clear about severing ties with me."

My mother had no such qualms. "Almost putting you out of business in the process."

A couple of women seated at a nearby table nodded as though in agreement. I didn't recognize them right off the bat, but that wasn't unusual for me. I tended to know people's pets better than I knew them personally. Without a Biscuit or Rex on the other end of the leash, I had a hard time identifying the owner.

"Well, that didn't happen." I tried to sound matter of fact, to quell any gossip mills that might start up because of this conversation. "Dr. Shively was happy to act as my referral practice."

No doubt because the number of cases I sent his way had grown. It might have been petty of me, but instead of giving Dr. Burnham a chance, I referred all my surgical procedures and cases needing hospitalization to Jamie now.

Asking my mother if we could continue this conversation at another time in private would be an exercise in futility. My mind scrambled for something to distract her, and for the briefest of moments, I thought of saying, *did you know Joe had been shot on his previous job?*

But I rejected that diversionary tactic almost as soon as it occurred to me. It wasn't my story to tell, and besides, how would I explain seeing such a scar where it was located without raising all kinds of speculation in the minds of anyone listening in? It didn't help that a Google search had been thin on details. The only thing I'd been able to discover was that Joe had been injured during the apprehension of a killer, and that there had been at least one fatality at the scene. I'd meant to ask Joe about it, only I'd barely seen him in weeks.

"I still say you should be making plans to open your own clinic. You know how long these things take. You should be scouting locations, lining up contractors, and pricing equipment. Fall will be here before you know it."

She had a point, but I hated to concede anything to her. The truth of the matter is I had a terrible head for business and was lousy at organization. Taking over Doc's practice would have been challenging, as I would have had to modernize it—Doc hadn't even had computers—but the bones of the operation were already there. The idea of starting from scratch to build my own clinic was overwhelming, and until I had access to my inheritance, I kept making excuses not to do the groundwork.

"I'm not entirely sure I want to open a clinic in Greenbrier. I don't think the town can support two veterinary hospitals right now."

"I'm sure it can't," my mother said tartly. "Which is why you need to do it. Run that harpy out of business."

Though I don't think she'd timed it on purpose, I'd just taken a sip when my mother spoke, and I nearly snorted ice water up my nose. "Harpy? Don't you think that's a bit strong?"

"I do not." My mother leaned back as Kim set her tray on the edge of our table and dispensed our food. "I heard she's seeing Sheriff Donegan."

My fork hit the side of my plate with a clatter as it slipped out of suddenly frozen fingers. Kim met my gaze for the briefest of moments, and I thought I saw sympathy in her eyes. I couldn't tell if it was because Julia Reese was my mother, because of what she'd just said about Joe and Rachel Burnham, or both.

Probably both.

Conscious of the twitching interest of the ladies at the next table, I picked up my fork and speared my collard greens. "Joe is allowed to date whomever he likes."

The fact that I hadn't seen much of him since the day I saw his scar was completely beside the point. Completely.

Though Joe was starting to remind me of a feral cat. Shows up at infrequent intervals for food and attention, only to disappear for days at a time, especially if you get too close. No doubt tomcatting around.

"I don't think she's actually seeing him," Kim volunteered. "More like she ran into him here at the diner and they shared a booth. I'm sure Joe was just being neighborly."

"Is that what they're calling it these days?" My mother's lips pursed, and her eyes narrowed in an expression of patent disbelief. "Was she dressed like a tiger or a leopard this time? I guess it doesn't matter when you're a maneater."

Kim outright sniggered at that one while I counted to ten and tried to decide which was more upsetting: my mother's needling or the notion that Joe might be seeing the Anti-Me. Given the way Kim teased her peroxided hair and favored skin-tight jeans on her days off, it was a case of Ms. Pot enjoying the slander of Ms. Kettle anyway.

One of the ladies at the next table leaned over. "You know, she hired Rayna Hanson's daughter, Amber, to work as an assistant. My understanding is those short skirts are part of the office uniform. All of the sudden, my husband wants to be the one to take Sadie in for her annual check-up."

The other woman at the table joined in. "Wendy is lucky Dr. Burnham only makes her wear a tiger scrub top. I can't imagine having to wear one of those tight outfits all day long."

My mother snorted inelegantly. "Dr. Burnham probably knows how ridiculous such a uniform would look on someone of Wendy's age. Mark my words, Wendy won't hold that job much longer. That woman can hire two young people for what she has to pay Wendy."

"No one is firing Wendy. She's irreplaceable." I pretended my greens needed more salt, which they certainly did not, before continuing calmly. "Wendy has been with Doc for years. She knows every client and every patient on sight. She's one of the clinic's biggest assets."

"Tell that to Burnham." My mother cast a knowing glance at her audience.

Calling Dr. Burnham by her last name only was a huge sign of disrespect on my mother's part, and given the way the ladies around us nodded, it was clear they'd picked up on this fact and were ready to run with it.

It was time to change the subject.

Before I could, however, Amy Burdette crossed over and took a seat in the booth behind us, turning so she could join in the conversation. "You talking about the new vet? Olivia Cantrell is fit to be tied over what they did to her cat."

Amy, like myself, took care of several feral cat populations, but unlike me, tended to have a blind spot about what could be saved and the best use of limited resources. We'd butted heads before over her tendency to house sick animals in the same space as healthy ones, but her heart was in the right place. Dressed in a bright yellow shirt that proudly proclaimed her as a "crazy cat lady," I wasn't surprised she'd wedged herself into the discussion.

"What happened to Olivia's cat?" my mother asked.

"She left Snowball for boarding one weekend," Amy began, but I interrupted.

"Since when does Greenbrier Vet Clinic board animals?"

The facilities simply weren't set up for that kind of thing. There were a few cages and kennels for patients staying the day for treatment or hospitalization, but there was more to boarding than a stainless-steel cage and an old towel for bedding. I knew because I'd looked into expanding GVC's services in that direction when I took over. It would have required relocating the practice to a new site or leasing the property next door and doing some major renovation. The market was there, however. With the new subdivision drawing more and more residents every day, it was only a matter of time before a boarding kennel opened in the area.

Burnham was being smart about cornering the market early, but I doubted she had suitable facilities.

Oh, great. Now my mother had me calling her Burnham too.

"They've offered boarding ever since they reopened for business. Grooming, too. That's how the big blow up with Olivia happened." Amy looked all too happy to share the story, leaning in to speak in a loud whisper, "You know Carolyn Price, right? She was grooming over at the pet store in Clearwater, but she jumped at the chance to work locally when Dr. Burnham approached her."

I knew Carolyn peripherally. She had frequently suggested to clients they contact me when she noticed a flea problem or an ear infection when grooming for the big chain store, but we hadn't actually met.

Amy, seeing she had a captive audience, continued with patent glee. "Well, she was grooming the Gardener's cat, Cotton..."

I had a bad feeling where this was going.

"And Wendy sent Snowball home with the Gardeners by mistake. The worst part is the Gardeners never realized they had the wrong cat! Can you imagine? It wasn't until Olivia went to pick up Snowball that they realized the switch had been made. Oh, Olivia was hot!"

"Wendy wouldn't have made such a mistake. She knows every patient on sight—even one white cat from another. Besides, they all wear paper name tags when they are in the clinic. Like hospital bracelets for human patients," I said.

"That's just it." Amy slapped her hand down on the back of my mother's seat for emphasis. "Carolyn had removed the collar to bathe Cotton, and the cage ID card had fallen on the floor. Wendy put the card back on the wrong cage, and Snowball went home with the wrong people."

"And the Gardeners never noticed?" One of the ladies at the other table clearly couldn't believe her ears.

Amy looked amused. "They thought 'Cotton' was acting a little weird, like she didn't know them, but they didn't think anything of it until Olivia came back to town."

I cringed just thinking about it. What a PR nightmare. "But both cats got returned to their rightful owners with no harm done, yes?"

Amy nodded slowly. "Yes, but Dr. Burnham fired Wendy."

Exclamations of dismay and disbelief broke out around us, but I couldn't help noticing the smug look of satisfaction on my mother's face. She did love being proved right.

"Poor Wendy." There had to be more to the story than that. It seemed impossible to believe Dr. Burnham would throw away years of experience and dedication over an understandable mistake, given the circumstances. Had I been in charge, I would have held an office meeting to determine how the error had occurred and what could be done to prevent such accidents in the future. I'd create a system that would double and triple check patient identity. The changes in routine, combined with the influx of more animals than typically seen at the clinic, was bound to lead to some problems. Though upsetting, no harm had been done this time and the mistake had been unintentional. Perhaps my mother had been right, and Dr. Burnham had been looking for an excuse to fire Wendy.

Amy wasn't done, not by a long shot. "Olivia went to Facebook to leave a nasty review, but Greenbrier Vet Clinic doesn't have a Facebook page."

"What kind of practice doesn't have a Facebook page in this day and age?" my mother huffed.

"Doc has never had any sort of presence on social media. He didn't need it. And to be fair, I almost never go to my own Facebook page." I don't know why I was playing the devil's advocate. Maybe because the ladies in the diner seemed so hostile to Dr. Burnham.

"Yes, but you *have* a page, even if you don't keep up with it." My mother lifted her chin. "I say if some stranger comes to a small town to buy a business and doesn't feel the need to create a social media presence, then she has something to hide. It would be different if she had family here, but she doesn't."

Oh, now I *had* to put a stop to this.

"Hold on there." I held up a hand to the women nodding around me in silent agreement with my mother. "There's plenty of reasons why she may not have started a page yet. There's a lot to running a vet practice, and I'm sure she had more important things to do first if she wanted to open on time. As for the mix up, we all make mistakes. What's important is what we do to try to prevent them in the future."

I hated to think of the things I'd gotten wrong, misdiagnosed, or screwed up in my years in practice. Some of my mistakes still haunted me. Failures happen to the best of us because no one is perfect. Worse, sometimes a case goes badly despite doing everything right. It was one of the reasons I tried very hard not to get sucked into someone's complaints about another vet because I knew that one day, I could be on the receiving end of someone's unhappy rant.

"That's very generous of you, dear. But there's one question no one seems to be asking. Why *did* Burnham come to Greenbrier?"

My mother delivered her question with the air of Miss Marple nailing a key observation in an Agatha Christie story.

At that moment, the door to the diner opened, and Dr. Burnham walked in.

A hush fell over the room, and all eyes turned to her. Dr. Burnham had to be aware that she'd been the topic of conversation, based on the sudden silence. It was strange that someone like her would be caught dead in Sue's greasy spoon in the first place. She froze at the chilly reception before pretending not to notice everyone staring and walked up to the counter.

"I'm here for takeout," she said, somewhat louder than necessary, given the quiet.

My mother stood up. "I'm going to give her a piece of my mind."

No! Anything but that!

I reached across the table for her arm, managing to press into the mashed potatoes and gravy on my plate as I did so, but just like a cat who didn't want to be caught, my mother slipped out of my grasp.

Indecision paralyzed me. What should I do now? If I joined my mother, I'd look like I supported her actions in whatever was about to go down. If I remained seated at the booth, I also looked as though I condoned her confrontation with Dr. Burnham. The rest of the women were no help. They were fixated on the scene about to unfold as though watching a daily soap opera. Kim paused in the act of chewing her gum. Amy leaned forward to see and hear better, and suppressed excitement gleamed in her eyes.

Had this been a room full of men at a sporting event, money would have begun changing hands. Though anyone who knew my mother would never bet against her.

A couple of construction workers seated at the counter appeared to pick up on the tension in the room. As they weren't members of the Linkous family, they must have been subcontractors hired to work on the new subdivision. One nudged the other, and both half-turned to watch Burnham approach the cash register. Though given the shortness of her skort—leopard print this time—they could have been focused on her for other reasons.

"Dr. Burnham," my mother's voice rang out pleasantly. "How are you finding your time in Greenbrier?"

The look of blank incomprehension on Burnham's face was all too familiar. I probably looked the same when cornered in the grocery or the bank by someone who wanted to talk to me about their pets and I couldn't place them out of context. Burnham's instinctive frown flipped into a kind of pasted-on smile as she faced my mother, even though you could practically see the wheels turning as she tried to figure out if she knew my mother or not.

I could have told her Julia Reese wasn't someone you forget.

"Very much, thank you." Burnham's smile was fixed in place. "There's a lot to be said for life in a small town."

My mother's smile, on the other hand, resembled that of a shark that had just spotted a wayward seal. "Indeed, though most young people can't wait to leave for the bright lights of the big city. Tell me, how *did* you find out about our little secret paradise? Do you have family in the area?"

Sue came out from the kitchen carrying a several white bags—clearly more food than one person would eat. Dr. Burnham must have ordered lunch for the clinic. Sue set the bags on the counter behind the register and shot my mother a wary look before switching her gaze to me.

I gave a helpless little shrug.

As a result, I almost missed the look of uneasiness that crossed Burnham's face at my mother's innocuous question.

She turned away from my mother to hand her card to Sue.

"No, I'm not from around here." Burnham spoke lightly, without looking back at my mother.

"I didn't think so." Maybe I was the only one who could hear it, but an edge of satisfaction seemed to slide into my mother's voice. "So how did you find out about Doc's practice being for sale? It wasn't like he advertised it. In fact, he was already in negotiations to sell his clinic to someone else when you swooped in."

Come to think of it, my mother had a point.

Sue froze in the process of handing the card back, her mouth hanging open. Burnham plucked the card from nerveless fingers, pocketed it, and signed her receipt with stabbing strokes. When she faced us this time, her gaze traveled past my mother's shoulder to lock eye contact with me in the corner booth.

"Swooped in? That's an unfriendly way of putting it. I don't like your implications." Burnham flicked a dismissive look up and down my mother's frame. "You must, of course, be Mrs. Reese. The likeness to your daughter is unmistakable."

Which was a little unfair. Sure, we both had red hair, currently in pixie cuts, but that's as far as the resemblance went. My mother was petite, with dark eyes and olive skin. I had my father's Scots Irish coloring with freckles and muddy green eyes. In comparison to my mother's birdlike frame, I was an Amazon. The running joke around town was that the stork broke its back delivering me. I'm not really all that tall. I just seem like it next to her small but fierce frame. With flaming red hair not seen outside of an episode of the X-Files, she favored polyester pantsuit ensembles with perky scarves and sensible shoes, while I was a boots and jeans kind of gal.

The principal of Greenbrier Middle School, upon my mother's retirement, had been heard to mutter that all hurricanes should be named *Julia*.

My mother narrowed her eyes at Burnham's dismissal. If she'd been a bull, she would have pawed her feet and snorted. As it was, her fingers curled into fists.

Time to put a stop to this, even knowing my mother would ream me out later. I stood up and crossed over to her as she wound up for another volley.

"There's no other way to put it. Everyone here knows my daughter was planning to buy the clinic. I'd like to know how a young person such as yourself—you can't have graduated more than a couple of years ago—came to find out about Doc's practice and had the resources to buy it."

This time it wasn't my imagination. Burnham's face went sheet-white, before the color rushed back in an angry flush.

I caught up to my mom and laid a hand on her arm with the care I would have used to approach a barking dog. "I think we should go, Mother."

Burnham's nostrils flared as she spoke. "It's none of your business how I came to find out about the practice, nor how I was able to finance the purchase." She directed her glare at me now, noting the splatter of food on my chest with a curl of her upper lip. "Suffice to say, I was able to do so without having to wait for money from someone who had died. Furthermore, if I have a bone to pick with someone, I can do it myself. I don't have to send my mother to do it."

With that, she swept her order off the counter and marched out, the little bell over the door jangling raucously as she left the diner.

If I hadn't taken hold of my mother's arm, I believe she would have followed Burnham and punched her. As it was, she wrenched her arm away from me. Her face was an ugly hue, and I feared for her blood pressure.

"Are you going to let her speak to you like that?"

My mother, when livid, was a fearful thing to behold. I stood my ground, however.

"What do you expect me to do? She bought the practice. Maybe not fair, maybe not square, but it's none of our business. And you were the one who started it."

Probably not the smartest thing I could have said. Thwarted of her primary victim, my mother redirected onto me.

"That little harpy is right about one thing. I had to say something because it was clear *you* wouldn't."

I resisted the urge to slap my hands over my eyes and pull my palms down slowly, stretching my skin into a grimace. I did not want to have this conversation in public, but there seemed to be no way out of it. "How many times do I have to say this? By the time I found out about the sale, it was already a done deal. What did you expect me to do?"

My mother lifted her head with a snort. "I would have shot her."

She spun on her heel and stormed out. I hastily tossed a twenty at Sue and ran after her.

Chapter Six

It took three days before my mother stopped being angry with me for not standing up for myself with Rachel Burnham.

Irony, thy name is Julia Reese.

What had finally shut her up was telling her that having a confrontation with Dr. Burnham in public made me look unprofessional.

It was the one thing my father, the town's pharmacist, had been able to say to control some of my mother's more contentious altercations over the years. When I invoked the magic word, the reaction had been immediate.

Her mouth had snapped shut with the force of a steel trap, and though her rage still suffused her cheeks, she said not another word on the subject. Of course, for the better part of those three days, she said not a word to me. Apparently, the right to stand up for myself wasn't meant to include her as well.

Surely, there was no harm in prodding Mr. Carter again to see how much longer it would be before I could move into Amanda's place?

Ming, the elderly Siamese I inherited from Amanda, jumped up on the table next to the stack of records I was working on. Having been successfully treated for his thyroid condition with radioactive iodine, he was now back to his former magnificent self: twelve pounds of sleek muscle, his baleful blue eyes a stark contrast to his shining chocolate mask. Ignoring my admonition to stay off my papers, he flopped onto his side among them and began washing his face with one dark paw.

My cell phone rang and vibrated at the same time, spinning lazily on the tabletop, causing Ming's eyes to dilate. I snatched it up before he could bat it onto the floor.

Not recognizing the number, I almost let it roll over into voice mail, but as my own boss, that was a luxury I couldn't afford. Still, I answered the call warily. There were so many telemarketers these days. Sometimes I got more than thirty spam calls in a twenty-four-hour period.

"Hello?"

"Dr. Reese? Rachel Burnham here. I know this is short notice, but I have a favor to ask."

I pulled the phone away from my ear to stare at it in disbelief. Was she serious?

My reply was no less wary than before. I drew my response out into several syllables. "Yes?"

Dr. Burnham hurried on, almost as if she was afraid I'd hang up on her. "I find I have to be out of town for a few days starting the day after tomorrow. I need someone to cover for me at the clinic."

This *had* to be a joke. And yet Burnham didn't seem like the type.

"Excuse me?"

Just as surely as Burnham must have heard the incredulity in my voice, I heard the sigh in hers. "Believe me, I wouldn't ask if there was any other solution, but something has come up."

"Dr. Burnham." All at once, I seemed to be having difficulty speaking clearly, and I spoke slowly so I could enunciate without spluttering. "You made it very clear when we met that you had no need of my services."

"I know." This time she did sigh. "I regret that. If it helps any, I was acting on the advice of Dennis, my business manager. He felt, given your devoted fanbase, it was best if the clinic severed association with you from the beginning. I have to say, he may have been right. You have no idea how tiresome it is to have to explain to everyone who walks through the door that no, Dr. Reese won't be seeing their pet today." She paused for a moment before adding, "That said, I could have handled things better the day you arrived. You weren't exactly what I expected."

I had to ask. "What *did* you expect?"

She laughed at that, a sound without mirth. "A saint. Someone who walked on water. A modern-day James Herriot."

"Where on earth did you get that idea?"

I could almost picture her shrug. "From Dr. Smith, who obviously felt bad about selling to me when you expected to buy him out. From Wendy, who let me know that everything I did was wrong. From the clients who wanted to know when you were coming back. Even Joe was full of praise for you."

Joe? On a first name basis, I see.

"You know Sheriff Donegan?"

"Yes. We met in D.C. He used to speak fondly of Greenbrier, and when ... when I needed a change of scenery, I decided to come here. He made it sound so picturesque."

Joe never told me he'd met Burnham before.

"Uh-huh."

So. Not only did she come here to buy out my clinic underneath me, but she had eyes on Joe as well. None of which made me inclined to help out now.

"As you said, it's short notice. Perhaps you should consider closing the clinic for a few days while you are out of town."

My voice was professional, *not* frosty.

"That's just it. Under normal circumstances I would. But I have a hospital full of patients and while I can transfer some, I can't send them all to the emergency clinic in Birchwood. Most aren't critical, but I have Mrs. Oberstein's cat, Pirate, hospitalized to treat a urethral obstruction."

My heart took the express elevator down to my stomach. Pirate, an overweight, black, one-eyed cat beloved by the elderly Frances Oberstein, had been at high risk for an obstruction for years. As well as fatty liver syndrome, diabetes, and anything else that free choice feeding cheap, dry cat food could cause. I'd been after Frances to put Pirate on a healthier diet ever since she became a client. Now hospitalized, catheterized, forced to eat a prescription food, wearing a plastic collar, and on fluids, Pirate was at high risk for developing secondary problems. Frances was legally blind, but even if Pirate could be transferred to an out-of-town facility, he needed a high level of care. He needed someone who knew him.

I couldn't say no.

"Very well. I'll need you to reschedule any planned surgeries. I'd also appreciate case summaries before you leave. How long will you be gone?"

Relief was patent in her voice when she replied. "I will do as you ask. Thank you. I appreciate this very much."

We worked out the details. She'd do the final checks tomorrow evening. I was to be at the clinic at 7:30 am on Wednesday, the following day. Burnham expected to return after closing on Friday, but we left it so that if she was delayed, I'd cover the half-day Saturday as well.

"I'll arrange for Amber to meet you at the clinic Wednesday morning," Dr. Burnham said.

I almost told her that wouldn't be necessary because I still had a key, but I caught myself in time. No need to tell her that, especially since the odds were good that she'd changed the locks.

"Right then. I'll call if anything changes tomorrow. And Dr. Reese? If it helps, I don't have a problem with you seeing your own patients at the clinic if necessary. I realize this is an imposition on you."

Given the planned workload at the clinic, I doubted I'd have the time to do so, but it was nice to know it was an option, and I thanked her for it.

There was an awkward pause, and then she said, "Joe was right about you."

Immediately my spine stiffened. "Oh?"

"Yes." Her voice became breathy and amused. "He was the one who suggested I call you. He seemed certain you'd say yes. He said you were good people."

There were a lot of things I wanted to be, but I supposed that was better than nothing.

Five-thirty came far too early on Wednesday morning.

As a house-call vet, I'd gotten used to setting my own schedule, and rarely did a client want me to come to their house before 9 a.m. As such, I was used to having a leisurely cup of coffee with my bowl of cereal, and then heading out to Amanda's to feed the horses and feral cats. To get everything done and arrive at the clinic on time, I had to get up an hour earlier than usual, and I moved like a zombie through my morning chores. The only good part about being awake that early was that now we were in the full-blown dog days of summer, it was best to get the outdoor chores done before it got so beastly hot.

The other good thing about leaving the house at o'dark-thirty was that my mother was still asleep, and I didn't have to listen to another lecture on the wisdom of working for The Enemy.

In my mother's eyes, Rachel Burnham was the Devil Incarnate. No good would come from my agreeing to cover for her in her absence. My mother had harassed me about my decision to provide coverage until I pointed out I was doing it for the patients. At that, she'd had become strangely quiet.

When I'd glanced up from checking my messages to see why she'd gone silent, I'd found her staring at me with the oddest expression.

"What?" I'd asked.

"Nothing." Her usual briskness returned. "For a moment there, you reminded me of your father."

High praise indeed. My father had made good money running the town's only pharmacy before a chain store moved in, but he'd also given much of his services away. To this day, I still heard stories of the acts of generosity and kindness he'd bestowed on his clientele. For years, I'd walked the fine line between trying to live up to his legacy and hoping to make enough money to someday retire.

At least my inheritance from Amanda had made it easier to stop worrying about retirement.

On Wednesday morning, I grumpily reminded myself that I really didn't have to work as hard as I'd done my entire adult life, and that it was high time I learned to say no to people. Then I remembered how upset Mrs. Oberstein had been when she'd been hospitalized last Christmas, and though her doctor had agreed she could go home for the holiday, her daughter had been unwilling to "go through the hassle" of picking up Pirate from the clinic where Doc had made an exception to boarding him, when she'd have to turn around and bring him back the next day. I'd been filling in for Doc when Mrs. Oberstein had called in tears to explain she wasn't going to be able to collect the cat as she'd hoped, and Pirate had sent her a dozen yellow roses as a result.

Where that cat got hold of a credit card, I have no idea.

Regardless, Pirate would get the personalized care he needed now.

Yawning, I parked in the lot behind the clinic, and got out of the car. Fortified with an extra-tall dark roast coffee picked up from the local convenience store, I released Remy from the Subaru. He frisked his way to the back door of the clinic, happy to be going to work at the hospital with me again.

There was no sign of Amber, but as I was about ten minutes early, I wasn't particularly concerned. Juggling the coffee with one hand, I pulled out my keys and tried the old one Doc had given to me back when I first started doing relief work for him. The key slid into the bolt and turned, but the entire lock mechanism rotated with it.

Jeez. Either Burnham needed to replace the locks ASAP, or the new one was a piece of junk. But then again, she'd probably been too busy with all the regulatory things involved in taking over a vet clinic to worry about the locks just yet. Remy stood wagging his tail and nosing my hand when I hesitated.

What if Burnham had installed an alarm? It was something I'd recommended Doc do for some time, though he'd never seen the need. There were several controlled drugs that had street value, and they didn't call ketamine, a commonly used anesthetic, Special K for nothing.

I shook my head. If Burnham hadn't gotten around to changing the locks, it was unlikely she'd put in an alarm. I was being foolish. When I opened the door, I was proved right. No alarm system.

Remy galloped down the dark corridor in front of me as we entered the building. I turned on the lights as I went, so Amber would know I was here when she finally arrived. I could use the extra time to go over Burnham's patient list and familiarize myself with the care plans before Amber came in and we began the day's work.

The odor in the building was worse than I remembered. Even the cinnamon air freshener couldn't cover the stench. Honestly, had I been Dr. Burnham, I'd be seriously considering stripping out the flooring and replacing it altogether. The place smelled less of disinfectant, and more of a kennel that hadn't been cleaned in days.

The fluorescent lights seemed overly bright in the treatment room. Squinting, I set down my bag and coffee mug on the counter and gaped at the huge stack of records waiting for me. Beside the records lay a typed, three-page list of instructions. Written in pen on the top page was Burnham's cell number, along with a note that said she would be unavailable for a large part of her time away, and if there was an emergency, I was to call Dennis Montanaro.

Every cage in the treatment room was occupied, and a chorus of meows and barks greeted me.

What on earth?

Remy toured the room, stopping to sniff noses with patients, some of which didn't react kindly to a large German Shepherd crowding their space, even if his tail was wagging. I found one of his old dog beds stuffed above the bank of cages and pulled it down beside the exam table. I put him on a down-stay and began reading the case summaries.

What I read didn't make a lot of sense. Every cage in the hospital was filled, but most of the patients didn't need to be there. Buffy, the Emerson's plump, elderly cocker spaniel, had another ear infection, but for some reason, instead of being sent home with medication for her owners to use, she was being housed for the duration of her treatment. Same with Jake, the Stanley's Labrador, who was notorious for eating anything that wasn't nailed down. He was experiencing diarrhea, but instead of going home on a bland diet and something to settle his stomach after a workup didn't reveal any major issues, he was being kept at the clinic until his diarrhea resolved. One look at his big body cramped in a stainless-steel cage caused my lips to flatten. It was a good thing Burnham wasn't here or I'd have a thing or two to say about her treatment regimes.

I practically hissed, however, when I read the records on a pair of kittens housed in isolation for an upper respiratory infection. They'd developed diarrhea after being given high doses of antibiotics, and the notes indicated they were not to be discharged until the diarrhea resolved. I gasped out loud at the running total of their medical expenses so far. The kittens had been hospitalized for the better part of ten days, and their bill was over eight hundred dollars. Given that most respiratory infections were viral, the decision to use antibiotics was questionable, but it was also the likely cause of the stomach upset.

Another set of case notes indicated that a dog was being "hospitalized" in a crate in the employee's bathroom because it had presumptive kennel cough. Again, after diagnostics had indicated no serious complications. Why on earth would anyone keep a patient with a highly contagious but non-life-threatening condition in a hospital with a lot of other animals?

Livid, I dug through the records until I found Pirate's file. A quick scan of his treatment indicated it had been reasonable and appropriate so far, but the running list of charges made me wince. Mrs. Oberstein was on a fixed income, and her bill for Pirate's treatment had already topped a thousand dollars.

Burnham might be used to practicing in the Big City with metropolitan prices, but Greenbrier was as blue collar as they come. Dr. Burnham and I were going to have words on her return.

According to his record, Burnham wanted Pirate to remain catheterized until she came back, but it was already past time for his catheter to be pulled and for him to be monitored to see if he could urinate on his own. If he kept the catheter in much longer, he risked bladder damage. Biting my lips to keep from saying bad words, I decided as soon as Amber arrived, we'd pull Pirate's catheter.

Where was Amber, anyway? With all the animals clamoring for care, cages that needed cleaning, and medications to be administered, she should have been on the job already.

A small sound made me look up in time to see the door to the treatment room swing close. Instinctively, I turned to look for Remy, but his bed was empty, and he was nowhere to be seen. We'd been working on the "stay" command, and while he was becoming more reliable, clearly he'd blown me off today. A glance at my watch showed I'd been going over records at least ten minutes, so it was no wonder Remy got bored.

My watch also informed me Amber was late. Not by much, but still.

With a sigh, I went in search of my dog.

Stepping into the corridor on the far side of the treatment room, I was struck by the eye-watering odor of cinnamon as I had been the last time I was at the clinic. I'd have to ask Amber to shut those dispensers off while I was here. Another, familiar odor that I couldn't quite place lay under the overpowering scent of Christmas, and I frowned, wrinkling my nose.

To my right were the exam rooms, their doors open and waiting for patients. At the far end of the corridor, however, lay the private office. The door was also open, and the light was on.

"Remy?" I called.

To my relief, he came trotting out of the office, but his ears were flattened to his head, and his manner somewhat subdued. Still frowning, I ran my hands over his muzzle while he licked me. In the rectangle of light cast by the open door, there appeared to be faint black smudges on the linoleum where he'd walked. I picked up one of his paws and wiped my finger over the pad. Something tacky was present.

That's when I recognized the sickly, metallic odor.

Blood.

Alarm and anger flooded my veins. Surely, Burnham didn't have a critical patient stashed in her office! If she did, then it was in trouble.

Taking a firm grip on Remy's collar, I pushed the door further open and gaped at the scene within.

If I'd wanted to give Burnham a piece of my mind, I'd missed my chance. She lay face down at her desk in a pool of blood.

Chapter Seven

FINDING A BODY IS a lot like stumbling upon a snake.

There's that initial, instinctive reaction which freezes you in place while you process what you're seeing. Is it really a snake? Is it poisonous or not? If it's a copperhead or rattlesnake, adrenaline floods your muscles, preparing them for flight or fight. It's almost impossible to stay still after that point. You are compelled to move. But movement could prove fatal when dealing with a hidden threat.

This wasn't the first time I'd discovered a body. As a veterinarian, I was no stranger to copious amounts of blood. But the combination of the two—the realization I was looking at the corpse of someone I knew and that she was surrounded by great quantities of her own blood—that staggered me. I stumbled backwards out of the office, reeling with shock.

After I dragged Remy back to the treatment room and told him to lie down on the dog bed, sternly commanding him to *stay*, I called Joe. I suppose I should have called the sheriff's department instead, but I had Joe's number and he was the first person that came to mind.

To my frustration and embarrassment, I couldn't get a sentence out without stuttering.

"Hang on, slow down." Joe spoke without his usual good-natured drawl, his abrupt tone cutting through my panic. "Where are you and what's happened?"

I took a deep breath and tried again. "I'm filling in at Doc's. I mean the Greenbrier Vet Clinic. You know, for Dr. Burnham. She was going out of town, but she didn't go. She's here, only she's dead. In her office."

Well, that made a lot of sense. So much for staying cool in an emergency.

"Sit tight. I'm sending deputies and an ambulance right over." There was a pause while I heard the muffled sounds of him directing action with his hand over the receiver and then he came back. "Are you sure she's dead?"

An inappropriate laugh bubbled its way to the surface. "I didn't get close enough to touch her if that's what you're asking. But no one can lose that much blood and still be alive. Plus, the blood is black and mostly dried. Except where Remy walked through it."

"Is anyone else there with you?"

"No. Oh! Amber is supposed to be here. Amber Hanson. She was supposed to let me in, but she hasn't shown up. Joe! What if Amber is here somewhere as well?" My heart thudded painfully in veins. "She could be hurt!"

"Ginny." Joe spoke calmly, and every word was an anchor as my pulse pounded in my ears. "I need you to go outside until someone arrives to clear the building, okay?"

"The animals—"

"They can wait until we make sure no one else is in the clinic. Can you do that for me?"

I snapped my fingers at Remy, and he jumped up to cross over to my side.

"Yes. We're leaving now." My voice caught. "Are you coming too?"

"I'm on my way. Go outside. Don't hang up. Keep talking to me."

I grabbed my bag and headed down the corridor with the dog toward the back door, clutching the cell phone like a lifeline.

"You wouldn't believe the set up." Indignation strengthened my voice. "The clinic is jammed floor to ceiling with patients, most of which don't need to be here. The cages are filthy, and animals need to be cleaned, fed, and medicated. I don't see how—"

I was surprised by a low chuckle from Joe.

"That wasn't exactly what I meant by 'keep talking.' Never mind. Is there any sign of a break-in? Can you tell if anything is missing?"

"Oh." Remy and I burst out of the dark corridor into the bright sunlight and a wave of relief washed over me to be out of the building. "I don't know. I went straight away to the treatment room and began going over the case files."

His sharp reply interrupted me when I would have gone on about the patient situation in more detail. "How'd you get in the building?"

"Amber was supposed to meet me. When she didn't show, I tried my old key, which still worked. Well, kinda sorta. I think there's something wrong with the lock. You don't think Amber is still in the building somewhere, do you?" Dread assailed me at the thought that perhaps someone else lay dead or injured inside.

No sooner had I spoken than a red Honda Fit zipped into the parking lot. Reflexively, I grabbed Remy's collar as the car swerved into a parking space. A loud bass thumped through the closed windows until the engine stopped. The driver's door opened, and a pretty blonde in a plum scrub top and tiger-striped skort bounced out.

"Hang on, I think Amber just got here," I said to Joe.

"Golly. Sorry I'm late." The young girl—surely no more than a teenager—gave me a perfunctory smile as she hauled a huge purse out of the car and slammed the door. "I thought it was Erin's day to open but it's not. It's mine. Tony should have been here to let you in, though."

She crossed the parking lot without waiting to see if I was coming.

"Hold up there!" I shouted after her. "Are you Amber?"

She turned around to place a hand on her hip and tip her head to the side with an obvious sigh. "Yes. I need to clock in before it gets any later. The boss will have my head as it is."

"Yeah, about that." I hesitated. There was no good way to say it. "Something bad happened in the clinic. Dr. Burnham is dead."

Amber gawked at me for a moment and then said, "Shut the fu—er, fudge—up. You're not *serious*, are you?"

I nodded and lifted a finger in the air at the sound of sirens headed our way.

Amber fished her phone out of her purse, and with her thumbs flashing in mind-boggling speed, she began typing on her keypad.

"Hang on," I said. "Who are you contacting? I don't think we should be spreading the news until Dr. Burnham's next-of-kin has been notified."

Amber stuck a button with force and looked up at me with a smile. "Too late. No one's going to believe this. Oh, I'd better text Erin and Carolyn, too. She'll want to cancel her grooming appointments."

"Did you hear any of that?" I said to Joe, when Amber went back to her car, typing a mile-a-minute.

"Some. Not all. So, besides Amber, there are at least two other employees expected today, is that right?"

"Three including the groomer, but apparently neither she nor Erin are due in yet. Someone named Tony should have been here, however."

"Sit tight. We're almost there."

As proof of his words, Joe's SUV bumped into the driveway, followed by his deputies in their own cars and an ambulance. One advantage of a small town: almost all the emergency services were located near Main Street. Everyone immediately spilled out of their vehicles. I disconnected the call and walked over to where Joe had collected his team and was giving directions.

"We're going to go in first and clear the building for the EMTs. At least one victim, possibly more. Be careful, and mindful of the fact there could be an injured person inside somewhere." All business, Joe seemed like a total stranger, a man who barked out orders instead of the man for whom lazy charm was his primary mode of operation.

He caught sight of me. "Dr. Reese. What can you tell me about the layout inside?"

His professionalism steadied me. I indicated the back door. "This hallway leads to the treatment room. I went straight there, turning on lights along the way. There's a swinging door at the far end of the room; that opens into another hallway, where you can access the exam rooms on one side, as well as the pharmacy and stock areas. There's another door leading to the waiting room and reception area, or you can cut through the pharmacy to come in behind the front desk. There's a public restroom off the waiting area as well. If you keep on down the hallway, you'll come out at Dr. Burnham's office. The light was already on in that room. That's where I found her."

"You didn't come across anyone else in the building?" Joe asked, never taking his eyes off my face.

I shook my head. "No. But head's up. Records indicate Burnham was using the employee bathroom as a holding area for a patient, so it's possible you'll find animals in other, unexpected places."

"Good to know. Thank you." He shifted his gaze to Remy, who acknowledged the eye contact with an ingratiating wag of his tail. "You said Remy walked through blood?"

I nodded, feeling sick. "Just a little. Most of it was dried. It's what led me to Burnham's office, though. I was afraid she had another patient in there and there was something really wrong."

"There was something really wrong, all right," Frank piped up. "What's with you and finding bodies, Doc? This ain't Cabot Cove, you know."

Deputy Frank Talbot, a real laugh riot. His main partner, Holly Walsh, rolled her eyes behind his back.

"Let's clear the building first, Frank. Audition for *Last Comic Standing* later." The slightest hint of a drawl crept back into Joe's voice. "Frank, Holly, you're with me."

Joe unholstered his gun in such a fluid move, it was as if it were an extension of his arm. I couldn't help but think about his near-fatal scar and the situation that might have caused it. My breath caught as the three of them entered the building. What if I'd been wrong and there was someone hiding in there the whole time?

But though it felt like a lifetime, it couldn't have been more than a few minutes before Holly appeared at the back door and waved the EMTs inside. Not long after, they came out as well, and returned to their vehicle, presumably to wait for the coroner.

Probably the only reason the activity hadn't caught the attention of passersby was because of the early hour and the fact the employee parking was behind the strip mall, and out of sight of Main Street. Still, it wouldn't be long before clients began showing up.

"Now what?" Amber had appeared by my side, shading her eyes with one hand. "Do we wait here or what?"

"At some point they'll need to let us in to take care of the animals, so don't go anywhere. When is Erin supposed to get here?"

"She comes in at ten. I got a hold of Carolyn. She keeps her own schedule, so she's calling her clients and telling them not to come." Amber cast a baleful look at the sky. "It's getting hot out here."

"Yeah, I know." I felt the heat too, and Remy had begun to pant, even in the shade. "But the coroner needs to come before they can move the body. Until he makes a determination as to the cause of death, Dr. Burnham's office is a crime scene."

Amber's eyes widened and her mouth formed a perfect little O in surprise. "You saw her, right? What do you think happened?"

The scene was imprinted on my retinas every time I closed my eyes. Though I hadn't seen a weapon, given the spattered blood across the desktop, I suspected Dr. Burnham had sustained a gunshot wound to the head. But I didn't want to tell Amber that. "I'm not sure. I didn't get that close. It's useless to speculate anyway." Another thought occurred to me. "You said earlier you expected someone named Tony to be here. Have you been in touch with him this morning?"

She made a face. "Like I'd give him my number. Ew. No. Anyway, Erin said he quit last night, so I'm not surprised he didn't show."

"He quit?" Just another headache to deal with. "Do you know why?"

She shrugged in the manner of someone who didn't particularly care. "He probably got a better offer elsewhere. It's a crap job."

"No pun intended," I said, trying for a little levity.

She looked at me blankly, completely missing the point of the joke. Given that she didn't seem particularly upset that her boss was dead, trying to lighten the mood was probably a moot point.

Holly came over, notebook in hand, to take our statements. As soon as she was done, I said, "We've got to get in there as soon as possible. Animals need to be fed and medicated, cages need to be cleaned."

"I know you're itching to do your job, Doc." Holly lifted her shoulders in a shrug. "But we've got to do ours first."

"Tell Joe that it won't be long before the first appointment gets here. If you could let Amber and me into the treatment area, we could cancel the day's schedule and I could go through the cases and discharge everything that can go home. That would make a big difference in the number of people who'd have to go in and out of the building to take care of patients later." I wasn't too proud to beg. "Please. Just talk to him."

Holly tapped her notebook a few times in her hand before speaking. "I'll see what I can do."

We watched as Holly went back inside.

"Do you know why Dr. Burnham was going out of town?" I asked.

Amber's ponytail bounced as she shook her head. "Nope. But whatever it was, she wasn't looking forward to it. Something she was supposed to do later, but it got bumped up on the schedule or something. She wasn't easy to work for at the best of times, but she'd been biting our heads off left and right for the last couple of days, ever since she found out she had to go. Tony's not the only one who was thinking about quitting."

Hopefully, the rest of the team would hang on until we got the patients sorted or transferred.

"Tell Erin she will probably have to come in anyway," I told Amber. "If Sheriff Donegan will allow it, we could use her help manning the phones while you and I go through the cases."

The person I'd really like to call was Wendy, but it was unlikely I'd get permission for her to enter the building, seeing as she wasn't an employee any longer. Still, if anyone could help me efficiently treat and discharge patients, it would be her.

After Amber finished texting Erin, I told her what I had in mind, should we be granted access to the building.

"Just you and me? It will take us *hours* to finish everything," Amber wailed.

"Which is why I'm hoping the sheriff will authorize Erin coming in to help," I said. "Look on the bright side, if we clear the decks of non-urgent cases, then the workload will be much lighter until things get sorted out."

As if my words had conjured him, Joe appeared at the back door of the clinic. He paused for a moment to glance out over the parking lot, and then strode toward us. Messy, dark hair stood up in all directions, as though he'd just tumbled out of bed. The chocolate brown sheriff's uniform might not have been his best color, but it certainly fit him as though it were tailor-made. In deference to the heat, he wore a short-sleeved shirt, and I had to blink to banish the sudden image of him in swim trunks that somehow became superimposed on his presence now.

"Holly says you need to get in the building," Joe stated without preamble on joining us. "As soon as the coroner releases the scene, I'll authorize your access to certain areas, but only with one of the deputies present. Understood?"

Remy had gotten to his feet when Joe approached, and Joe now patted his head absently while fixing his gaze on me with a hint of disapproval, as though he expected me to mess up his crime scene.

I chose to ignore his subtle attempt at intimidation. "We told the groomer not to come, but there's another employee due to arrive at ten. We could really use her help. I told you earlier about the other staffer, Tony, who works in the kennels, but Amber here said he quit last night."

"Did he now?" That infamous half-smile tugged at one side of Joe's mouth. He flipped open a small notebook and shifted his gaze to Amber. "You would be Amber Hanson, correct?"

Amber twisted the hem of her scrub top between her fingers and giggled. "That's me."

I glanced at her with a lifted eyebrow. If she'd been a cartoon character, fat red hearts would be pulsing out of her eyes right now.

Joe was seemingly oblivious to his effect on her, but his lips twitched briefly, as though reeling in the full power of the Donegan smile. "Could you give me the full name of the employee who quit yesterday?"

Amber happily obliged. It turned out Tony was a member of the ubiquitous Linkous family. Present in Greenbrier since the first Linkous had opened a sawmill on site back in the day, the Linkouses had their good and bad branches. Given that Tony had been scooping poop at a vet clinic and not working for one of his uncles or cousins in construction or plumbing, odds were high Tony wasn't one of the more ambitious family members.

"We'll follow up on that." Joe flipped his notebook shut and pocketed it. "Thank you, Ms. Hanson."

I swear the kid blushed.

Before she could simper herself to death, the coroner pulled into the parking lot and Joe excused himself.

Amber fanned herself with her hand as he walked away. "Is he hot or what?"

There was something to be said for a man in well-fitted slacks. I tipped my head sideways to better appreciate the view, only to stop when I realized Amber was doing the same thing in perfect unison.

A text alert chimed, and Amber checked her phone. "Uh-oh," she said on reading the message, her fingers flying in response.

"What now?" I asked.

She never looked up from her viewscreen as she typed. "Erin's not coming. Totally freaked about Dr. Burnham. She says she can't do it. Come in, I mean. Not with the boss lying dead in the office."

God save me from the dramatics of teenagers. Bad enough I had to deal with my mother's theatrics.

"Unless Erin killed Dr. Burnham herself, I don't see what the problem is," I sniped. "She's not being asked to view the body. Neither of you will be allowed anywhere near the actual crime scene." I held out my hand. "Get Erin on the phone. I need to speak with her."

"You mean actually *call* her?" Amber looked aghast.

"Yes, Amber. Sometimes the professional thing to do is to speak to someone over the phone, rather than text or Facetime them."

Casting me side glances as though I might be the bogeyman from some slasher film, Amber called Erin. When Erin picked up, Amber ducked her shoulder and half-turned as though to shield her from me. Her lowered voice was urgent when she spoke. "Hey. Dr. Reese wants to speak with you."

Squawking sounds came out of the speaker as Amber handed the phone to me.

"Hi, Erin," I began, exchanging my annoyance for calm understanding. "Look, I know what happened here at the clinic is very upsetting to you, but we really need your help today. Amber and I need to take care of the patients and send as many home as possible, since the clinic will be closed for some time. You mostly work the front desk, right? Your assistance on the phones, answering questions and so forth, will be invaluable today."

"But I don't know anything!" Erin wailed.

Lord give me patience.

After counting to three, I said, "Of course not. I didn't mean about Dr. Burnham. I meant about the patients and how we're going to manage things over the next few days."

"But there's dead body in the clinic!"

"Not for much longer," I said with a briskness I didn't necessarily feel myself. However, one of the nice things about having other people fall apart around me is that it tended to stiffen my own spine. "The police are on the scene taking care of things. You'll never be alone at any time in the building. What do you say? We really need your help."

It took some more back and forth with me, along with Amber chiming in with her support, before Erin agreed to come. When I handed the phone back to Amber, she said, "They might not even let her in once she gets here."

I'd thought of that too, but figured if I shared that concern with Erin, it would have put the final nail in her refusal to come.

"I'm sure the sheriff will see the advantage of getting enough people in to get the work done as quickly as possible."

When you're waiting in an unshaded parking lot, even a few minutes can seem like hours. Amber gave up standing watch with me and sat in her car with the driver's door open, her eyes glued to her phone. I took up a post with Remy at the end of the lot under a small oak that cast feeble shade. The minutes crawled by slowly on my watch. But eventually, the coroner returned to his car, and Holly waved the EMTs back inside.

I stood up when Amber came to join me.

"What's happening now?" she asked.

"The EMTs will take her body to the hospital morgue. The coroner will do the autopsy and rule the death as either accidental, a suicide, or a homicide. Until he does, the building will be treated as a crime scene. If it weren't for the patients, we wouldn't be allowed back in. As it is, expect to get fingerprinted."

"What?" Amber's mouth fell open in surprise.

I grimaced, remembering with distaste how the crime scene specialists had left fingerprint powder all over my supplies when I'd discovered Amanda dead in her swimming pool. That would be one more thing to deal with before we ended up with it on everything, including the patients. "Routine, I'm sure. As long as your fingerprints aren't any place they aren't supposed to be, it's no big deal."

A furtive look skated across Amber's face before her features slid into wide-eyed innocence again. "Oh, yeah. Right. No big deal."

My mother would have no doubt recognized that guilty expression after all her years as a schoolteacher. Where exactly was Amber concerned her prints might show up without a reasonable explanation? On the deposit bag for the bank? The lockbox for controlled drugs?

Would you listen to me? I was looking for trouble where probably none existed. Too many nights falling asleep to TV crime dramas, that was my problem.

"Do you know if Dr. Burnham kept a gun at the clinic?"

No sooner had I asked the question than I wished I'd bitten my tongue off first.

"Oh. Em. Gee." Amber pronounced each letter with great exaggeration. "Are you saying she was *shot*?"

She whipped out her phone again. Given that I was the only one to have seen the body, there would be no doubt where this leak sprang from when word got out.

I stopped her with an outstretched hand. "I didn't say that. Like I said, I didn't get that close to the body. I was just thinking out loud. I didn't see an alarm system. Vet clinics get broken into all the time."

But Burnham's position at the desk, combined with the presence of blood spatter, was certainly suggestive of a gunshot to the head.

"Well, if she had a gun, *I* certainly didn't know about it."

Amber spoke with an odd sort of confidence, and I wondered again where her prints might show up. Bit of a snoop, eh?

I might have questioned her further on the subject, only the throaty roar of a V8 engine erupted behind us, and we both turned as a bright sports car entered the parking lot. If it had been a pickup truck, I could have told you if it was a dually or not, and what its towing capacity was, but all I could say about the sports car was that it was eye-blindingly yellow, and the slant of its headlights made it look like a mean hornet. That, and it looked brand new. It was a little disconcerting to see a car that cost more than my last house headed toward us.

Without bothering to line up in a parking space, the yellow car came to a stop, angled in front of us. The driver's side door opened, and Dennis Montanaro got out. Shades blacked out his eyes, but there was no disguising his anger.

Oh crap. I should have thought about contacting him.

"What the hell is going on here?" He snapped at me, waving a hand at the emergency vehicles. "And where's Dr. Burnham? She was supposed to meet me over an hour ago, and she isn't answering her phone."

Amber turned a face toward me that shone with gleeful hostility. "You want to tell him, or should I?"

Animosity toward Montanaro or reveling in the drama of Burnham's death? Maybe a little of both? It was hard to tell with Amber. Making a mental note to figure out later which emotion was driving her reactions, I stepped forward. "I'm sorry to have to tell you this, but I found Dr. Burnham dead in her office when I arrived."

"Dead?" He took off his sunglasses to glare at me. "Are you sure?"

No, I just called the sheriff's department and the coroner for fun.

Just then, the back door to the clinic opened, and the EMTs rolled out a stretcher with a black body bag on it.

"Pretty sure," I said, working hard to keep any hint of sarcasm out of my voice.

Without another word, Montanaro pulled out his phone and called someone on speed dial, holding up his index finger in an imperious gesture for me to stay in place. I shot a look at Amber, but she was watching Montanaro with simmering dislike. When the person on the other end of his phone picked up, he said, "Nadine? Change of plans. Call the Board and cancel. Dr. Burnham is dead. You heard me. No, I don't know anything more than that. I just got here myself."

He hung up without acknowledging Nadine and said, "Right, then. How long will it take you to clean up the mess and open the doors?"

Chapter Eight

AMBER GASPED LOUDLY, WHICH had the benefit of covering my own sharp intake of breath.

"Now you listen here," Amber exploded, her voice quivering with rage. "If you think for one moment that my job description includes cleaning up the place after the boss offed herself, you've got another think coming."

She pushed forward to stab the air in front of Montanaro's chest with her forefinger.

I couldn't afford to have another employee quit on me today, so I cut in front of Amber and shot her a quelling glance. "I'm sure Mr. Montanaro didn't mean for you *personally* to clean Dr. Burnham's office, Amber. There are professional services for that." I shifted my gaze to Montanaro. "That said, we have to wait for the sheriff's office to clear the scene. In the meantime, the clinic will be closed. We don't have a choice in the matter. I'm sure you understand."

"We'll see about that," Montanaro snapped. "We have a business to run here. Every hour the doors are shut, we're losing money. Who's in charge here? I need to speak to that sheriff right now."

"Then today's your lucky day," I murmured, as Joe exited the building with Frank, saw us standing together, and made a beeline in our direction.

In a pissing match, I'd rank Joe's odds over Montanaro's any day. Burnham's business manager might be a Doberman in a fancy suit, but Joe was a wolf masquerading as a farm dog. Some of the tension oozed out of my shoulders at his approach. I looked forward to seeing Joe put Montanaro in his place.

"You'll be able to enter the building to take care of the patients in a moment, Dr. Reese." Joe addressed me first, with the continued professionalism from before. "I'm assigning Deputy Walsh to escort you.

I've authorized her to allow Erin Deveraux to assist you and Ms. Hanson in discharging and rescheduling patients."

"How long will we be kept out of the building, Sheriff?" Montanaro didn't wait for an introduction but pushed his way into the conversation. "We need to make plans for the business."

Joe tipped his head back and slightly to one side as he lifted an eyebrow. "And you are?"

"Dennis Montanaro. I'm overseeing Dr. Burnham's assets here."

He did not offer his hand for a shake.

"I see," Joe drawled, his smile polite. "Are you her lawyer then?"

"Not exactly. Think of me more in terms of a business manager." Montanaro cut his glance in my direction and leaned toward Joe. "Perhaps if I could have a word in private with you?"

"Certainly." The amusement in Joe's expression suggested he knew exactly how much it was going to frustrate me to be shut out of this part of the conversation. "As a matter of fact, I have a few questions for you. Ah, here comes Deputy Walsh. Holly, if you could escort Dr. Reese and Ms. Hanson to the treatment area, I'll join you momentarily."

With a brisk nod, Holly indicated we should follow her. I would have to find out what Montanaro's relationship to Dr. Burnham was some other way. In the meantime, I had a slew of patients to see.

The crime scene techs stopped us just outside the door. With my assistance, they took photos of Remy's feet, and using a roller, inked his pads and pressed them down on a piece of paper. We then had to clean his paws before he was allowed into the clinic. The whole process looked as though he was being booked for a crime, and his woebegone expression during the procedure didn't help. I was sorely tempted to snap a picture of the proceedings myself. It was social media worthy.

I thought we'd never get the ink off his feet. Amber fidgeted and scrolled on her phone, punctuating her boredom with loud sighs while Deputy Holly waited impassively for the two of us to go inside.

The odor of death seemed more potent on re-entering the building, but perhaps that was because I knew the reason for it now. Amber had barely set foot in the treatment area before she exclaimed, "What *is* that smell?" and covered the lower half of her face with her sleeve.

I couldn't come up with a suitable answer before she gagged and bolted for the bathroom.

"Hey, you can't do that!" Holly exclaimed, chasing after her.

I closed my eyes to the sounds that followed and tried to outline a plan of action. Unfortunately, I'd been right about the work cut out for us. The crime scene techs had left evidence of their investigation all over the clinic, and before we could begin to see patients, we had to break out the dust buster and vacuum to clean the treatment area.

Amber had also been right. It would take us the better part of the day to work through the caseload and discharge as many patients as possible. Until Erin arrived, I had a slightly-green-around-the-gills Amber contact clients to cancel or reschedule their appointments—not easy when we didn't know when the clinic would open again, or have a vet to see patients, for that matter.

After persuading Erin to come in early for her shift, I was able to examine and assess all the hospitalized patients and initiate discharges for every animal whose owner we could reach. Once the priority cases had been dealt with, we fed and medicated the remaining animals. After that, we tackled cleaning cages, which would have been easier if there had been outside runs or spare cages to shift patients around while we worked. As it was, there were no empty dog runs to kennel Remy, and more than once I had to tell him to go lie down again when he became too interested in what we were doing. He wanted to jump on every newcomer as well, leading to apologies on my part and a silent vow to be a more consistent dog trainer in the future.

We worked straight through lunch, ordering pizza and eating in the parking lot in between discharging patients. By late afternoon, there were only a handful of clients unable to pick up their pets. Several were out of town, and had left healthy animals for "boarding", though I suspect most would be appalled if they'd known of the inappropriate conditions. We'd pulled Pirate's catheter, but he still needed to be monitored for urine output before he could safely return home. Another critical case was a little Pomeranian recovering from pancreatitis. Tiffany's people were in the habit of slipping her greasy tidbits from their plate, and her most recent illness had been quite severe. If they were lucky, she wouldn't develop diabetes as a result of the organ damage.

The toughest part of the patient discharges had been presenting clients with bills I hadn't generated. Many of the owners were understandably shocked by their final invoices, and I felt compelled to adjust their totals, particularly when so few of them had been given any idea of what their charges might be. By the time the final patient had been sent home, I wanted nothing more than a giant glass of Merlot by the swimming pool with my favorite playlist blasting in the background.

None of which would happen at my mother's house.

The only good thing about the workload was the fact it had left me with little time to stew about Burnham's death.

As soon as the local gossip mill got rolling, thanks to Amber's early morning text alert to her friends, gawkers and ghouls had shown up at the clinic seeking the (literally) gory details. Since we were operating on a curbside basis, with clients coming in and out of the lot to pick up pets, we couldn't exactly turn anyone away, but Holly's stern presence had sent most of the rubberneckers packing.

But that hadn't stopped the phone calls. Erin had fielded most of those by telling the truth: she didn't know much about the situation except that Dr. Burnham was dead, and yes, all routine appointments were canceled for the time being. Anything else she referred to Clearwater, or the emergency clinic in Birchwood Springs.

After the third time my cell had rung with the dramatic *dun-da-dunt-da-duna* personalized tune, Amber had asked curiously, "What's that ringtone? I swear I've heard it before."

"The Wicked Witch of the West's theme from *The Wizard of Oz,*" I'd replied, gritting my teeth.

Her brow had cleared for only a second. Frowning again, she'd asked, "Aren't you going to answer it?"

With a sigh, I'd pressed "accept" on my phone. "Hello, Mother."

"There's been a death at the clinic and I'm just *now* finding out that my daughter is still alive?" My mother had begun without preamble. "The very least you could do is call me and let me know that I can stop planning your funeral now."

If you were wondering where I'd learned to count to three before speaking, it was from dealing with my mother. "Since you've heard about Dr. Burnham's death, I assume you also know I was the one who found her."

"I would have still liked to hear from you myself. You didn't answer my calls."

With any luck, she hadn't heard my sigh. "I'm sorry. Things have been really hectic here. Listen, I'll fill you in this evening. But right now, I have to sort out patient care for the next few days, and the sheriff's department is limiting our access to the clinic."

"Do you need me to come down there and straighten them out?"

Ye gods, the last thing I wanted. I'd envisioned my tiny mother, dressed in one of her black pantsuits, laying down the law to ... the law. The image was terrifying.

"No, we have it under control for now. But I have a lot of work to do. I'll talk to you this—"

She'd hung up without saying goodbye.

I hated it when she did that. The irony is that if my sister Liz or I had dared to call her when she was at work for anything less than the immediate threat of bleeding out or the house being on fire, she would have crucified us when she got home. Now that my mother had retired, she seemed to think the world should stop spinning at her convenience.

I couldn't afford to let her get under my skin just then.

At long last, we'd checked out the final patient who could go home.

"Good job, you two," I announced to Erin and Amber when the last client pulled out of the parking lot. "I really appreciate your hard work today."

Erin wore her natural curls pulled off her face and held in place with a leopard-spotted headband. Unlike Amber's short skort outfit, it seemed Erin preferred to wear a black scrub set, decorated with a fringe of leopard spots.

Where *did* these jungle-themed uniforms come from?

Erin exchanged a look of faint surprise with Amber. If I had to guess, compliments hadn't come their way very often under Burnham's command. After her initial rough start, I'd been pleasantly surprised to find Erin capable of doing her job with a minimum of supervision, leaving me to work with the patients. I'd only had to shore up her confidence and tamp down her anxiety about being in "a place of death" a couple of times.

"What's going to happen now?" Erin indicated the building behind us. "Do we come in to work tomorrow as planned or what?"

From the way she fidgeted, it was clear she didn't want to come back.

"That's a good question," I agreed. "I need to talk with the sheriff, but I don't think so. Until they release the scene, the police are going to limit access to the building. Since we sent most of the patients home, I can handle taking care of the rest. I honestly don't know what this means for the future of the clinic. I guess it will depend on who Dr. Burnham's heirs are and what they decide to do with the practice."

"You don't have to come in tomorrow," Amber said to me. "I can do the treatments. I used to do them on the weekends all the time."

Damp tendrils of hair hung limply around her pale face. She definitely wasn't as perky as she'd been this morning, but I appreciated the offer, especially since we were all hot and tired. No doubt, she was looking to add as much to her paycheck as possible, particularly if it was potentially her final one. There didn't seem to be any point in telling her that as an unlicensed assistant, it was illegal for her to administer medications unless under the direct supervision by a veterinarian. Another black mark for Burnham in my book.

"No, it's my responsibility right now. I was contracted until Saturday. I need to stay on at least until we get all the sick patients discharged. Besides, I'll have to coordinate with the sheriff's department for them to send a deputy to meet me. No one will be allowed in without an escort."

From the guilty look that flashed briefly across Amber's face, I wondered what she was so anxious to gain access to.

"Well, at least we had a good day on the books." Erin rolled her shoulders to stretch them out. "That will have to please old Monty. He can't fuss about money for a change. I hate checking clients out though. They're always so upset about their bills."

"Yeah." Amber narrowed her eyes at me before adding, "Why did you send everyone home anyway?"

Not wanting to share my opinion of Burnham's practice management style, I merely shrugged. "It only seemed to make sense. There's no telling how long it will be before we get another vet in here."

"So, you're saying there's a good chance we're going to lose our jobs," Erin asked, shooting another meaningful glance at Amber.

"I don't know. It all depends on how Dr. Burnham left things."

Last time I checked, you had to be a veterinarian to own a vet practice in Virginia, though the regulations changed all the time. It was quite possible Burnham's heir would find themselves find themselves in the unenviable position of having to sell the business on short notice because they weren't legally allowed to operate it. Was there an opportunity for me to purchase the clinic on the rebound?

I didn't want the only employees to walk out but the truth was, they probably needed to look for other work, at least temporarily. "Anyway, if you want to clock out, I can take it from here. It was good working with you both today."

We exchanged cell numbers so I could keep them informed of any changes to the schedule.

"Better give me Carolyn's number as well," I added as afterthought, and placed the contact information in my phone when Amber gave it to me.

The engine of Montanaro's sports car announced its arrival before the bright yellow vehicle came into view. It swung into the lot and barreled up to where we stood. For a split-second, I thought he wasn't going to stop and we'd have to scatter like pigeons in the park. Instead, he pulled to a sideways stop and killed the engine.

As Montanaro sat in his car, texting on his phone without looking at us, Erin said in a low voice, "At least we won't have to deal with *him* anymore."

Amber said nothing but shot daggers with her eyes at Montanaro's car as she toyed with her necklace.

"Tough guy to work for?" I asked with some sympathy. "What exactly does he do, anyway?"

Erin exchanged glances with Amber, and an uncomfortable silence followed until Amber said, "He acts as though he owns the place."

"He doesn't seem particularly upset about Dr. Burnham's death," I observed. "Were they close?"

"Dennis Montanaro doesn't care about anything but the bottom line."

Amber's assessment was delivered with a burning glare of dislike in Montanaro's direction.

"He won't be our problem much longer." Erin sighed and added, "Good riddance, I say. He gives me the creeps."

Montanaro's exit from the car was the impetus Erin needed to leave. It might have been my imagination, but I got the impression Amber wanted to speak to Montanaro. She seemed to change her mind after a glance at me and hastened off after Erin as Montanaro removed his sunglasses and made his way over.

"Nice car," I said by way of appearing friendly.

For the briefest of moments, his face transformed, and he looked like a man in love. "It's a brand-new Chevy Corvette. Zero to sixty in two point eight seconds and 470 foot-pounds of torque. I went for the dual exhaust, which gives me 495 horsepower."

Which was meaningless to me. All I knew is that it was a *Look at Me* yellow. With a hefty dose of *I'm Richer than You* as well. And, if we were being completely honest, a tincture of *I'm Compensating for Something* to boot.

My lack of enthusiasm must have showed because his look of animation faded back into cool superciliousness again. "I'm glad I caught you, Dr. Reese. There are things we need to talk about."

He scowled briefly at the sky, shading his eyes with one hand as he did so. "Can we move this inside? It's too hot to hold a decent conversation out here."

"I'm sorry," I lied. I wasn't sorry at all. "But the clinic is still off limits."

"How long is *that* going to last?"

Whatever his relationship had been with Burnham, it hardly seemed to be a close one, based on his level of annoyance at the inconvenience of her death.

"Hard to say." The back of my neck prickled, the heat of which reminded me I'd forgotten to put on sunscreen, and I was probably turning pink now. "I have to coordinate with the sheriff's department on coming back to treat patients, so I'm sure they will update me as soon as possible."

Montanaro didn't *quite* sigh. "I suppose that's to be expected."

He suddenly turned on a mega-watt smile. "In that case, may I take you to dinner? I have some things I'd like to discuss with you, Ginny. May I call you Ginny?"

Was he coming on to me? It had been so long since I'd been on a date, it was hard to tell. Or did he intend to ask me to continuing covering for Dr. Burnham beyond the days I'd already been contracted? I wasn't sure about the legality of that, and I doubted Ethan Burrows, my mom's lawyer, would know. It was possible Lindsay Carter might, however. He seemed to be on the ball for a small-town attorney.

Either way, it wasn't a conversation I wanted to have right now. I was hot and sweaty, probably reeked of things best not mentioned, and it had been a long, stressful day.

"I'm sorry, but I have my dog with me. I can't go to dinner this evening."

Montanaro frowned. "Can't you leave him here in one of the kennels?"

I pretended to consider that idea. "Normally, it wouldn't be an issue to do that. But I can't ask Deputy Holly to hang about waiting for me to come back from dinner."

"Is there a time when you *don't* have your dog with you? How about—"

"Oh, look!" I said brightly, pointing out the obvious as Joe pulled into the parking lot. "Here comes the sheriff. We can ask him about getting back into the building."

The look Montanaro shot me seemed to speak volumes, but unfortunately, it was in a language I didn't understand.

Joe parked the department SUV in a bona fide space, quite close to where Montanaro's Corvette disdained the use of designated lots altogether. He got out of the vehicle and ambled over with the lanky grace I'd remembered from his days as the King of Track and Field in high school. My sense of relief at seeing him was disproportionate to the situation. Like I was the assistant cornered in the circus cage by the tiger, and the lion tamer had just walked in and taken control.

"Sheriff." Montanaro hailed Joe before he reached us. "I hope you have good news."

"That depends," Joe drawled in his best Sheriff Andy Taylor manner. "If you're hoping to have full access to the clinic tomorrow, I'm afraid I can't let you do that just yet."

When Joe pulled out the golly-shucks-Mayberry routine, his intent was to disarm and mislead those around him into thinking he was nothing but a country hick. I knew better. He'd won a full scholarship to the University of Maryland and had gotten a degree in criminology. He was no slouch in the brains department.

"I think I made it clear to you this morning how important it was for things to get back to business as usual around here." Montanaro bristled at the roadblock. "When *can* we expect to get into the building?"

"That's not up to me. The coroner has to sign off on the cause of death." Joe rubbed the corner of his temple, and for the first time, I noticed how tired he looked. Sweat stained the collar of his uniform, suggesting he'd been out in the sun for a good bit of the day. "There's only one man to cover the entire county. Unfortunately, there's a bit of a line at the moment, so I doubt you'll get any answers before Monday."

"We'll see about that." All former hint of affability was gone. Montanaro fixed his gaze on me and said, "I need to meet with you at your earliest convenience."

"How about first thing in the morning? Six-thirty at Sue's diner? I can meet you there before coming here to check on patients."

I'd hoped the early hour suggested would put him off, but no such luck.

"Until then, Ginny. Sheriff." With a stiff nod, Montanaro slipped on his dark sunglasses and headed for his car.

The Corvette's engine seemed to roar with annoyance as Montanaro drove off. There was no point trying to speak until the sound subsided. As we watched him drive out of sight, Erin and Amber exited the building, but instead of joining us, they got into their own cars and sped out of the lot as though I might stop them and demand several more hours of drudgery.

"Dennis Montanaro calls you Ginny?" Joe's voice went silky-smooth, like a fine whiskey before the heat of alcohol hit you. "Did I miss something?"

"Doubtful," I snorted. "Old Monty, as the girls call him, probably wants something from me."

"Hmmm." Joe's murmur was noncommittal, and yet sounded somehow disbelieving at the same time.

"Holly's still inside. I need to check one of the patients and collect Remy, but then I'm done." I gave Joe an assessing once-over. "You look about as beat as I do. Do you want to meet me at Amanda's for a swim? Beer's on me."

He shook his head wearily. "No can do. Wish I could, but I wasn't kidding about the waiting list at the morgue. Tommy Detweiler's kid smashed up his brand-new pickup truck this afternoon. Trey was dead at the scene, along with Randy Cook. Lilly Jung had to be airlifted to Birchwood Springs."

"Oh no!"

I didn't know the local kids well, but I knew most of their parents. We'd all gone to high school together. There was at least one horrific car crash every year, usually involving new drivers, alcohol, and a high rate of speed: a bad combination on the narrow, winding roads in our area. The community would be devasted. I foresaw the outpouring of grief, the roadside memorials, the sermons on how these kids were in a better place now. I couldn't help but think their parents would have preferred them to be in this imperfect world a bit longer. Perhaps my mother's prohibition on our riding with anyone who'd had their driver's license less than a year wasn't quite as draconian as it had seemed at the time.

Joe rubbed his face with both palms. "I hate this part of the job."

I touched him on the arm. "I'm really sorry."

His sad smile, which held none of its usual devastating charm, somehow wormed its way into my heart as though it had.

Belatedly, a thought occurred to me. "Oh hey, I'm sorry about Rachel Burnham too. I understand you knew her. Outside of Greenbrier that is."

Was it my imagination, or did a portcullis just drop in front of Joe's face?

"Not well, but yes. We'd met in D.C. She used to have a practice there."

"Yeah. That's what she said. Only, I wasn't sure because you didn't seem to recognize her name when I mentioned her that day at the pool."

"That's because she'd gotten divorced and reverted back to her birth name before moving here. But I wouldn't have recognized her from your description of her anyway."

Nope, not my imagination. Not only had the portcullis clanged shut, but I could detect archers on the walls, and perhaps even some of those guys with pots of boiling oil.

Predictably, my own back went up.

"What was wrong with my description of her? Given her fondness for jungle cat prints, the spots alone should have been a dead giveaway."

"You know," Joe began, his eyes narrowing, "I can understand why you'd be somewhat hostile to Rachel, given that she bought the clinic, but I didn't expect you to be so judgmental."

"Excuse me, what?" Gaskets began to leak steam. "Okay, for starters, she didn't just buy the clinic, she bought it out from under me! I was negotiating—"

"She bought the clinic in good faith. If you're going to be pissed with someone, then be angry with Doc."

Joe folded his arms across his chest, and there was a time when I'd have found that posture extremely sexy, given the sheer masculinity of his bared forearms and the stretch of cotton over his biceps, but I wasn't having any of it now.

"Putting aside the question of how I should feel about someone who snatched away a business opportunity that I've dreamt about for *years*, how on earth have I been judgmental?" I punctuated my sentence by putting my fists on my hips.

"The first thing words out of your mouth about her was how you felt about the way she dressed. Because she liked pretty clothes and wanted to look nice, you found fault with her as a veterinarian." The look Joe flicked in my direction shouldn't have stung, but it did. "Even today, with her lying dead in her office, you couldn't wait to tell me what you thought about her professionalism and competency."

"The only time I ever said one word to you about her idea of what passed for appropriate work attire was barely an hour after I'd met her and discovered she'd stolen my business. Excuse me for being less than thrilled with her at the time."

In retrospect, I probably shouldn't have exaggerated the words *excuse me* with excessive sarcasm.

Joe's glare drilled me with disapproval. "People around here like you, Ginny. You're respected and your opinion counts for a lot. A word from you would have gone a long way to making Rachel feel accepted. Instead, you let your mother mount a witch-hunt against her—"

"Now hold on. Since when have I been able to control my mother?"

Since when had anyone, save my father? And what witch-hunt was Joe talking about?

"Fair point." Joe nodded grudgingly. "But I *defended* you to Rachel."

Rachel, was it?

I ignored that little spurt of annoyance. Rachel could hardly be competition now, could she? Not that I'd been competing for Joe's attention. Besides, I didn't care what Joe thought about me except as a friend.

Right. Keep telling yourself that, honey.

My inner monologue made me a tad sharp when I said, "Her practices leave a lot to be desired. She was gouging her clients. I know how much it costs to do business, and how narrow the profit margin can be, but she had to have a two hundred percent markup on her fees. And then there was the fact she was hospitalizing patients that could have easily been treated by their owners at home. That's just a money grab right there."

"Well, maybe some people want to make a living at their jobs, Ginny." He spoke with an uncustomary snap. He seemed to lay sarcastic emphasis on my name. "Maybe some people don't want to live on a shoestring out of some misguided notion that undercharging for their services is a noble thing to do. Just because someone doesn't do something the Ginny Reese way doesn't make it wrong. And maybe, just maybe, if people like you hadn't been so judgy about her choices, she wouldn't have decided to blow her brains out."

He left me, mouth open in shock, and stalked back to his car.

Chapter Nine

"WELL? WHAT HAPPENED? THEY'RE saying Burnham was murdered during a break-in."

My mother met me at the door with an elevated eyebrow. Impatience emphasized the fine lines on her face, which were still less than noticeable than that of most women her age. Sometimes I thought my mother and I were like *The Picture of Dorian Gray*, but instead of a painting that aged because of the subject's actions, it was me growing old on behalf of her.

Lord knows most days I felt like the adult in the relationship.

"What? Drat it, those girls must have started that rumor." I could guess who put that thought in their minds, too. Me, that's who. One more thing for Joe to lay blame at my feet. "That's not what happened at all. Let me get the animals settled, and I'll catch you up. It's been a perfectly beastly day. Is there anything to eat?"

A pipe dream, to be sure. My mother was even less of a cook than I was. Growing up in her household had given me an appreciation for the species-specific foods Purina made. "People Chow" would have made my life a lot simpler as a child.

"There's some egg salad in the fridge. You can make yourself a sandwich."

I made the blech face and pretended to retch when she headed back into the living room. I hated anything with mayo in it (I know, how could I truly be a child of the South?) and my mother knew it. I'd have to make do with whatever was in the fridge. At least one advantage of temporarily moving back in with my mother was the positive effect it had on my weight. The negative effects on my psyche were another thing altogether.

From the entrance to the living room I could see that half the drawers to the credenza were pulled open, and their contents scattered on the floor.

"Are you looking for something?" I asked.

Flustered, her face reddened as she wheeled toward me. "No. Not at all. I'm just re-arranging a few things."

"Mother, it you've mislaid some important papers, just say so. If you recall, we re-did the files after Dad died. Whatever you're looking for is probably there."

Her features stiff with indignation, she said, "I'm fine. I can manage perfectly on my own."

No doubt she would continue to tear the house apart to find whatever it was she was looking for until she gave in and asked for my help. Hopefully it was only something as innocuous as the warranty for one of the appliances and not receipts needed for this year's taxes.

With a shrug, I followed Remy down the hallway toward the kitchen.

Ming was waiting there, meowing hoarsely in the manner that only a cat dying of starvation could manage. Remy leapt forward on seeing him, but then skidded to a halt when Ming turned an imperious stare on him. It was a bit funny to see a ninety-pound German Shepherd back down to a twelve-pound cat, but I was grateful Remy respected Ming's age and general meanness.

Ming jumped on the settee at the far end of the room, ran along its length, and then up the arm to a small cabinet where I'd established a safe feeding station for him. His meows reached an ear-splitting pitch as I opened a can of smelly cat food and dumped half of it in his dish.

Remy began pogo-sticking around the room in anticipation of getting his kibble, but I made him sit and wait while I filled his bowl.

"I don't know why that animal can't eat dry food like any normal cat," my mother groused with a curled lip on entering the kitchen behind us. "His food *reeks*."

My mother had a nose like a bloodhound. I suspect she would have made a good perfume tester in another lifetime, only she'd have forbidden anyone to come within thirty feet of her carrying a spritzer bottle of scent. Growing up under her unbelievable sense of smell meant there'd been little my sister and I could get away with. Five minutes in the company of someone smoking or drinking and the evidence rode home with us. I was only a little sorry Ming's preferred dinner made her want to gag.

"As I've said before, cats are true carnivores. They need to eat meat." I switched into professional explanation mode from long habit. After all, I *was* the expert on this subject. "Dry food is too high in carbs for cats and sets them up for all kinds of health issues as a result."

"Yes, yes, I know." My mother rolled her eyes. "So, you've said. Repeatedly."

Remy inhaled his kibble and then went to the base of the cabinet to stare hopefully at Ming on the off chance he would spill his food. A thin stream of drool trickled out the side of his mouth.

My mother casually opened the catch-all drawer under the counter and began rummaging around in it.

Sympathizing with Remy's hunger, I scrounged for my own dinner. The freezer held three low-calorie frozen dinners that consisted of a sad little piece of compressed meat and fake mashed potatoes with your choice of a spoonful of vegetables. The fridge was mostly empty as well, except for a large bowl of egg salad that my mother most certainly did not make. Her longtime school aide and now general employee, Betty, must have been by earlier. There was also a partial loaf of white bread, part of a tomato, a small jar of peanut butter, and two apples.

I guess I was having cereal again for dinner. If nothing else, it had the advantage of being fast.

Apparently not finding what she was looking for, my mother settled herself on the other side of the table and waited until I'd poured milk on my cereal to ask, "Are you sure you wouldn't rather have a shower before you eat?"

Her timing, as always, was impeccable. As if I would abandon the already prepared cereal to shower now.

"This won't take long," I said as calmly as possible.

As soon as I'd taken the third spoonful, she asked, "So if Burnham wasn't killed by an intruder, then what happened?"

I filled her in between mouthfuls of the tasteless, high fiber, low flavor bran flakes she favored.

"I know what Mr. Montanaro wants to speak with you about." She cast a knowing glance in my direction. "He's going to make you an offer. Well, you be sure to snap it up this time. Don't let him leave that diner without a signature on a contract."

"That's not how it works. Montanaro probably has limited authority to act on Dr. Burnham's behalf, now that she's dead." I rubbed my forehead wearily and wrinkled my nose at the scent on my sleeve. Well past time for a shower and a fresh change of clothing.

"You need to make it work. You lost the clinic the first time because you weren't forceful enough. Don't lose it again." She stood up and smoothed the front of her pantsuit.

"Where are you going?" I asked as I chased the last flake of cereal around the bowl. Even though I was ravenous, I couldn't face a second helping.

"Trey and Randy were students of mine in middle school." She gave a deep sigh. "Their parents are going to be overwhelmed tonight. I thought I'd go and offer my help with the arrangements."

"Oh." I'd known in theory that she'd probably taught both kids when they were younger—she'd taught almost everyone in town at one point or another—but the reality of their deaths struck me afresh. "I'm so sorry. Give me a moment to freshen up and put on clean clothes, and I'll come with you."

"That's very thoughtful of you, dear, but not necessary. I'll be gone for several hours, and you have your own work to do this evening."

Whatever force field that held the appearance of eternal youth in place—her energy, her sheer force of will, Oil of Delay beauty products, whatever—slipped for a moment, and for the first time in my memory, my mother appeared to be an old woman. Just for a second. Then time blinked, and the shield was back in place.

"Be careful," I admonished, as she picked up her purse.

She gave me the oddest stare. "Why wouldn't I be?"

Yep. Everything was back to normal.

After she'd gone, I rummaged around the cupboards looking for something else to eat. I was always starving in my mother's house. There was probably a metaphor in there somewhere.

"You have it easy," I told Remy as I gave him a dog biscuit from the box I kept in the cupboard. "At least you'll never go hungry around here."

Apple slices slathered with peanut butter quieted my grumbling stomach. After I'd finished eating, I went upstairs to the spare room I'd been using, with Remy at my heels. When I opened the laptop, he jumped up on the bed with a sigh. He knew the routine. Once I got online, odds were good I was probably going to be there a while.

However, this time, instead of wasting time bouncing from site to site, I had a purpose in mind. I texted a good friend of mine, Michelle Seavey, and asked if she was available to Zoom with me. A few seconds later, she responded with a "Yes!" and a smiley emoji.

I set up the call, and when it went through, Michelle was sitting at her computer. Since I'd last seen her, she'd dyed her asymmetrical bob a vivid blue, and I exclaimed over the dramatic effect I'd never dare to pull off in Greenbrier. As we spoke, a fluffy orange and white cat leapt up to the desk and draped herself in front of the keyboard with a flick of her tail.

"Who is this?" I asked.

"That's Honey," Michelle said with a fond smile, stroking the cat as she spoke. Honey arched up into her touch, obviously enjoying the attention. "We recently adopted her."

"She's gorgeous. Very regal. I suspect she and Ming are having conference calls when no one is looking."

We laughed about that and caught up on each other's lives for a bit. Then I got down to the reason for my call. I'd told her about losing the practice to Burnham in an email back when it had happened, but Michelle was shocked when I related the events of the day.

"That's horrible," she exclaimed when I finished recounting everything: finding the body, Montanaro's insufferable attitude, and the state of things at the clinic.

"I didn't call you up just to be a shoulder to cry on," I said. "I need some of that Google Voodoo that you do so well."

Michelle and I had met during a medical conference nearly a decade ago, and despite living on opposite sides of the country, remained friends ever since. She worked for the Veterinary Resource Database, and as such, had access to information I'd never find on my own. She also had a gift for ferreting out facts. I'd often tagged her for difficult cases, and one of my proudest moments of collaboration with her was when we managed a treatment protocol on the fly for a hamster with wet tail. Kiki the Hammy had lived, despite all odds.

"I'm happy to help, but what do you hope to find?"

I explained about my fear that my mother and her friends might have contributed to Burnham's suicide.

Michelle sucked her breath in through her teeth. "You may be right. Online bullying is a serious problem for veterinarians, and one of the reasons the suicide rate is so high among the profession. It doesn't help that vets have easy access to lethal drugs."

"That's just it. I did some checking earlier today, and I couldn't find much of anything about Burnham on social media. Well, not before her death, that is."

Michelle shifted the cat to one side. Switching her focus from my face to her screen, her fingers flew over the keyboard as she typed. "Let's see ... I'll go back further. Rachel Burnham. A small mention of her buying the practice—that's in your own paper, the *Greenbrier Gazette*."

I nodded. The *Gazette* printed a weekly paper and maintained a low-key website for daily news.

"Okay, I'm pulling up the clinic's website now." Michelle shared the screen so I could see what she was looking at as well. "Looks like it's mostly about services offered and plans to expand. Not much about the staff."

"Given the recent changes, I'm not surprised."

"Huh," Michelle said, more to herself than to me. "No social media links for the site. Which is unusual. At the very least, you'd expect some kind of "follow us on Facebook!" kind of thing."

"Yeah, my mother said the same. But maybe Burnham didn't have the time. Her caseload was ridiculous, and I'm sure she had her work cut out for her modernizing the practice. Honestly, it's more than one person can do. If I was running GVC, I'd hire someone to manage the social media."

"Like your mother, perhaps?"

Michelle dropped the screen share to shoot me a foxy grin that made me forgive her for the suggestion.

"Perish the thought. Can you imagine how she'd handle a negative review? She'd torpedo the reputation of the clinic in a flame war."

"Speaking of reviews," Michelle added, and the screen changed views. "I'm pulling up the clinic pages from Google and Yelp. Oh, my. Yikes."

On screen, the page scrolled slowly. Initial reviews for GVC were mostly positive, with five-star reviews for the level of care and thoughtfulness of the staff. The most recent reviews, however, had taken a nosedive. Together, Michelle and I read some of the comments, which ranged from annoyed to vitriolic.

"Some of these comments are nasty, but hardly the kind of thing you kill yourself over. I mean, I've never even checked my own reviews. No one makes you look, right?" I said when we reached the end of the current ratings.

"You have a Facebook page for your business, right? Why doesn't she?" Michelle was scrolling so fast now, it almost made me dizzy. "No Facebook page as far as I can see."

A thought occurred to me. "Look up Olivia Cantrell. See if she has a profile."

We hit the jackpot there.

Olivia had posted in outraged detail about the Great Cat Mixup, and her post had hundreds of comments. I recognized the names of many of my own clients and members of the community among the dogpile. Some of their suggestions as to what should happen to Dr. Burnham were shocking. I felt sick reading them.

"Okay," I said, taking a shaky breath. "That makes a little more sense. But still, it's not like this stuff was on Burnham's own page. She didn't *have* to read it. She might never have known it was out there."

"Someone could have sent her a link. I wouldn't put that past some people." Michelle looked thoughtful for a moment. "Put another way, if you found out that there was something ugly posted about you online, wouldn't you check it out? Even if you had the sense not to respond to it, human nature would compel you to look."

She was right. Back in vet school, someone started an anonymous forum where students could complain about professors and classmates. Virtually everyone I knew had come under fire, including me. Against my better judgement, I'd gone to see what was being said, and some of the cutting remarks left scars I bore to this day. I'd laughed it off in public. After all, my mother had said worse to my face. But I wished I'd never peeked at the forum.

"But this would have blown over. In fact, it probably already has." Even as I tried to convince Michelle, I cringed at the vitriol behind the comments.

"Yeah, but these things tend to snowball, no pun intended. The next time someone is upset, they remember what happened to poor Snowball, and it concentrates their anger even more. Also, you don't know what kind of pressure Dr. Burnham was already under. Something like this could have been the final straw."

Her words made sense. Snapping my fingers, I said, "Can you look further back into Burnham's past? Before she came to Greenbrier. Maybe this isn't the first time she's had something like this happen to her."

"That's just it." The screen share stopped, and Michelle's frowning face appeared. "I can't find any mention of her before a few months or so ago. It's like she doesn't exist."

For a split second, the notion that Burnham was in WITSEC flashed to mind. Perhaps something in her past had caught up with her. Then I remembered what Joe had told me.

"She got divorced recently and changed her name. At least, that's what Joe said."

"Oh. Well, that's simple enough. Get him to tell you her married name and we'll go from there." Michelle leaned back in her seat and smiled when Honey stood, stretched, and jumped into her lap.

Shame heated my cheeks. "I don't think Joe would be amenable to sharing that information right now."

"Oh?" Michelle lifted a questioning eyebrow, looking like a severe, blue-haired Vulcan from *Star Trek* as she did so.

I told her what Joe had said. "The worst part is, he may be right," I concluded.

"Hold up there. Did you post horrible things about Dr. Burnham online? No. Did you run around whipping up hard feelings against her in town? No." Michelle's brow furrowed in anger. "I think Joe's being unfair to lay any blame for this at your feet."

Having someone in my corner made me feel a bit better. "In his defense, he'd had a terrible day. But the truth is, I didn't do anything to make things easier for Burnham either. And I bet my mother *did* go around stirring up trouble."

"You are not responsible for your mother's actions," Michelle said, not for the first time in our friendship. "As for not making things easier for Burnham, suppose instead of being about to buy a clinic you were getting married. Everyone in town knew you were engaged. You'd tentatively picked out a date. Then, out of nowhere, this other woman sweeps in and elopes with your fiancé. Would you then tell everyone to give her a chance because she might be a nice person? Would you show up at their place with a housewarming gift?"

"No." I snorted at the thought. "I'd be far more likely to egg their house in the middle of the night, only everyone would have a pretty good idea who was behind it."

"Give yourself a break," Michelle said calmly. "You had a major disappointment and you handled it with more grace than most people I know."

"Only because my mother has taught me not to waste time on fights you can't win."

"And because you go out of your way not to be anything like her. Sometimes too far. You *are* allowed to stand up for yourself, you know."

"I stand up for myself when it's important." Annoyance prickled in my voice.

"No one doubts that, not after the way you handled Amanda's ex-husband in the bar that night." Michelle grinned and I knew she was thinking of that embarrassing viral video. The last time I checked, it had over half a million likes. "But your line that no one should cross is practically at your feet. By the time someone hits it, you have no room for anything but to go ballistic. It wouldn't hurt to set your boundaries a little farther out, you know."

Remy sat up abruptly, jumped down off the bed, and rushed out of the room.

I glanced out the window and saw Joe's SUV crawling down the gravel drive.

"Hey, I've got to go. Looks like Joe is here."

"Joe the Sheriff or your friend Joe?"

Ugh. It was hard to say in which capacity Joe might be at the moment. My uncertainty must have showed on my face because Michelle added, "Maybe he's coming to apologize. Keep me posted. In the meantime, I'll keep poking around to see if I can find anything else about Dr. Burnham. Remember, set your boundaries!"

Keeping Michelle's advice in mind, I decided to meet Joe on the porch. Remy spoiled my attempt at cool indifference by wagging his tail so hard his entire back half swung from side to side. The sun wouldn't set until nearly eight p.m. but it felt even hotter than earlier in the day.

When Joe got out of the car, however, he didn't appear to be in a conciliatory mood. Dark aviator sunglasses blocked his hazel eyes from view, making it hard to read his expression.

"Is your mother at home?"

Not the words I expected.

"No."

I wasn't in a conciliatory mood either.

Joe's lips flattened and he nodded several times, as if he hadn't expected any other response.

"Your mother has several weapons, I believe," he said at last.

Weapons? As in plural?

Frowning, I responded, "To my knowledge, my mother only has the one gun: a long-barreled revolver."

A slight smile appeared. "I've seen that one. A little Colt Cobra. Blue metal finish? Practically an antique. I think they stopped making those in the early eighties. I'm not talking about a pocket pistol, though." The smile faded as though it had never been there. "She bought another gun more recently, however. An automatic. Something a little easier for her to handle, no doubt. A thirty-eight."

I'd been processing the fact my mother had a second gun I knew nothing about—something that had been a big point of contention during my dad's final days of dementia as she wasn't a believer in gun safes or the appropriate storage of said firearms. But then the implications of Joe's visit hit me.

"Hold on a minute. Why are you asking about her guns?" No sooner had I spoken then I answered my own question. "Wait, are you saying Burnham didn't kill herself? That she was murdered? And you think my *mother* had something to do with it?"

My voice had risen with every sentence until Remy cocked his head sideways at the pitch. Picking up on my tension, he whined and pressed his shoulder against my leg.

"I need to speak with your mother right away. Where is she?" Joe asked, working his jaw slightly with the effort of not saying anything more.

"She went to see the Detweilers," I said, biting off my words with a snap. Taking Remy by the collar, I went back in the house, letting the door slam behind us.

Chapter Ten

Once Joe had driven off, I called my mother. Naturally, she let her phone roll over to voice mail; if she didn't want to be disturbed, she wouldn't pick up, despite the fact I was supposed to be available to *her* night and day.

On my third attempt, she answered, her voice sharp with annoyance.

I bulldozed through her irritation. "Where are you?" I demanded.

"I'm just leaving the Cooks and am headed to the Detweilers now."

The way she yelled at the phone made me confident she was using the hands-free holder I'd gotten for her, which was one good thing about the evening so far. At least I didn't have to worry about her running into a ditch while talking on the phone.

"Joe is looking for you. He's asking questions about a .38 automatic. Is there something you want to tell me?"

There was a long pause before she said faintly, "I don't know what you mean."

"I mean that I have the strong impression that Burnham's death wasn't a suicide after all, and they want to talk to you about it." Truly pissed now, I rolled on. "They seem to think you have a second gun that you never told me about, and that somehow, this weapon seems to be important to the case. So, I'm asking you again, Mother. What's going on?"

"It's none of your business if I bought another gun. I have the right to purchase the means to defend myself!"

"From what? Killer groundhogs?" I asked. I knew better than to antagonize her, but I couldn't help it. The last time she'd fired a gun, it had been over a marauding whistlepig that kept eating her tomatoes in the garden.

"Yes, if necessary." She huffed a little. "I'll have you know, thanks to my superior marksmanship—"

I couldn't let that one slide.

"It was less than three feet away! You missed him with every shot!"

"That was a deliberate choice on my part," she said with great dignity. "I know how you feel about killing things, and I *chose* to miss my target."

"You almost shot me in the foot!"

"Ridiculous," she announced with icy disdain. "You were nowhere near the groundhog."

Which was kind of my point.

I repressed a loud sigh and wiped my face. Counting to five, I said, "I don't care that you bought another gun." It was a miracle lightning didn't strike me on the spot. "But for some reason, Joe is asking about it. That can only mean one thing; he must think Dr. Burnham was killed with your weapon."

Suddenly the ransacking of the drawers and cabinets came to mind. I pressed my forehead into my palm.

"Mother, have you *lost* your gun?"

"I know I had it the other night. It was in the glove compartment of my car." Words flowed out of her in a torrent. "But it's not there. I thought maybe I'd brought it inside, but I can't find it."

I made a fist and thumped my forehead several times.

"Okay, this is what we're going to do. I'm going to call Ethan Burrows and tell him to meet us at the sheriff's department." Ethan was the family lawyer. He'd probably be about as useful as a screen door in a submarine in this situation, but he was the best I could do on short notice. "You're going to go straight there, so you don't get picked up by one of the deputies. We'll tell Joe your gun went missing. When did you last see it?"

"Yesterday evening. I went to the church for the meeting about the literacy program."

Only my mother would think that it was necessary to pack heat to go to a church meeting.

"Which means you parked in the church lot off Main Street," I said. "Did you lock your car?"

"Did you not hear me? We met at the church."

"Right," I said firmly. "You didn't lock your car. Someone could have taken the gun out of the car at any point during the evening. How did it wind up with Dr. Burnham?"

There was a suspiciously long silence before my mother said, "I'm sure I don't know."

Have you ever watched any of those crime shows where the main character is good at reading people? Can spot a lie from a mile off, based on a choice of words or tiny alterations in someone's expression or voice?

The addition of the word "sure" to the sentence "I don't know" changes its meaning entirely.

"What aren't you telling me, Mother?"

"Oh dear." She sounded distracted, and a moment later, I found out why. "There's a deputy's car behind me flashing its lights. I have to go."

"Don't say anything without your lawyer," I shouted before she could disconnect the call. "We'll meet you at the sheriff's office."

As soon as she hung up, I called Ethan and told him what was going on, asking him to meet us downtown. He was decidedly unenthusiastic, but I wouldn't take no for an answer.

In the end, his services hadn't been needed. Joe tried to shut me out of the interview process, but my mother refused to answer any questions unless I was present. After reiterating that his specialty was really tax and estate law, Ethan had sat in his chair wearing a frown and saying little. Finding out the gun that had killed Burnham belonged to my mother didn't exactly come as a shock; given that it was missing, and Joe had been asking about it had been a dead giveaway, but my stomach twisted at the news just the same. And when questioned as to why her fingerprints were on the weapon along with Burnham's, my mother had observed with her usual acerbic bite that of *course*, her fingerprints would be there. It was her gun after all.

When asked how the gun had wound up in Burnham's possession, my mother had said, "I don't know. The only person who could answer that is Dr. Burnham herself."

She admitted to having lost track of the gun after she left it in her unlocked car. When Joe tried to push further, I interrupted. "There you are then. The worst you can charge my mother with right now is failure to safely secure her weapon." I glanced at my watch. "Unless you have any further questions, we all have better things to do."

The tic in Joe's jaw signaled that he wasn't happy with my intervention, but you know what? Tough noogies.

"We're done for the moment, but we may have further questions in the future." Joe sent a single, burning glance in my direction before he said smoothly, "Don't leave town, Mrs. Reese."

Needless to say, I didn't get a lot of sleep that night.

After leaving Joe's office, I'd met Deputy Holly at the clinic and performed my evening checks in near silence, not speaking unless I absolutely had to. This seemed to work for Holly as well, who'd said next to nothing herself, merely chewing gum like a placid cow. I'd gotten the distinct impression she was relieved by my silence, and suspected she'd been given orders not to discuss Burnham's death.

One could guess who'd issued them.

On returning home, I'd found a note from my mother waiting for me on the kitchen table. She was tired. She'd gone to bed. She didn't want to be disturbed. She had nothing further to say to me about Rachel Burnham.

I confess, I was relieved. Surprised, but relieved.

And a little suspicious to be perfectly honest. I'd fully expected to be up until all hours rehashing the day's events. Not one to look a gift horse in the mouth, I'd retreated to my own bedroom with the animals in hopes of getting some sleep.

Sleep was fragmented between spending far too much time staring at the ceiling and unpleasant dreams where I was trying to get someplace important only barriers kept leaping up in my way: flooded streams, boulders blocking the road, vines catching at my legs when I tried cutting through the dark, wet woods. I woke once with a start to find Remy licking my hand, and I buried my fingers in his soft fur, stroking him until my heart stopped pounding in my chest. It was a relief when my alarm finally went off.

Mother's door was still closed when I tiptoed past it. Ming's raucous meowing made me toss food at him and dash to the car with Remy before the noise woke her. After stumbling about in the dark feeding the animals at Amanda's place, I made my bleary way to Sue's diner. The delectable odor of frying meat, coupled with the heavenly scent of strong coffee, hit me as I pushed through the door of the diner.

I might just live after all.

Despite the early hour, all the seats at the counter were taken, and a good many of the booths were filled as well. Workers coming off shift from the arsenal in Goose Creek and the construction crews for the new subdivision were polishing off their breakfast plates, accounting for the early morning rush. The sweet smell of maple syrup awakened my hunger from the night before with a vengeance. I waved to those customers I recognized, but at that hour most people were concentrating on eating, so I snagged one of the last booths and sat down without having to start a conversation before my brain came online.

"You're here early," Kim said, yawning as she filled my coffee cup. "What'll it be?"

Poor Kim. She worked almost the same hours as Sue. During the summer, the staff expanded with high school students, but it was hard to find help that wanted the six-a.m. shift. I knew Sue was also on the lookout for a good short-order cook. I hoped she found someone soon.

I didn't need a menu. "Give me the Lumberjack special. Scrambled eggs, bacon, toast. No butter on the pancakes, please. Oh, and a glass of OJ."

"Mighty big appetite for someone who found a dead body yesterday," Kim said, not needing to write down my order.

"Still staying with my mom. You know how it goes." I shrugged and changed the subject. "I'm meeting Mr. Montanaro here shortly."

"I'll put your order in and send him back when I see him."

It wasn't like the diner was so large I'd miss him, but it was nice of her just the same.

While I waited for my food, I scrolled through my email. It was too soon to expect any word from Michelle, but I was still disappointed there was nothing in my inbox from her.

The bell over the door jangled, and I looked up to see Deb enter the diner. I waved to her, and she came over to slide in the seat across from me.

"Hey, what's up?" I asked, blowing on my coffee before taking a sip. Kim liked to keep the pots at volcanic temperatures.

"You're not usually here this early," Deb observed wryly. She was dressed for the heat to come, in a tank top that showed off her muscular arms, with her dishwater blonde hair pulled back in a ponytail. She wore cut-offs and heavy work boots, suitable for a day at the barn. "Let me guess, no food at your mom's house?"

"Only egg salad," I replied, making a face.

Deb looked amused. "But you hate egg salad."

"See?" I pointed emphatically at her. "Anyone who knows me knows that. What about you? What brings you here this morning?"

Deb yawned and rubbed her temples. "Taking some students to a combined test this weekend at Westfall Manor. Had to pick up some new hay nets and buckets from the feed store. Dad asked me to get breakfast for him."

I nodded. Westfall Manor put on a horse trial every summer. Eventing is a sport that features a single horse and rider combination competing over three different disciplines: dressage, cross-country, and stadium jumping. A combined test was a type of trial that featured only two of the three disciplines, in part because it took a lot of land to be able to host all three. Westfall was one of the few facilities in the area that had a cross-country course, and most of the local eventers tried to get there as a result.

Deb had been a surprise baby, born twenty years after her oldest brother. Like my own family, her siblings had moved away, leaving her eighty-five-year-old father in her care.

"It's too late for you to go to Westfall, but I'm headed to Lexington at the end of August." Deb's smile was sly as she added, "The cut-off for entering isn't until next weekend."

I shook my head. "I haven't been riding. Too hot. Maybe something in the fall."

Maybe when I wasn't worried about my mother being arrested for murder.

"I'm going to hold you to that. As for it being too hot, you could get up early and beat the heat."

As far as I was concerned, no such time existed. I just wasn't as tough as Deb. Truthfully, there'd been a time when I wanted to take my mare, Scotty, as far as I could as a competition horse. I'd dreamt of competing at recognized events, moving up through the levels, taking seminars with Olympic riding coaches, the works. These days, I just wanted to have fun. Which meant showing up at the local shows once a year and beating the pants off everyone. Scotty *rocked* at dressage and could clear a four-by-four oxer with ease. Her success was limited only by my lack of dedication as a competitive rider.

"Right now, I'm tied up with this situation at the clinic. I'm headed there now after breakfast," I said, reaching for another packet of sugar. Kim also liked to make the coffee strong enough to dissolve spoons.

"I heard you found the body. Pretty bad, huh?"

"You have no idea." I shuddered as the memory of Burnham lying face down on her desk sprang to mind, complete with the sharp tang of blood in the air. "I know you do the social media thing even less than I do, but you're tied into the sport dog community now. Have you heard any rumblings about Dr. Burnham? Angry clients, that sort of thing?"

Deb twisted her mouth to one side as she thought. "Actually, I've got a website and a Facebook account now."

"You do?" I was astonished. The only people more off-grid than Deb were the hippie-types in the commune on the other side of Goose Creek, or the die-hard local farmers in their eighties.

Deb's grin turned sheepish. "Yeah, since I'm adding dog training to the horse side of things, I needed to have a place where people could contact me. But I still don't spend any time on Facebook. I hate that site."

"Same here. But do me a favor, will you? If you run across anything, will you let me know?"

"Why?" Deb's eyes narrowed. "You don't think she was murdered, do you?"

"Heavens no." I waved off her suggestion, despite doubt trickling down my spine like drops of sweat. Just because my mother had picked a public fight with Burnham and later Burnham had been found dead with my mom's gun in her hand didn't mean it was murder. Right? If it was murder, I didn't *really* think my mother capable of killing someone, did I? "I'm just wondering why someone moves to a town where she has no connections, buys a practice—which is not cheap, by the way—and then commits suicide. I guess I'm trying to make sense of it."

"You're assuming she didn't bring her troubles with her. Most people do." Deb tipped her head to one side like a wise owl. "People seem to think that they can just start over in another place. But you tend to cart your baggage with you."

"Ain't that the truth."

However, Rachel Burnham had known at least one person in town. Joe.

"As for getting up early to ride, it's all I can do to finish my chores before going into the clinic for the next few days. If I got up any earlier, there would be no point in going to bed," I added. "I'm meeting the business manager here any minute now. I imagine he'll want to talk about me managing the current caseload until everyone is discharged from the hospital."

"Huh." Deb didn't sound impressed. "Make sure he pays you what you're worth."

Before I could respond to that, Kim headed in our direction with my food, and Deb stood up. "I'd better get my dad's breakfast before he starts calling looking for me. I'll let you know if I find anything out about Dr. Burnham, but don't hold your breath."

Deb waved to Kim on her way to the counter to pick up her takeout as Kim set her tray down on a nearby table and began unloading plates in front of me. I gave a happy sigh and reached for the little jug of maple syrup to drizzle on my pancakes. "Thanks, Kim."

I didn't wait on ceremony but snatched up a slice of crisp bacon and took a bite.

"You talking about Dr. Burnham?" Kim asked as she set the orange juice beside my plate.

"Hard not to, you know?"

And I didn't want to talk about her now. I wanted to tuck into my food while it was still hot.

"It must have been awful finding her like that. Was she all bloody?" Kim's avid expression suggested she might not have found the experience as terrible as I did. "Did you see a gun?"

The easiest way to get people to stop asking me about Burnham's death was to be clear how little I knew. Sooner or later, word would get out that my mother's gun was involved, but if I could put off that moment a little longer, I would.

"Once I realized she was dead—and there was no mistaking *that*—I hightailed it out of there and called the sheriff's department. I couldn't really tell you what was in the office besides Dr. Burnham slumped over her desk."

Kim looked disappointed. "You don't have any idea how she killed herself?"

I closed my eyes, which proved to be a mistake when I pictured Burnham again. "All I can say is there was a lot of blood."

"So, she used a gun, then." Kim nodded as though this was the only solution that made sense. "Clearly, she didn't hang herself, or you'd have mentioned it. And there wouldn't be any blood if she'd injected herself with pentobarbital or overdosed on pills. Though that would have been a better way to go, don't you think? Nice and quiet, just go to sleep in her own bed, maybe with an alcohol chaser..."

I must have looked at Kim as though she'd sprouted a couple of extra heads, like a peroxided version of Cerberus, the three-headed dog. "Where on earth did you hear about pentobarbital?"

Pentobarb is traditionally used as part of euthanasia protocols for pets, but it wasn't the sort of thing the average person knew by name, and certainly not someone like Kim, who as far as I knew, didn't even own a goldfish.

"*Greenbrier after Dark*. It's a podcast. You haven't heard of it?" Kim looked over her shoulder at one of the construction workers who was trying to catch her attention. "I'll be right there."

"Someone's doing a podcast about Greenbrier? I'd think most weeks they'd have little to say." I adopted a narrator's voice. "Dave Henley's Holstein, known for her ability to jump a three-strand barbed wire fence in a single bound, was seen eating the flowers on the Main Street window boxes again. Meanwhile, join us for our exciting segment on watching paint dry."

I made a little puddle of syrup on one side of my plate and pushed a forkful of pancake into it. Pancakes soggy with syrup were disgusting in my book.

Kim picked up her tray. "Are you kidding? There's a lot more going on than you think around here. Who's been arrested, where the meth houses are, all that controversy about the new subdivision ... Amanda Kelly's murder—and your inheritance of her estate—was the main topic for over a month."

I paused with my fork partway to my mouth. "Me? The subject of a podcast?"

Kim's face split into a wide grin, making her look younger than her actual age. "Especially after that viral video."

There was no way to hide my face with a fork in my hand, so I sighed and continued eating.

"You should check it out. I'm sure they'll do another episode on you since you found the body." Kim broke off to call back to the impatient customer, who'd signaled her again. "Keep your shirt on. I said I'd be right there."

She stomped off to attend the rest of the patrons.

The bell over the door rang again as Montanaro entered the diner. He paused at the entrance, seemingly taken aback by the crowd, until he spotted me and made his way over. He looked out of place in his expensive suit, leather briefcase in hand and wearing dark sunglasses. Those he removed as he sat down and placed them on the table between us. He eyed my breakfast spread and said, "That's a lot of food for one person. You must be hungry."

I smiled sweetly at him. I'd grown up hearing my mother comment about my eating habits my entire life, and his comments were benign by comparison. "I *am* hungry. And if you reach for a slice of bacon, I'll stab you."

I made several jabbing motions with my fork.

He gave one of those uncertain laughs, the kind that said he couldn't tell if I was joking or not but thought it best to believe that I was.

"I can call Kim over to take your order," I said.

"No need. Coffee will do for me. You don't mind if we get down to business, do you?" He snapped his fingers in the air in Kim's general direction, gesturing for her to come over when he caught her attention. He turned away before he saw the look of outraged incredulity on her face.

Without acknowledging her presence as she poured him a cup of coffee, he began speaking. "As you know, we have to do something about the clinic. What's the status of the patients there?"

He was oblivious of the hard glare Kim shot at him when she'd topped off his mug.

I thanked her instead, lifting my eyebrows and making a face when she made eye contact. She snorted softly and said, "You're welcome, Ginny," laying sarcastic stress on the first word in her sentence.

Montanaro in the meantime had taken a sip of coffee, grimaced, and was in the process of dumping large quantities of sugar and cream into his mug when Kim left us. He finished doctoring his drink, took another sip, and then watched me eat as though I were the lead carnivore in a nature documentary: with equal parts fascination and revulsion.

I could have told him a lifetime of dining out with my mother had made me impervious to being guilted out of eating something I'd already ordered. I was, however, glad I'd started without him. Between bites, I caught him up on the status of the hospitalized patients. Barring any setbacks, I planned to discharge Pirate and Tiffany within the next twenty-four hours. Ironically, it was the healthy boarders that posed the biggest problem, as their owners were out of town. We hadn't been able to reach all of them, either.

It didn't take me long to finish my breakfast, and I stacked my empty plates on the corner of the table with their silverware, to make it easier to bus the table later.

I concluded with my round-up, "So, I can continue to oversee the animals remaining at the clinic until their owners return to pick them up, but I have my own clientele to take care of as well. If the building wasn't off-limits to the public, I could meet some of my clients at the clinic, but there's no telling when the police will release the scene. I'm assuming they won't let anyone else in the building to take care of the boarders except those who have been cleared, like me."

Especially if they were starting to question if it was suicide or not.

That reduced me to kennel help, but unless Montanaro balked at paying for my time, his only other alternative was to ask Amber or Erin to take care of the boarders, and I had mixed feelings about that. If any of the boarders ran into trouble during the remainder of their stay, they would need veterinary care.

"It will jam up my schedule, but I can manage going to the clinic three times a day to feed, water, and clean up after the boarders." That was an understatement, but I had to let him know caring for the remaining patients was more than just popping in twice a day to make sure they had food. "What's going to happen to the clinic in the long run? Do you know?"

Montanaro aimed his megawatt smile at me and said, "That's why I wanted to speak with you. I'd like to discuss the future of Greenbrier Vet Clinic."

I frowned at him. Wasn't he overstepping his rights?

"Er, isn't that a matter for Dr. Burnham's heirs to decide? I have to tell you, I'm not likely to be able to afford to buy the practice at the price Dr. Burnham paid for it."

While I didn't want another vet taking over, I refused to shell out the difference Burnham had offered to scoop the business out from under me.

Montanaro's smile took on an air of pleased secrecy, like the Grinch when he'd formulated his evil plan to sweep into Whoville disguised as Santa Claus. He leaned forward as though sharing something private, just between the two of us.

"Dr. Burnham's heirs don't come into it because she wasn't the owner of the business. We are." He placed his briefcase on the table in a smear of syrup, but there didn't seem a great need for me to point that out. He popped the clasps on the case and took out a brochure. The shiny trifold paper featured a beaming veterinarian holding a spaniel puppy as she stood in front of a sparkling veterinary clinic. Above her head a banner read, "Welcome to CVC!"

I didn't take the offered brochure.

"Champion Veterinary Corporation? *You* bought the clinic?" Indignation raised the pitch of my voice several octaves. "No wonder Burnham was able to offer so much money. What was she, your shill?"

Montanaro frowned and, glancing about, flapped his hand a few times in a gesture for me to lower my voice. "It's a perfectly acceptable business practice. Most young veterinarians graduate with too great a debt load to be able to buy into a clinic. They spend half their working lives paying off their student loans before they can even consider running their own practice. With CVC, you are still your own boss, but have the benefits of being part of a franchise. I want to make that same offer to you, Dr. Reese. It's a mutually beneficial arrangement, and you know it."

"If it was such a reasonable, standard business practice, then why not say so up front? Why hide behind Dr. Burnham?"

I folded my arms across my chest and waited for an answer.

Montanaro took another sip of coffee and made a tsking sound. "Come now, Dr. Reese. We're both adults here. You know as well as I do, it's all about perception. Your 'Doc' Smith isn't just a highly respected member of the community, he's a veritable institution around here."

The finger quotes Montanaro made around the word "Doc" caused me to bristle.

"Then there was the expectation that you, his protégé, would take over the business." Montanaro shook his head with practiced sadness. "Anyone coming in behind this would find it a tough act to follow. Big shoes to fill."

I waited him out on the cliches. When I said nothing, he continued, "Dr. Burnham gave a face to CVC's purchase of Greenbrier. Humanized it. With time, we would have gone public with the connection. Within a couple of months. That's our policy when transitioning clinics in sensitive situations. People in smaller communities such as this one need time to adapt to change."

"Are you saying we're all local yokels here?"

He traced the rim of his coffee cup, chuckling to himself without meeting my glare. "Of course not. We're just being practical in setting up the new owner for the best chance of success."

Tempted as I was to ask him how that had turned out for Burnham, I clamped my lips over the snide remark before it slipped out. My dad always used to say, "Don't burn your bridges until you're sure you don't want anything on the other side of the river." Growing up in a river town, my dad's version of the truism always made a lot of sense to me.

Montanaro took a sheaf of papers out of the briefcase and pushed them across the sticky surface of the table toward me. "We'd like to make you the same offer we made Dr. Burnham. Become a franchise owner when you buy into the clinic but start out with a salary of over seventy K a year. Most business owners can't pay themselves a salary for the first couple of years when they open a practice. As part owner of the clinic, you'll continue to reap the benefits when at some future date, you sell to another CVC associate. You'll also be able to draw on CVC employee lists to staff the clinic with additional practitioners when you expand. You'll have a stable of relief vets to call on when you want to take time off. You *can* take time off. As much as you like! Not to mention you'll have the weight—and financing—of the corporation behind you when it comes to bringing Greenbrier Veterinary Clinic into the twenty-first century. Access to stellar lab equipment. The finest supplies at contracted prices. Healthcare and benefits for the entire staff. You know you'd have trouble providing all of that if you had to do it on your own. I'm aware you inherited money, but do you really want to spend it all on buying and rebuilding this practice as an independent practitioner? You could have the best of both worlds here."

He reached across the table as though he might take my hands and I instinctively withdrew, struggling to hide my disgust in the process. The problem was, in many ways he was right. I'd been a vet for nearly twenty years, and I'd never come close to bringing home the kind of paycheck he offered. Certainly not in Greenbrier. The very disadvantages to being a solo practitioner he'd listed were among the fears that had kept me up late at night trying to decide what I wanted to do. Had my doubts come through to Doc? Had that been why he decided not to wait for me any longer but took Burnham's deal?

"I'm listening," I said slowly.

I feel certain Satan had the same expression on his face when Eve paused to glance at the proffered apple.

Montanaro indicated the papers on the table. "That's a standard NDA. Sign it, and I can share with you the details about what it means to be a CVC associate." He leaned back and spread his hands, palms up. "Until then, this discussion is all theoretical. I've disclosed all I can at this time. Speaking of the time," he paused to glance at his smartwatch, and then looked up at me with a self-satisfied smirk. "We both need to be going."

He took out a pen from the inside of his suit, clicked it, and handed it to me.

With a feeling of deep reluctance, I took the pen from him and pulled the papers over to read them. As he'd said, it was a standard non-disclosure agreement, which prohibited me from sharing the details of CVC's business model.

"Signing this doesn't mean I'm committing to being a franchise partner," I said, clicking the pen several times as I looked over the documents.

"Quite right." Montanaro became quite expansive now, learning back to rest one arm behind him on the back of the booth. "But CVC reserves the right to keep their operating protocols private as proprietary information. I'm sure you understand."

I didn't really, but I wasn't going to learn more without signing the NDA. I brought the papers closer to me and signed the forms.

When I handed them back, it felt as though I'd sold my soul to the devil.

Chapter Eleven

BREAKFAST SAT LIKE A lead weight in my stomach as I headed toward the clinic. It didn't help that Montanaro had given me a thick binder of CVC guidelines that he'd asked me to read. He'd wanted to meet again that evening to go over the details of the offer CVC was making me, and suggested I join him at the Mossy Creek B&B where he was staying so we could discuss the matter in private.

The thought of meeting Montanaro in his room at the B&B had made my skin crawl.

"I have to meet Deputy Holly at the clinic this evening for treatments. Perhaps you could join me there when I've finished taking care of the patients for the night? We could grab a bite to eat at *Calliope's*."

If it was after dark, I wouldn't have to take Remy home first. I preferred to keep bringing him with me, if possible.

Montanaro hadn't been happy about the change in plans, but I was already stretched to the limit with all the running around I had to do. The last thing I wanted as a little tête-à-tête all the way out in Mossy Creek.

I still felt as though I needed a shower.

On my way back to my car, a little red hatchback pulled up in front of Montanaro as he crossed the parking lot. He seemed reluctant to stop at first, but then leaned in the open window to speak to the driver. I couldn't see who he was talking to, but the car could have been Amber's. Asking about the status of her employment, perhaps? Who knew?

Remy was highly disappointed that I didn't bring him anything from the diner and sniffed me thoroughly when I rejoined him in the car. Since I'd never give him anything greasy to eat, I'm not sure where the disappointment stemmed from, but a dog's hope always springs eternal when it comes to food.

Deputy Holly was waiting for us at the clinic, and I felt my own sense of disappointment before I reminded myself that the Sheriff had better things to do that babysit someone at a crime scene. Besides, I was still mad with him, right? No, it was best that I *didn't* see Joe just then.

Remy greeted Holly like a long-lost friend, and to my embarrassment jumped up on her, causing her to release her breath with an 'ooof' of surprise.

"I am *so* sorry." I hauled Remy from her with a stern "off" command. "He knows better. Really. Believe it or not, he passed his Canine Good Citizenship test."

"I don't mind." Holly ruffled his ears while Remy wriggled with glee, his tongue hanging out his mouth like a roll of salami. "He's just being friendly."

"I mind though. Can you imagine if he barreled into my mother like that? He'd break something."

"I'm sure it would never cross his mind to jump on your mother." Holly's snort was not very ladylike. "She would quell him with a single glare."

She had a point.

To my surprise, Holly then offered to help take care of the boarders.

"You don't have to do that, though that's really nice of you. Pretty sure scooping poop isn't in your job description."

She grinned at that. "Yours neither, I suspect. But the way I see it, the sooner we take care of the animals, the sooner we both get out of here."

I couldn't argue with that logic, and so accepted the help.

Jaeger, a big yellow Lab who spent most of his time leaping up and down in his run like a deranged jackhammer, had gotten an upset stomach. I prescribed something to settle his gastrointestinal tract, surprised that more of the boarders hadn't done the same in such a high-stress environment. Reducing the numbers in the clinic no doubt had helped with that. I was pleased to see that Tiffany was eating her bland diet without any further signs of pancreatitis. Pirate was also doing well, having used the litterbox normally. He'd been unhappy and not eating until I'd provided him with a cardboard box to hide in. During the night, he'd eaten his prescription food and was even purring when I opened the cage to check on him.

Once I was finished with the rounds, I called both Tiffany's and Pirate's owners to let them know they could come pick up their pets.

Mrs. Oberstein's voice was tremulous with either age or emotion when I contacted her.

"Oh, thank you my dear. You're so good to us." She paused for a moment, then went on breathlessly. "I'm afraid Pirate will have to stay at the clinic a bit longer. My daughter, Karen, says she can't come pick him up until Monday at the soonest. And it will have to be after 5 p.m. Her job is quite demanding, you know."

Having a demanding job myself, I was pretty sure I did know. I also knew that Karen was a schoolteacher, and her classes were out for the summer.

I had to think about how best to phrase my next question. "Mrs. Oberstein, you're not going into the hospital any time soon, are you? You're doing okay?"

"Oh yes." Her voice steadied as she went on, "I'm doing fine. I just don't drive anymore, you know."

"Well, at this point, I think Pirate would be better off in his own home. He's eating his special diet and urinating normally. He actually likes his medication, so I don't think you'll have trouble giving it to him. If you think you can take care of him, I'll drive him out to your place later today."

"Oh, would you mind? I hate asking you do to that, but I've missed him so much."

I could picture her clasping her hands with joy.

"It's no trouble at all. As a matter of fact, you'd be doing me a big favor. With Dr. Burnham's death, we're trying to send as many patients home as possible, and I think he's ready."

"Oh dear." She faltered again. "I'm not sure I have the money to pay his bill until the first of the month. That's when my social security check comes in."

"Don't you worry about that right now. The most important thing is getting Pirate home."

I rang off, only to find Holly watching me from the treatment room door.

"You're a real softie when it comes to little old ladies, aren't you?" Her smile suggested she'd caught me in the act of committing a crime.

"Because I know I'll be a little old lady someday." I sighed as I opened Pirate's record. Fortunately, most of his charges hadn't been invoiced yet, and I would be able to slash his fees.

"Softie," Holly repeated, patting Remy on the head. "You sure you want to be in charge of the clinic? You'll probably be bankrupt within a year."

"Doc did all right for himself," I said sharply.

"Doc has a strong practical streak as well as a big heart." Holly looked around the treatment area. "What's next?"

With Holly's help, it had only taken me about an hour to care for the patients still in the clinic. We arranged to meet around lunchtime and again at eight p.m. or so. My own patient schedule had been freed up in anticipation of filling in at GVC while Dr. Burnham was out of town, but I still had my own clients to call and messages to answer. Had I not known Deb was off to Westfall Manor in the morning, I'd have asked her to feed the animals at Amanda's just to reduce the amount of running around I had to do, but her schedule would be even crazier than mine for the next twenty-four hours.

Pausing only long enough to fire off a text to Michelle seeking any information on the Champion Veterinary Corporation, I decided it was best to head back to my mother's house until time to meet Holly again. As soon as I hit "send", I winced. I'd forgotten the time difference. Hopefully, Michelle wouldn't hear the text alert until a reasonable time on her end. Meanwhile, I would look over the Hospital Policy Handbook Montanaro had given me, as well as find out the status of the gun situation.

No sooner had I pulled up at the house, then my text alert went off. It was Michelle. I let Remy out of the car and sat with the driver's side door open, hoping for a breeze as I picked up the phone.

What do you want to know about CVC?

I typed as quickly as I could.

Turns out they own the clinic. Burnham just a front. They want to offer same deal.

Her response was almost immediate.

WTH??

I snorted at that and typed some more.

Supposed to meet with Monty tonight. Had to sign NDA to even discuss.

She practically screamed her reply.

DON'T SIGN ANYTHING ELSE!!

If the all-caps hadn't caught my attention, the emphatic punctuation would have. I would have defended my decision, but another text came through.

Much to say on this. Too much to text. Call me later.

I glanced at my watch. With the three-hour time difference, I hadn't expected her to respond to my text so quickly, and I felt bad for contacting her so early. Regardless, I should probably talk to her before I met with Montanaro this evening.

Will do, I texted.

Seeing that my mother was out when I entered the house, I made myself a cup of coffee and sat down with the CVC employee's manual. I needed room to open the heavy binder and spread it out on the kitchen table.

Remy made a beeline for Ming, who was sleeping on the settee near the back door. After swiping the cat's head with several licks from his tongue, Remy oozed onto the settee as well, causing Ming to growl as he refused to shift over to make room for the large dog moving into his space.

"Sort it out, you guys," I cautioned as I began flipping through the book. I skimmed the first bit, which was largely an ode to the wonders of working for CVC and how signing with them would make all your professional dreams come true. The accolades even implied being a CVC associate would fulfill all your personal dreams, too.

I'd just worked my way through the mission statement and had begun the first of the treatment protocols when my cell chimed. Another unknown caller. With a sigh, I picked up.

"Ginny Reese here."

"Dr. Reese? This is Carolyn Price. Amber Hanson gave me your number."

Carolyn's voice was like warm honey, syrupy and sweet.

"Of course." I crossed over to the coffeemaker to pour myself another cup. "I imagine you're calling to see when the clinic might open back up."

"I thought you might know."

I added a dash of milk to my mug, replaced the carton in the fridge, and carried the coffee back to the kitchen table. "Unfortunately, no word yet. They're allowing me inside under supervision and with restricted access to take care of the patients. But even if they release the scene, there's no saying when there will be another vet there to see animals. I wouldn't count on the clinic being open for business any time soon."

"Darn it." The sound of her heavy sigh blew through the phone's speaker. "I was afraid of that. Which shuts me down completely in the meantime. My clients schedule their appointments six to eight weeks out. This is going to upset a lot of people."

"I hear you," I said with sympathy. "I don't suppose you can operate out of your home for a while?"

"I wish." Carolyn's laugh was bitter. "I don't have the zoning, so I even if I had the set-up to groom here, I can't legally run a business out of my house. Even so, I could probably get away with it if it weren't for my next-door neighbor. She's always looking for something to complain about, and she'd be happy to report me if she caught me operating a business in a residential area."

"I've been through zoning hassles myself, so I get where you're coming from."

"I've been saving for a mobile van, but those things cost a fortune. By the time I pay out forty percent of my income to rent space in somewhere, there's not much leftover to invest back into my own business."

"Forty percent!" That seemed excessive to me. "But you're only making what? Fifty or sixty dollars a pet in the first place, right?"

That was a lot of scissoring and nail trims.

"Tell me about it. At least Donnie gets health insurance through the foundry. I'm covered on his policy. But no sick days, no paid vacation for me."

"I'm so sorry to hear this. Can you get your old slot at the pet store back again if you need to?"

"Maybe. If I grovel a bit. They only took a thirty percent cut, so perhaps this isn't such a bad thing after all." She sounded more resigned than angry now. "When I moved my business to Greenbrier, I thought having Dr. Burnham taking a bigger cut of my wages would be offset by less wear and tear on the car, and in gas money. More convenient for my clients, too. But it seems like I made even less money than before."

"Did you ever think about leaving? I got the impression tensions ran high the last few days."

"You're not just whistling Dixie," Carolyn said with a laugh. "You could cut the tension with a knife. I probably would have left, only I signed a non-compete contract. Can't work as a groomer anywhere within seven miles of the town limits for two years."

Whoa. That was a heckuva non-compete. And for a groomer? That was more restrictive than most clauses for veterinarians. Something else to think about if I was considering signing a contract with CVC. If things fell apart, I could find myself prohibited from working anywhere in my own hometown.

"That seems a bit strict," I said slowly.

"That's what Donnie said. You're both right, but I didn't see as I had much choice." She made a *tsking* noise through her teeth and said, "Anyway, that's neither here nor there now. I've got to come by the clinic and pick up my grooming kit."

"Er, I don't know if that's allowed. In fact, I'm pretty sure they won't let anything other than pets and their medications leave the clinic right now." I hated being the bearer of more bad news, but my hands were tied. "You probably need to call the sheriff's department."

"Are you kidding me?" The syrup in her voice hardened into resin. "Bad enough I'm out of work but I can't afford to replace my equipment, too. Do you know that Montanaro creep tried to tell me my tools belonged to the clinic? The grooming table alone set me back six hundred dollars, and it was another three hundred for the power dryer. To say nothing of my shears and clippers."

"Yikes," I said in sympathy. "Can you prove what belongs to you?"

"You bet your booty I can," Carolyn snarled. "I have receipts."

"Good. I'd call the sheriff's department and lay claim to your stuff now. Once Montanaro gains access to the clinic again, who knows what will happen?"

"Wait." Suspicion darkened her voice. "Do you know something I don't about what's going to happen with the clinic next?"

"No, no," I said, hoping I didn't sound too insincere. "Just reasonable speculation, that's all."

I ended the call with the promise to let her know if I heard anything. It certainly seemed that Burnham's death caused more problems for Carolyn than they solved, but with any luck, her contract with GVC was now void.

I went back to reading the binder. I hadn't gotten more than a third of the way through it before my eyes began to glaze over, and I decided it was a more reasonable time to call Michelle.

She picked up on the third ring.

"Hey, hope I'm not bothering you, but I've been reading the employee manual, and I think I know why you didn't want me to sign anything with CVC," I said by way of greeting. "They are ... quite strict ... aren't they?"

"You don't know the half of it. Corporations like CVC own approximately ten percent of all vet clinics in the country right now, and something like fifty percent of all referral clinics. I think as more veterinarians look to retire, we'll see an even bigger proportion of clinics being bought out by chains."

"Montanaro said it was because so few graduating vets are in a position to open their own clinics or buy into an existing one." I turned another page, struck by the rigidity of CVC's operating rules. "I can believe that. Most millennials are struggling to make ends meet regardless, and that's not counting the ridiculously high student loan debt the average new graduate carries."

"Right?" Michelle's annoyance came through loud and clear.

"I don't know how to say this without violating the NDA, but the organization's operating protocols are very specific."

Michelle snorted at that. "I wouldn't be too concerned about the NDA. There's an anonymous forum in the Veterinary Resource Database where people can vent about any number of things. There are quite a few threads dedicated to the problems with working for a chain vet practice. Without naming names, it's pretty clear which organization most people are talking about. Let me guess, it's the patient treatment protocols that are bugging you, right?"

As though she'd released a dam, the words flooded out of me. "There's a written protocol to follow for every conceivable situation. Every case must be approached diagnostically in the same way! There is no room for doctor judgement. It doesn't matter if your patient is visibly battling a flea infestation, you can't just prescribe flea control and treat any secondary problems. Come on, a fungal culture and biopsy on every skin case? Medicated shampoo regardless if the owner can bathe the dog or not? Pricey fatty acid supplements bearing the CVC brand name and marked up fifty percent over cost? And don't get me started on the vaccine protocols! Do you mean to tell me a Walker hound used for bear hunting and a tiny Chihuahua that never actually touches the grass both need every vaccination in the book? There shouldn't be a one-size fits all approach when it comes to vaccination plans."

Michelle's chuckle grew quite evil. "I'm guessing you're unaware of the contests CVC holds within the organization. The clinic that sells the most vaccine packages gets an all-expenses paid trip to Cancun. Every employee. That sort of thing."

"Ugh. I want to throat-punch someone. Aren't there any allowances for veterinary experience?"

"My understanding is that if you deviate from the protocol, you have to justify it to management. Too many deviations, and they penalize you monetarily. But playing devil's advocate for a moment, they argue that standardized protocols allow them to move doctors from one practice to another almost seamlessly. Plug and play veterinary medicine." Michelle's sigh was clearly audible. "Please tell me you aren't considering taking this Monty guy up on his offer."

It was my turn to sigh. I pushed my hand through my short hair, making it stand up on end. "I'm not sure I have any choice here. They already own the practice. They're going to install another vet in there one way or another. Maybe it makes sense for it to be me, so I can mitigate some of the damage it will do."

"You're deluding yourself if you think that will happen. Once you sign, they will control every aspect of how you run your practice. Not to mention, that high salary they offer? It's based on a production model. You only get paid that amount if you hit target productivity goals. I bet he told you that taking time off wasn't an issue, right? Well, it isn't as long as you hit your goals. Heck, you get penalized for taking a lunch break on this system."

I thought of the way the clinic had been jammed with animals, many of which hadn't needed to be there. What if that had been an attempt to make some sort of financial quota?

"What's weird is that CVC bought the Greenbrier clinic in the first place," Michelle said, without waiting for my response. "Normally they don't buy solo practices. They want at least two vets in place."

"Maybe that's how the clinic was represented to them." The more I thought about it, the more likely it seemed. "After all, I worked there at least a few days a week. They could have crunched the numbers based on that."

"Well, either way, I think you should stay clear of them. You don't need their money. Remember that." I could hear Michelle typing in the background. "I've got to get back to work but I'll do some more digging. Still haven't found anything on Dr. Burnham yet, but I have a few ideas as to where to look. The weird thing is, even with the name change, I should be able to find *some* link to her former name. I swear, if I didn't know better, I'd say her internet presence has been scrubbed."

"People can do that?" I asked in disbelief.

"For a pretty penny. It's not something the average person can do, however, so I doubt that's what's happened in this case."

We ended the call, leaving me to think about what she'd said. No, I didn't need the money, but I could go through the reserves of Amanda's estate pretty quickly if I bought GVC. Even more if I built my own practice from the ground up.

Did I really want to do that? One of the reasons I'd been toying with my own clinic was to better serve the town while decreasing the amount of time I spent on the road, and with the hope of hiring an associate to share the workload. But if the Champion Veterinary Corporation had established themselves as the animal care center in the area, there was nothing to say I had to work at all.

Nothing except it wasn't in the Reese family nature to be idle. Nothing except the gnawing guilt I would feel if my clients had no other options than to pay the inflated fees at the only show in town.

The cell chimed, loudly announcing the approach of the Wicked Witch of the West.

"What's up, Mother?" I asked when I picked up the call.

"I'm only allowed one phone call, so I made it to you. I knew you'd answer," my mother said without preamble. "I've been arrested for the murder of Dr. Burnham."

Chapter Twelve

I MIGHT HAVE BROKEN the current land-speed record on my way to the sheriff's office.

As usual, however, my mother had been exaggerating.

"We haven't arrested her," Joe said when I blew into his office, breathing fire. "We're merely holding her for questioning."

"Based on what grounds?"

Joe indicated the chair across from his desk, which I took with barely contained fury. He sat down in his own chair and picked up a pencil from a notepad on his desk. He rolled it between his fingers and tapped it on his notebook a few times before speaking. "Before I get into that, I have a few questions for you as well."

That took me aback. I recognized his casual interview mode from the time he'd questioned me about Amanda's death. Relaxed, conversational. A discussion between friends.

It was the playing with the pencil that gave him away. The tap-tap-tap of the pencil on his notepad underscored the tension he tried to mask.

"I've already given you a statement about finding Dr. Burnham."

He nodded. "Yes, but I'd like to know more about how you were hired in the first place."

"What can I say?" I held up my hands, palms outward. "She needed someone to cover for her while she went out of town. It's not like there are that many people she could have called on to fill in."

"I suppose not," Joe agreed. "Any idea why she had to go out of town?"

"She didn't tell you?" I lifted an eyebrow. "She said it was your idea to call me."

"Really?" The pencil hovered over the pad a moment, then resumed tapping. "She didn't talk to me about this trip. If we discussed your covering the clinic at all, it was more in general terms. Did she tell you where she was going?"

I narrowed my eyes with a slight purse of my mouth. "It's not like we were BFFs. She didn't say, and I didn't ask." Remembering Montanaro's outrage the morning of her death, I added, "Check with Montanaro. He was looking for her yesterday morning. Said she was supposed to meet him and hadn't shown up."

"Yes. So he said."

I just stared at Joe. If he'd already spoken to Montanaro, then he had to know what the out-of-town meeting had been about. Something to do with a Board. Perhaps in relation to CVC's ownership of the clinic? Either way, Joe wasn't looking for answers. He was looking for *my* answers.

I sat in silence and waited for him to break it.

When he did, it wasn't what I expected.

"Can you tell me what you were doing the night before last? Say, between eight and ten p.m.?"

"Tuesday night?" I frowned as I thought about it. I know I'd taken advantage of the fact my mother had gone out. "I got home around seven thirty or so. I ordered takeout from the Chinese place and had it delivered."

I checked my phone. "They texted me at ten after eight to say they were almost there. I probably met them at the door by eight-fifteen at the latest." I kept scrolling through my alerts. "Okay, the Hursts called around eight-forty to say they desperately needed a refill of JuJu's seizure medication, as they were headed to the airport first thing in the morning. I had to drop everything and call the pharmacy before they closed. You can check with Mabel. She said in no uncertain terms she wasn't staying one minute past nine p.m., as her drive home took her nearly an hour."

Joe made a note. "Will do. What about from eight-forty-five on?"

"Let's see, after I finished eating—" I broke off when I recalled I'd colored my hair. Nothing major, mind you. Just a little boost of its natural red, which tended to fade in the summer's sun. But Joe didn't need to know that.

He latched onto my hesitation just the same. "Yes? You did what?"

"Girl stuff," I said repressively. Watching his face contort as he tried to figure out what that meant was a bonus.

"Anyone who can vouch for your whereabouts? Any other phone calls with clients?" A hint of a smile crossed his features and the tapping of the pencil stilled for a moment.

No doubt he recalled the last time he interviewed me regarding a suspicious death, and I was saved by virtue of the fact I'd been enticing an evil chihuahua out of a hole in a wall at the time in question.

I shook my head. "Quiet night for a change. I caught up on emails and Netflix."

"I suppose if necessary, we can get a warrant to go through your streaming history. Though a good prosecutor would contend that you could have turned on the TV and left the house. I will, of course, be verifying your statement."

My mouth fell open and I began to sputter.

Joe, however, acted as though he'd said nothing out of the ordinary. "What about your mother? Where was she during this time?"

"As she already told you, she had a meeting at the church. She was gone when I got home and didn't return until sometime after ten. Not long after, but I'm not sure of the exact time." I leaned forward, slightly grinding my teeth. "I've answered your questions. Now you answer mine. Was Dr. Burnham murdered?"

Joe tossed the pencil down and his lips flattened almost to the point of disappearing. "There are inconsistencies with the positioning of Rachel's fingerprints on the gun. We also found a little piece of latex in the gun's slide, which suggests someone was wearing disposable gloves when it was fired. Then there's the question of how Rachel came to have your mother's gun in the first place."

"Anyone could have taken it from her car."

"Someone would have had to know it was there to begin with. And somehow, Rachel gained control of it." He leaned back in his seat and rubbed his face with both hands. "That's my big stumbling block, Ginny. If Rachel committed suicide, how did she get her hands on your mother's gun? Explain that to my satisfaction, and I'll release your mom."

"I'll do just that," I said, standing up to glare down at him.

He lifted a hand in a gesture of abeyance. "Hold up there. I didn't mean for you personally to explain it. You know what I mean. Look, the last time you got involved in an investigation, you nearly got yourself killed. We don't need a repeat performance of that." He shot me a piercing look. "If it comes down to it, you have a pretty good motive for wanting Rachel dead as well. You'd know about the gun in your mother's car, and you don't have an alibi for the entire time in question."

"Oh, so I suppose you think I'd be stupid enough to use my mother's gun? When it could implicate her? Let me tell you, bucko, there are a lot of ways I could kill someone that wouldn't require a gun. An injection of insulin would do nicely and be completely untraceable unless you knew what to look for. Heck, I have an entire pharmacy at my disposal. How about—"

Joe pinched the bridge of his nose and sighed. "Please tell me you aren't going to list all the ways in which you would be the perfect suspect."

"What do you want me to do?" I inhaled sharply. "You expect me to do nothing while you hold my mother as long as you possibly can without charging her?"

The look he flashed me was layered with frustration and annoyance. "The D.A. thinks we have enough to charge her now. Your mother isn't exactly known for her sweet temper, and she was heard threatening to shoot Rachel at Sue's diner. Unless your mother can explain the latex in the slide, it's looking like murder disguised as suicide. Then there's the matter of finding your mother's fingerprints at the clinic, too."

That piece of information took me aback, but only for a second.

"Oh, for heavens sakes." I jabbed my finger in the air at him. "I've been working at Doc's for years. In all that time, you think my mother never came by the clinic to visit me? Heck, my dad's prints are probably there, too. Besides, if my mother took it into her head to shoot someone, there wouldn't be any doubt about it. There wouldn't be any sloppy attempt at covering it up, and she would be the first one to march into the station and admit she'd done it because she'd have believed she had every right to do so."

If my mother's prints had been found in Burnham's private office, they would have arrested her already. But they must have found something to warrant further questioning, and that's what made me uneasy.

"You really aren't helping her case, you know." Joe's wince said it all. "But I know what you mean. She's about as subtle as a freight train."

"You've already questioned her as to her whereabouts the other night. Asked and answered. She was at the church."

"Your mother's being vague about what time she got to the church and how long she was there. I've talked with some of the church members, but no one can recall seeing your mother for the entire meeting. The church is only three blocks away from the clinic. In theory, she could have slipped out when no one was paying attention. I'm just trying to pin down where she was during this time." He shook his head. "I can't say any more than that. It's not helping that your mother is refusing to answer even the most basic questions. I put her in holding just to let her cool her heels a bit."

Now I knew how the bull felt behind the gate when someone in the arena waved a red flag at him. I turned on my heel to leave.

"Ginny, wait," Joe said, rising to his feet.

When I faced him, he ran his hand through his hair and down the back of his neck. "You understand I'm just doing my job right? The D.A. is new. He moved here from Atlanta, and he's eager to put his mark on things. He's putting a lot of pressure on me to close this case as soon as possible." Joe's grin twisted wryly. "I suspect he has political aspirations. You realize I have to treat your mother like any other potential suspect, right? We're talking murder here."

"Perfect. Just what we need, some out-of-town Big Shot thinking they know best." My response was clipped and precise. "Of course, you have to do your job. I expect nothing less."

"Then why are you so angry with me?" The frown that furrowed his forehead was more confused than annoyed.

He really had no idea, did he? How could he possibly think I'd forgotten the nasty insinuations about my attitude toward Burnham that he'd made just yesterday?

"If you think I'm mad with you for detaining my mother, then you're a bigger idiot than I thought."

Leaving him to chew on that one, I stalked out of his office.

I ran into my next problem when Ethan Burrows refused to come down to the sheriff's office.

"I am not qualified to represent your mother in this matter." He'd been firm in his refusal. "I can give you the name of a good defense attorney, however."

Hiring Matthew J. Sampson, Esquire proved harder than I thought it would be. To start off, he was based in Birchwood Springs, which meant at least an hour drive to reach Greenbrier. Then there was the matter of his being on his way out the door to court. I locked horns with his administrative assistant, and it was only by invoking Ethan's name was I able to get five minutes of the lawyer's time. I explained the situation as best I could and held my breath while I waited for his response.

In a rich, deep voice that would have landed him work as an audiobook narrator, he asked two brisk questions: could my mother account for how the deceased got her weapon and had she been formally charged?

"Not charged as yet," I replied. "She left her car unlocked in a public area. Anyone could have taken the gun. Her fingerprints were also found on site where the murder took place, but as someone who would have visited me at work, there's a reasonable explanation for her prints to be in any of the public areas inside the clinic, and in a few of the places off-limits to the general public as well."

Sampson made a non-committal sound and said, "My retainer is five thousand. I'll transfer you to my assistant to work out payment. In the meantime, tell your mother not to answer any questions until I arrive. I'm afraid that won't be until very late this afternoon, however."

I practically choked at the fee—and to think I could have gone to law school instead of vet med—but there was no question of not paying it. I gave his assistant my credit card information. Fortunately, it was only a matter of time before I had access to my inheritance.

Then I had the joy of telling my mother she had to be something she hated more than anything: patient. As Joe, Frank and Holly had all gone out, I was able to talk Deputy Rusty Linkous into escorting me to the holding area, though he shouldn't have. In his late twenties and green as grass, Rusty didn't even check me over for prohibited items, so I hurried through my task in order to be gone before Joe returned.

"I don't need a different lawyer." Another woman might have looked diminished sitting in the small closet that served as an interview room, but fuming rage only empowered my mother. She gripped her mug of coffee as though she might crack the ceramic with her bare hands. "I *have* a lawyer. You tell Ethan to come down here and get me out right now."

"He says he's not legally qualified to represent you. Mr. Sampson came highly recommended. He's on his way just as soon as he finishes up with another case in Birchwood. In the meantime, he doesn't want you talking to the police."

"I have things to do," my mother said. She gave a wave to the room around her. "I can't sit here all afternoon waiting to be released."

"I'm afraid you must." I told her what Joe had said about the slide. "You can't think of any reason for there to be latex stuck on your gun, can you?

Did you by any chance borrow some of my gloves to use while cleaning the gun?"

I tended to use blue nitrile gloves in my work, and almost always had a box in my car. Joe hadn't said anything about what color the material on the gun had been, but it was worth asking. Nitrile gloves were latex-free. Some people used "latex" as a generic term for disposable gloves, though I doubted Joe would make that kind of mistake.

"It's a new gun." My mother frowned. "I haven't cleaned it yet."

Seeing as I hadn't ever observed her clean and oil her weapons in all the years I'd known her to have one, this didn't surprise me.

Remembering her penchant for spy novels, I said, "I'm certain keeping you here is merely a tactic to wear you down. We both know you're tougher than that. Simply refuse to speak until Mr. Sampson gets here and everything will turn out all right in the end."

I hoped.

Surprisingly, this appeal to her inner Mrs. Pollifax, the little old lady turned CIA spy, worked. She mimed locking her lips and tossing the key over her shoulder. I felt slightly better about leaving her until Matthew Sampson could arrive.

Before I knew it, it was early afternoon, and time to meet Holly at the clinic again.

"Remy's not with you?" Holly asked, by way of greeting as she unlocked the back door.

I shook my head. "I had to go down to the sheriff's office first and didn't know how long I would be there."

"Ah."

The single word was packed with implications and Holly lapsed into silence after that.

I didn't waste any time: after taking care of the boarders, I discharged Tiffany to her people and then packaged up Pirate, along with his special food and medications, to return him to Mrs. Oberstein.

"How much longer is the clinic going to be off-limits?" I asked when Holly showed signs of restlessness.

She seemed less friendly than she had earlier, if her narrow-eyed assessment was anything to go by. Or maybe she was feeling the pressure of not discussing the fact my mother was a person of interest in Burnham's death.

"Since the general consensus is that it's murder, not any time soon, I would think." She fixed me with a cool stare. "You should know by now how these things work. However, the crime scene units are done with some areas." She consulted her notebook. "The kennels, reception, pharmacy, treatment area, and employee bathroom have been cleared for use with supervision."

"I'm just asking." I shrugged off her animosity, real or imagined. "I'm thinking in terms of going forward from here. Carolyn Price contacted me about retrieving her equipment. Montanaro will also want to know, and there's the issue of the boarders. Some of their owners aren't due back for a least a week. That means someone will have to continue to meet me down here three times a day."

"Tell me about it," Holly said without enthusiasm. "Are we almost done here?"

"Pirate's in his carrier. I just need to dump his litterbox and grab his medication."

"Right. I'll carry him and his food out to the car if you like."

Her willingness to help again felt like a peace offering, so I took her up on it. While she took Pirate out the back door, I carried his litterbox into the kennel and opened the large trash can there. Inside, I spied a large ball of paper towels, and made a note to tell the girls not to be so wasteful when cleaning in the future. As I tipped the litter pan into the can, the stream of litter hit the paper towels and turned them over.

An oblong white plastic device fell out of the wadded paper towels.

I stared at it for a long moment, thinking it was the oddest feline leukemia test I'd ever seen, and wondering if it was being made by a new company. Then my brain switched gears and I saw it for what it really was: a home pregnancy test.

It was positive.

Chapter Thirteen

I COVERED THE TEST strip with the rest of the cat litter, running various scenarios through my head as I did so.

The test surely hadn't been there in the trash the day of Burnham's death. For one thing, despite being hidden in a can no one in their right mind would poke through, it was the job of crime scene specialists to go through everything. They would have found the test if it had been present when they were processing the building.

But after the kennel had been processed and we were allowed back into it was another story altogether.

The only people who'd been in the building today were me and Holly, and I felt reasonably sure neither of *us* had deposited the test in the trash. I tried to recall if I'd seen the paper towels in the waste container this morning but remembered that I'd taken charge of hosing the runs while Holly had cleaned the smaller cages. For all I knew, the test could have been there this morning. Chances were good that it was, given I was finding it now.

Which only meant one thing: someone had to have put the test in the trash after the kennels had been processed but before now. I had a hard time picturing Holly carrying a home pregnancy test with her to dump it at a crime scene. But I could think of several reasons why a young girl such as Erin or Amber might not want to run such a test at her parent's house and be looking for a way to hide the results.

When I'd been in the same situation as a senior in high school, I'd tossed the test out the car window while speeding along Route 7. It had been a terrible time: first recognizing that my period was late, driving to Birchwood to purchase a test from one of the big pharmacy chains where no one knew me, and then working up the nerve to take the test itself. Given the fact that my mother regularly read me the riot act for failing to load the dishwasher in a timely fashion, I couldn't imagine telling her if I'd been pregnant.

Fortunately, in my case, the results had been negative. My period put in an appearance, and I went on birth control pills.

I never told Joe. Sometimes I wonder what would have happened if I had.

Amber had become quite green at the odor in the clinic yesterday morning. Granted, the smell was pretty bad, but most people who work with animals adapt to such scents. I shouldn't jump to any conclusions, however. It could have been she was more upset by Burnham's death than she appeared.

Either way, the positive test didn't seem to be connected to Burnham's death. I didn't need to make a big deal out of it or call attention to something someone probably desperately needed to keep quiet until she decided what to do about it. Neither Erin nor Amber were in high school, but they weren't much older than that. Shining a light on their sex lives when it had no bearing on the case seemed unnecessarily cruel.

"You coming?" Holly shouted from the treatment area.

"Be right there!" I called back. I left the litterbox in the sink to be cleaned and hurried to join Holly before she came looking for me.

She cursed and fiddled with the key as she locked the back door behind us.

"Something wrong?" I asked.

"This doorknob should be replaced." She struggled to get the key out of the lock. "The lock looks new, but it's so cheap it's already falling apart."

I spared a passing thought to wonder who was being the penny-pincher here, Burnham or CVC.

"That's weird." I'd already mentioned it to Joe, but it couldn't hurt to say it again. "I thought the locks hadn't been changed because my old key worked. But come to think of it, the entire mechanism rotated when I tried it."

The doorknob released the key unexpectedly, causing Holly to stumble backward. She fixed a stern look on me. "You *did* give up your key yesterday, didn't you?"

I smothered a sigh. "Yes, of course. But you realize what this means, right? Just about anyone could have gotten into the building."

"We're aware of that," Holly said repressively. "We should probably put a padlock on this door. And by 'we', I mean the sheriff's department, not you and me."

I held up my hands in a gesture of peace. "I didn't say anything."

Holly muttered something to herself under her breath as we walked to our cars. I only got a wave when I reminded her of our plans to meet back at the clinic that evening.

Pirate gave me a plaintive meow when I got in the car.

"Let's get you home, buddy," I said, starting the engine. "I've got people to see."

Dropping off Pirate took longer than expected. Living alone made Fran Oberstein chatty, and it was clear she seldom had company. Try as I might to shove Pirate at her and dash off again, I found myself accepting an invitation to come in, as she'd been baking. Who could say no to chocolate chip cookies? Besides, I had to make sure she understood how to take care of Pirate during his recovery. I left with a tin of warm cookies and a stern injunction to call me if she was in any way concerned about Pirate. When I drove off, the two of them were sitting together on her little sofa, the big black cat making biscuits with his paws as she stroked him and told him how ridiculously handsome he was.

Next on the agenda: killing two birds with one stone. I needed to pick up groceries, and it just so happened that Wendy now worked as a cashier at Bucky's. If I were lucky, she'd be on shift now. Knowing I had Mrs. Oberstein's cookies as a fallback made it easier to load up the cart with real food for a change. The beauty of shopping at Bucky's was the fact that the layout never changed. I could run in and grab exactly what I wanted and be back on the road in no time flat. The disadvantage was that items were often in short supply and prices often reflected that. I made a conscious effort to steer clear of the frozen pizzas and concentrated on the produce aislc instead.

As soon as I filled my cart, I wheeled it to the checkout. As I'd hoped, Wendy was behind one of the registers, so I got in her line. Another cashier with no line tried to persuade me to switch lanes, but I gave her a big smile and pretended to be enthralled with something on my phone. Eventually, I made it to the register.

"Hey, Doc," Wendy said as I began unloading items onto the conveyor belt. She wore an oversized navy and white uniform that could have doubled for a bowling league outfit. Come to think of it, I wouldn't be surprised if it did. "You having people over to the house?"

I glanced over the abundance of food I'd picked out, mostly fresh fruits and veggies. I laughed at her comment. "Nope. Just made the cardinal sin of shopping while hungry."

She nodded at the truism and kept ringing up my items. Dark circles accentuated bags under her eyes I'd never noticed before. Her uniform was a little too large and hung badly as a result. She looked tired in a way she'd never seemed when working at the clinic, despite how stressful it could be at times.

"How are you doing?" I asked impulsively.

Something fiery lit in her eyes, only to be immediately quenched.

"As well as can be expected. Not used to being on my feet all day."

"They won't let you sit down behind the register?" There didn't seem to be any reason why a cashier couldn't be seated; there was plenty of room behind the counter.

She rolled her eyes. "Nope. Jenna had to get a note from her doctor when she broke her foot, otherwise they would have made her stand when she was supposed to stay off it."

Yikes.

A woman got in line behind me, huffed when she saw how much I was buying, and wheeled her cart into the next line over. Good. I didn't want to be rushed. However, Wendy whipped my groceries across her scanner with brutal efficiency, and before I knew it, she'd read off my total.

While punching in my pin number in the card reader, I asked, "Is there some way I can talk to you? I have a couple of questions about the clinic."

Alarm widened Wendy's pupils and she glanced around as though someone might be listening.

"I don't think—" she began, but I cut her off.

"I only need a few minutes of your time."

With a sigh, she checked her watch. "I guess I can take my break early."

"Excellent." I beamed at her. "Let me run my groceries out to the car. Can I meet you in the lot?"

She cast a wary look about her and spoke out of the corner of her mouth, "Meet me around the back of the building in five."

I'd never been behind Bucky's. I left my car in the lot out front and walked along the narrow strip of pavement that allowed trucks to drive back to the delivery entrance. Several feral cats flattened themselves and ran at my approach, scattering from where they'd been rooting around near the dumpster. Wendy waited for me on a concrete loading dock behind the store. As I climbed the short flight of stairs to her level, she took out a crumpled bill from her pocket and stretched it against the edge of a drink machine, pulling it back and forth several times in an effort to flatten it. The machine refused to take it, however, spitting it back at her every time she tried feeding it into a slot.

"Let me buy you a soda," I said as I walked up to the battered drink machine and inserted my card into the slot. "What'll you have?"

She selected a Coke. When I didn't get one for myself, she asked, "Aren't you having one?"

I chose a bottle of water instead. "Trying to quit."

She made a derisive snort and accepted the cold can from my hand. "You make it sound like giving up cigarettes."

I shrugged. "I think it's just as addictive, if not more so. I read something recently that said eating cookies hit the same receptors activated when you do cocaine."

She raised both eyebrows at that and raised the can of soda in a toast. "Here's to cookies and soda, then." She took a swallow and asked, "What is it you wanted to see me about?"

Faced with the actual question, I wasn't sure how to answer. What was I hoping to get from Wendy? I stalled for time by unscrewing the top from my bottled water and taking a swig. "I was sorry to hear you'd been let go from the clinic."

Her lips briefly flattened as she tightened her jaw. "She'd been looking for a reason to fire me from day one."

"But that's crazy," I exclaimed. "You'd been with GVC for what—fifteen or so years? You were one of the clinic's most valuable assets moving forward. You did all the ordering, knew all the vendors, and knew where everything was. You know the clients on sight, which is better than I can do, and you remember all the little details about their pets. Which cats won't touch canned food, and which animals have had bad reactions to what meds, and which dogs won't drink water from a metal bowl ... not to mention that in a time of transition, you'd be a familiar face. Kind of like how they don't change the Doctor and the Companion at the same time."

The *Doctor Who* reference drew a smile from her, as I knew it would. We'd often talked about our favorite sci-fi shows when I'd worked at the clinic. The smile was brittle and tight, however, and disappeared almost as soon as it had appeared.

"Try telling *her* that." Wendy ground out her words with an unfamiliar harshness. "You couldn't tell her anything."

The hostility rolling off Wendy took me aback. I aimed for a diplomatic approach. "I imagine it couldn't be easy for either of you. No doubt she wanted to put her own stamp on things, but you had a better idea of what would probably work best on any given day."

Wendy drank from her can and set it on the railing beside her to fish out a pack of cigarettes from her pocket along with a lighter.

"What?" She shot me a sour glance. "Don't look at me like that."

I lifted a hand in a gesture of peace. "I'm not saying anything. I didn't know you smoked, that's all."

She lit the cigarette, puffing several times until it caught, then taking a long pull as though she needed it to live. "I'd quit but when you lose everything, there's not much point to staying on the straight and narrow, is there?

Everything seemed to be a bit of an exaggeration. I didn't know how to respond to that. Fortunately, something about the nicotine seemed to release Wendy's tension.

"Look, I'm not saying I was against all the changes Dr. Burnham was making." The end of her cigarette glowed red as she took another drag. "Modernizing the record-keeping system? Updating the lab equipment? Getting computers to run the business? I was all on board for that. Expanding services, too. But then she jacked the prices up like crazy. Six hundred dollars for a dog spay. Nine hundred dollars for a dental. She also acted like no one was capable of taking care of their own pets. She started leaving little nasty notes all over the place, saying how she wanted this thing and that thing done *her* way. And making me look bad in front of clients, blaming me for everything that went wrong. When she started stuffing animals in airline kennels and calling it boarding, I drew the line."

She puffed angrily between each sentence, the smoke wreathing her head as she spoke. I very nearly told her about Burnham being funded by CVC and my theory about the quotas, but I stopped myself in time. It didn't seem right to spread the word before I'd come to a decision about CVC myself. Or told Joe about it, for that matter. I should have done so earlier, but I'd been so mad about him holding my mother for questioning—and other things—that I'd simply forgotten.

"But you didn't quit," I pointed out.

She crushed out the cigarette and chugged down some soda before fixing me with a hard stare. "No, I didn't. Because she wanted me to. Because I cared about the clients and their pets. Because I'd invested fifteen years of my life in that clinic. Because good jobs are scarce in Greenbrier. You think I *want* to be working at Bucky's for nine dollars an hour? Oh, and just under forty hours per week, too, so Bucky doesn't have to pay any benefits."

I grimaced in sympathy. "That truly sucks, Wendy. I'm sorry."

Her frown was almost suspicious. "What are you sorry for? None of this is your fault."

"Maybe not directly." I let my hand shrug for me, turning palm up in a helpless gesture of apology. "Perhaps if I'd moved faster, gone to the bank and asked for a loan based on my expected inheritance—"

Wendy snorted. "Wouldn't have made no difference. Once Doc's wife got wind of a much better offer, nothing short of taking the money and running would have made her happy."

Since I'd come to pretty much the same conclusion about Hazel, I just nodded.

"But then the cats got switched," I observed.

Wendy's nostrils flared and her upper lip curled. She looked just like a snarling Pekinese. "I swear to this day, that mix-up was done on purpose."

"What?" I hadn't seen that coming.

She nodded vigorously. "Obviously, Carolyn had removed Cotton's nametag collar during grooming. And yes, those paper cage cards can fall out of the holders sometimes. But Snowball should have still been wearing his nametag. If he had, I never would have sent him home by mistake."

"What do you think happened? Surely the girls wouldn't have—"

"No, I can't see either Amber or Erin deliberately removing a collar. Putting the cage card back on the wrong cage by mistake, yes, but not switching things on purpose." Wendy's eyes narrowed as her anger blazed out of them. "Oh, no. Dr. High and Mighty did that herself so she had an excuse to fire me."

"Oh, Wendy." I shook my head. "You don't really believe that do you? The negative publicity alone isn't worth it. What a PR nightmare. You saw the stuff on Facebook, right?"

"I don't know what to think anymore." She rubbed her forehead tiredly, only to drain her can and chuck it into a bin labeled RECYCLING. She then fixed me with that unnerving stare again. "I heard they brought your mom in for questioning. That she's down at the sheriff's office, fit to be tied. Word is, your mom's gun was the murder weapon."

"Word gets around," I said slowly. It was unlikely anyone on Joe's staff was the leak; they knew better than to talk about cases. But I imagined my mother had blown a gasket on being asked to stay for questioning and anyone who'd been in the sheriff's office for any other reason probably heard the subsequent explosion. It suddenly seemed ten times hotter out there on the dock, and I caught myself pressing the bottle of cold water against the side of my neck. "What else are people saying?"

"If you're asking if people think she did it, most of the town thinks she did, only it doesn't suit her style, you know?"

I thought I did. "Not enough sound and fury? Too sneaky, trying to pass it off as a suicide?"

"Exactly." Wendy cocked an index finger in my direction. "'Course, some people argue that your mom's a clever lady. That after she blew Dr. Burnham away, she realized she had a good chance of making it look like suicide, so she took it."

"She could have taken the gun with her and no one would have been the wiser that it belonged to her."

Wendy shrugged as though conceding the point, but without much conviction. "But then it would have been obvious it was murder."

Well, that was discouraging. The fact that the gun belonged to my mother, and she'd been public about her dislike of Burnham combined with the lack of an alibi and prints at the scene ... I could see why the D.A. thought he had a case against her. Worse, I didn't see any way of proving otherwise. It was a wonder Joe *hadn't* filed charges yet.

"Everything they have is circumstantial," I said, more by way of convincing myself than Wendy.

She may have grunted in response, but her expression was sympathetic. Glancing at her watch, she said, "So what did you want to see me about anyway?"

I blew out my breath through my lips in a long sigh. "It's probably none of my business," I began, only to get interrupted.

"Whenever anyone says something like that, it's a given."

I shot a rueful smile at her. "Yeah, I hear you. Only I think someone at the clinic might be in trouble."

I told her about the used pregnancy test. Then it was her turn to puff and sigh a bit.

"Can't think anyone will thank you for interfering."

"Normally, I'd agree," I said. "But one of the girls said something about Montanaro being a creep, and it got me to thinking—"

Wendy's eyes went as round as an owl's. "You think he's involved? Seems like a pretty big leap to me."

"I hear you. But once it occurred to me, I just couldn't let it go." I shrugged, turning my palms up again. "That's just it. I don't know. But if he *is* involved, I don't think I can let that slide."

Especially after seeing someone who could have been Amber talking to him in the parking lot this morning.

Wendy made a dismissive noise through her nose. "I don't see why not. Both them girls are of age. I reckon he'd have had to move pretty quick to get someone knocked up so soon. Timing's not impossible, though."

"Well, that's just it," I said slowly. "Who then? Amber or Erin?"

The shift of Wendy's shoulders seemed to imply *who knows*?

"Erin's got a steady boyfriend. Amber's not picky who she dates as long as he's got money and pays her way." Wendy made finger quotes when she said *dates*. "Could be either one of them. But my money's on Amber."

"Yeah, I guess you're right."

I must have sounded defeated because Wendy said, "Don't worry. I'm sure it will turn out all right in the end."

"Thanks. I want to believe that too."

"I guess I'd better get back to work." Wendy shot a tired glance at the back door. "Say, I think I may have left a few things behind at the clinic. I was fired without notice and asked to leave on the spot. Any chance I could get in the building and take a look around?"

I shook my head. "Not just yet. They're not letting anyone in but me, and that's only with a police escort. Even if your stuff is there, no one is allowed to remove anything from the building right now. But I can keep an eye out and let you know when people are allowed back in. What did you leave behind?"

"I'm pretty sure I left a rain jacket. Can't find it anywhere. Light blue." Wendy shifted her feet a bit and added, "Also a scarf."

"I haven't spotted anything like that but if I do, I'll let you know."

"Thanks." She started back for the door, only to add over her shoulder, "Also, tell your mom thanks for me."

It wasn't until Wendy had gone back inside that I caught the first implication—that my mother had done her a favoring by killing Burnham.

It took me even longer before the second implication hit me—one that I'm sure Wendy hadn't intended on making.

She was happy Dr. Burnham was dead.

I had a lot to think about as I headed back to my car. After I took the sunshield down, I eased my way onto the broiling seat, grateful I wasn't wearing shorts to stick to the fake leather upholstery. I needed to get my groceries home ASAP, but I took a few minutes to look up the *Greenbrier After Dark* podcast on my phone. Apparently, they dropped a new episode every Saturday evening, but had done a special episode in light of the discovery of Dr. Burnham's body yesterday.

Was it only yesterday? So much had happened since then.

Tempting as it was to go back to listen to the older podcasts where I'd been discussed, I queued up the most recent episode on my tablet and played it through the speakers as I drove back through town. The hosts were young and male, prone to wise-cracking and wild speculation. Listening to their hyperbole was a waste of time. I'd been hopeful I'd learn something useful, such as a hint as to where they were getting their information, or some background on Burnham, but it was impossible to take anyone seriously who gave equal weight to a drug deal gone wrong and a botched alien abduction as possible motives for her death. At least I wasn't the only one who'd thought—even briefly—about witness protection. I just about to change over to music instead when a commotion in front of the sheriff's office had me slowing down.

At least twenty people—mostly women—marched up and down in front of the municipal building bearing placards and chanting something. As I pulled abreast of the crowd, I recognized several of the ladies, including Mary Boggs, the pastor's wife. When she saw me, she held up her sign and pointed at it for me to read.

"FREE JULIA REESE!"

I rested my forehead against the steering wheel. Joe would blame me for this too.

Chapter Fourteen

I PULLED OVER INTO the nearest parking spot and walked back to the crowd, joining it with no small amount of trepidation. Even as I reached the protesters, more people were stopping to see what the fuss was about.

I'm sure I had a sickly smile pasted on my face when I asked, "What's going on?"

"Ginny!" Mary marched over to me and took me by the arm, dragging me into the thick of things. "I'm so glad you're here. We're starting a campaign to have your mother's charges dropped."

"But she hasn't been charged with anything," I protested. "She's just being questioned. Which is only reasonable. It *was* her gun that killed Rachel Burnham."

"Oh, pish," Mary said. She pushed graying curls back off her face and fanned herself with her placard. "Being questioned? For hours? That's nonsense and you know it. It's police brutality, that's what it is."

Several women around us nodded vigorously and muttered words of agreement.

"It's *nothing* like that." If anything, the people being brutalized were the deputies themselves—by my mother. "You know she wouldn't allow that to happen. She's just been advised not to say anything until her lawyer arrives."

"Stuff and nonsense." Sharon Bartlett, the high school principal, spoke up. Even in this heat, she looked every inch an administrator, down to her crisp cotton blouse and navy skirt. How she managed to wear pumps all the time without killing her feet was a mystery to me. "Ethan Burrows came and went hours ago."

"That's because he's not qualified to represent her in this matter." Desperation made me shout over the grumbling voices. "Look, my mother has a lawyer coming down from Birchwood. Until then, she's not saying anything. Really, there's nothing to protest here. Please go home."

The door to the municipal building opened, and all heads turned to see who was coming out. When it proved not to be my mother, a general sigh ran through the crowd.

"Julia Reese is a pillar of the community," Mary raised her voice over mine, speaking to the crowd. "She taught most of our children. She's a leader in all our charitable drives. She runs the afterschool programs at the church. She's one of *us*. We will not let her be railroaded by outsiders into taking the blame for the death of an outsider."

The crowd burst into a ragged cheer, and the protesters shook their placards vigorously.

I turned to Sharon. "I can't believe you're taking part in this."

"Your mother and I might have had our differences." Sharon fixed a gimlet eye on me. "But she's not a cold-blooded murderer."

No, she wasn't. If my mother killed someone, it would be in plain sight, at the height of an altercation, and she'd present her wrists for cuffing with pride when the deputies showed up.

"Are you Dr. Reese?"

The speaker was the woman who'd exited the building. She was tall and slim, with her black hair done in long, thin braids with brightly colored beads at the ends. She extended her hand. Her nail art was *amazing*. Tiny black pawprints danced over a powder pink base, and on her ring finger, a little pug face peeped out. "I'm Carolyn Price, the groomer from the clinic."

"Oh!" I took her hand instead of shaking it. I am such a sucker for pretty nail polish, but I'd never seen anything as cute or clever. "Who does your nails?"

Carolyn laughed and presented both hands for inspection. "I did them myself."

"Honestly, Ginny, this is important." Mary frowned. "Anyone would think you wanted your mother in jail."

I bit my lower lip while I thought about that answer, and realized I'd waited a hair too long when I saw Carolyn struggling to hide a grin.

"Of course, I want my mother released from jail," I said to Mary. I did. Eventually. Desperate to change the subject, I addressed Carolyn directly. "Did you get things sorted out about your equipment?"

Her amused smile turned into a grimace at the mention of the grooming supplies. "No, I didn't. The clinic is still a crime scene, and the sheriff is refusing to release my stuff. Dennis Montanaro won't answer my calls. Do *you* have a way of contacting him?"

"I probably have the same number you do." I scrolled through my contacts and showed her the number when it came up.

Her mouth tightened and she clenched her fist. "Yes, that's the number I have."

"I'm meeting him tonight. He wants to talk about the clinic. I can bring up your situation if you think it would help." I didn't think it would. I might have better luck bringing it up with Joe instead.

"Would you?" Relief eased the tension in her face but worry still creased her brow. "I hate to be a nag about this, but I can't afford to replace my tools and I'm losing business every day the clinic is closed."

I didn't mention her non-compete. The only one who would care would be Montanaro himself, and what he didn't know wouldn't hurt him.

"I'll do my best."

"What's going on here? Why is everyone blocking the sidewalk?"

The new voice made me turn. Behind me, Doc's wife, Hazel, stood with a frown.

"A misguided attempt to help my mother." I indicated the crowd around us. "These nice people have got it in their heads that my mother is being unjustly held. Not to worry. Everything's under control. She's just waiting on her lawyer to clear things up."

Instead of clearing her expression, Hazel's frown deepened. Hazel had always been a little on the frumpy side, favoring clothing that didn't show dirt or hair, and sporting a no-nonsense practical haircut without makeup. Kind of like me, which was not a comfortable realization to make. But today she was dressed in a pretty cotton shirt and capri pants with espadrilles, and her hair had been trimmed into a saucy little asymmetrical bob and dyed the color of a nice glass of Merlot. If I wasn't mistaken, she'd pulled out the best of her *Avenue* makeup as well, which she no longer needed to peddle to make ends meet. Doc's retirement had treated her nicely.

"The police have questions about the night Dr. Burnham was murdered and how she might have gotten hold of Julia's gun." Sharon filled in the details. "Julia has been advised not to say anything until her new lawyer gets here. Whenever that might be. In the meantime, we're making our opinion on the matter known."

Hazel widened her carefully shadowed eyes. "Are they saying Dr. Burnham's death isn't a suicide?"

"That's right." Mary gave a short nod. The women closest to her began to shake their posters in agreement. "It's murder. And since she was killed with Julia's gun, that makes her the prime suspect."

"Despite the fact that *everyone* knows Julia carries a gun." Sharon rolled her eyes. "It's practically a fashion accessory for her. Though I did insist she leave it at home when she was teaching."

I wanted to sink through concrete and disappear beneath the sidewalk.

Hazel's cheeks turned redder than the blush she was already sporting. "That's ridiculous. So, let me get this straight. Julia won't say where she was the night of Dr. Burnham's death?"

"Well, yes and no." I felt compelled to explain. "She's already been questioned once. They wanted to talk to her again. But her new lawyer is held up and can't get here for a while."

"But the problem is an alibi for the time during which Dr. Burnham might have died. Right?" Hazel looked around at the women nearest to her. "That's ridiculous. Our Ladies Auxiliary meeting was about the new literacy program Julia is planning, which is a fine thing to be sure. She was front and center practically the entire time. I'm sure between us all, we can account for her movements that night. Sheriff Donegan might not want to release Julia until she answers his questions, but there's nothing keeping us from volunteering statements, now is there? He can hardly hold her after that."

"Now that is an excellent idea!" Mary pushed her glasses up the bridge of her nose and pointed her placard at the door of the municipal building. "Ladies Auxiliary! To the sheriff's office!"

The surge of people moving toward the building caused my heart to plummet like a free-falling elevator to my toes.

"Uh-oh," Carolyn said, catching my eye and pulling a sympathetic face at my expression.

Sharon looked back over her shoulder at me. "Aren't you coming?"

"I have groceries in the car," I said weakly. And bolted.

The last thing I wanted was for anyone in the sheriff's department to think I had any part of the Free Julia campaign, so I jumped in my car and roared away from the curb.

Chapter Fifteen

RIGHT UP UNTIL THE moment I was to meet Holly at the clinic for evening treatments, I had no idea what I was going to say to Montanaro about his job offer. I went back and forth on my decision all afternoon, waffling between an emphatic "no way" to "perhaps, but with certain conditions." It felt like a no-win scenario no matter how I looked at it. Either I was going to become CVC's lapdog, with little say-so in how I ran my business, or else CVC would become my main competitor, forcing me to use all my resources to fight to stay alive. What represented the sum total of all my assets would be a drop in the bucket to CVC. Did I really want to squander Amanda's inheritance in that fashion?

Or had I simply become comfortable with the idea of a large safety net and didn't want to go back to working as hard as I could to try to make ends meet?

Either way, I had to make up my mind, and soon.

While I was still trying to decide what to do, my mother pulled into the driveway. She swept into the kitchen, eyes bright with the stimulation of justifiable anger, and updated me on what had happened to affect her release.

The church ladies had been effective in establishing my mother's whereabouts for the time in question, and Joe wound up allowing her to go before the expensive lawyer arrived from Birchwood. She in turn fired Sampson, stating he'd done nothing to earn his high dollar retainer, and demanded my money back. I had to do some uncomfortable wrangling on the phone with Sampson to get him to agree to return the retainer. He insisted on billing me for the time he'd already invested. Even though I suspected I would get an extravagant charge for negligible work, I didn't argue with his stipulation, but asked that he send the invoice to me and not my mother. Oddly enough, he didn't question my request at all.

Once we sorted the lawyer's fees, I debated whether to tell my mother about Montanaro's offer. Surely it would be better to say nothing until I'd made my decision.

She was unusually quiet about her rescue at the hands of the Ladies Auxiliary, instead focusing her displeasure on the fact I'd given Sampson such a huge retainer. At this rate, I'd burn through the money Amanda had left me, and was that what I wanted?

I'd only been trying to deflect her—honestly, she was as persistent as a terrier digging after a rat—when I implied she might not have to worry about my inheritance after all. I realized too late she'd latch onto that statement with sharp teeth.

"Whatever do you mean by that?"

She was seated at the kitchen table drinking coffee, and the piercing look she'd given me was identical to the one I'd last seen the time I'd tried lying about going to a friend's house to watch a movie when actually, I'd been meeting up with Joe down at Bishop's Lake for a make-out session.

Mentally dope-slapping myself, I told her about Montanaro's offer.

I'd expected her to light up with enthusiasm over the notion I could buy the clinic after all, but instead she slapped her palm on the table so hard the coffee sloshed in her cup.

"I *knew* that woman was here under false pretenses!"

"Oh, come on. I hardly think that's fair. It's not like she wasn't a real vet or anything."

She glared at me over the brim of her mug. "You're telling me that it didn't make you angry when you found out the truth?"

I opened my mouth for an automatic protest, then snapped it shut. It *had* made me angry.

"She would have come clean eventually."

Even to my own ears, that sounded weak.

Mother sniffed in disdain and glared over the rim of her mug at me. "I don't think the people of Greenbrier would take kindly to the idea they'd been taken for fools. If she'd been up front with everyone in the beginning, it would have been bad enough, but to hide the source of her financing? She didn't belong here."

"That's not a reason to kill someone."

"Of course not, dear." For a moment, vindication gleamed in her eyes. "I'm just glad—"

She broke off without continuing her thought.

"You're just glad what?" I prompted.

"Nothing." She cradled her coffee in her hands, staring down into its depths.

Taking advantage of the lull in the storm, I collected Remy, and headed out the door.

Holly met me in the parking lot behind the clinic as the sun was going down.

I cleared my throat as she jiggled the key in the lock. "About this afternoon—"

She cut me off without ceremony. "I know, I know. You had nothing to do with the church ladies storming the department."

"I didn't," I protested. "I didn't find out about it until I was driving past."

"Relax." Holly's grin made a brief appearance. "I'm saying we *know* you didn't organize it. Pastor Boggs' wife was pretty clear on that front. Your mother has quite the fan club, doesn't she?"

"More like better the devil you know, I think."

"You might be right there." Holly grunted and wrenched the key so that the door opened. "The high school principal said something along the lines of 'she might be a witch, but she's *our* witch.'"

"I'm sure 'witch' was the nicer of the terms she could have gone with." I hesitated, not sure how far the friendliness went this evening. "So, I take it she's in the clear for now?"

"For now."

Remy and I followed her into the dark building. "Now that it's just boarders, hopefully, it won't take too long to feed and clean up. Any word on when the clinic will be cleared?"

Walking behind me, Holly's voice floated over my shoulder. "I imagine next week sometime."

We got down to it. Leaving Remy in the treatment room, I moved dogs and hosed runs, while Holly scooped out kibble and filled bowls. As much as I wanted to take the boarders outside to relieve themselves, there was no fence around the property, and I thought the risks of losing a dog too great. I was down to the last couple of patients when Holly's radio suddenly squawked.

"All units. 211-S in progress on at 1432 East Maple Street. I repeat, 211-S in progress at 1432 East Maple Street."

I turned off the hose. "Say, isn't that Crystal's Jewelry?"

"Yes." Holly's response was terse. She activated her radio. "Dispatch, this is Deputy Walsh. I'm just two blocks from the location of the 211. On my way. Send back up."

"Message received, Deputy Walsh. All units in the vicinity of 1432 East Maple, please respond to the 211-S in progress."

"I'm coming." I looped the hose back on the reel, but Holly held up her hand to stop me.

"I can't take you to a robbery in progress." Her tone was withering. "You'll have to wait here in the parking lot until I return."

"Go. All I have to do is move the last two boarders and fill their water bowls and I'm right behind you out the door."

She hesitated, obviously champing at the bit to rush to the break-in but at the same time, not wanting to shirk her duty supervising me.

"Go!" I pointed at the door. "They could be getting away!"

"I'll lock the door." She was already jogging for the exit. "All you have to do is pull it shut behind you."

"I've got this. Two minutes and I'm gone. Go."

True to my word, it only took me a matter of seconds to shift the two remaining dogs into their clean runs and make sure the water bowls were topped off. I switched off the lights in the kennel and re-entered the treatment room. Remy stood up from his mat on the floor and wagged his tail at my entrance.

"Ah-ah," I said, waving him back down. "I didn't say you could get up yet."

I was half-tempted to let the lapse in training pass, which is one reason I'm not the best dog trainer. Consistency is everything, and I tended to be a bit lackadaisical in my approach. But having a dog stay put where you leave it can potentially be a life-saving behavior, as I had reason to know from the time Amanda's killer tried to shoot me. Remy had been hidden under a table and came out at my command, a fact that had saved us both. So, I made him lie down again, counted to twenty, and then released him.

This is the part where the two of us should have left the building, as I'd promised Holly we would. I'm not sure what I expected to find that the police hadn't already discovered. What with my mother having been released, I didn't really have a good reason for my actions. I certainly didn't want Holly to get in any trouble, but as I was finally free of supervision, surely there was no harm in taking a look around.

I slipped on a pair of exam gloves and went out through the far end of the treatment room into the long corridor beyond. Remy padded along in near silence. Only the occasional click of his toenails on the floor gave away his presence in the gloom. The clinic was eerily quiet in the dark. Lighted EXIT signs illuminated the location of the doors, and another small light remained on over the reception desk.

At the end of the hallway, the door to the private office remained closed. I could make out the yellow crime scene tape across the door. My first roadblock. I hadn't realized the room would be sealed and there was no way for me to get in without breaking it. Disappointed, I cut through the pharmacy area to the reception desk, Remy close on my heels. I'd been in the pharmacy dispensing medications the day before, but there'd been no call for me to go to the reception area.

The usual clutter greeted my eye. Paper clips and rubber bands were stacked haphazardly in little dishes alongside staplers, tape dispensers, and white out. A jar of pens and pencils stood by the credit card reader. The two phones were silent, set to play the recorded message that that the clinic was closed, and any emergencies should be taken to Birchwood Springs.

I opened the appointment book, a large ring-bound affair with lined pages marked in ten-minute increments for appointments. Up until she'd been scheduled to leave town, the days had been booked from eight a.m. to six p.m. Three days a week, Dr. Burnham had done surgery. The rest of the week was given over to routine and sick appointments. Carolyn's grooming schedule had been full as well. I saw nothing out of the ordinary except the level of work one person was expected to carry out day after day.

I opened and shut drawers, finding stamps, business envelopes, labels for the printer, reminder cards to be mailed, and highlighters. Again, nothing unexpected. What had I been hoping to find in so public a space? Threatening letters? Illegal drugs? If someone had been siphoning off the controlled drug inventory, the place to look for discrepancies would be in the logbook, and I could easily examine that the next time I was legitimately in the building. I didn't need to sneak around to do that.

The back of my neck prickled the longer I poked around. Montanaro would be showing up soon, and I'd best be outside waiting for him when he arrived. Not to mention, if I got caught snooping, Holly would get in trouble. Worse, Joe would be extremely disappointed in me. Normally, I wouldn't let that bother me, except this time, what I was doing was wrong.

Car headlights passed by the main window in the waiting area, making me feel as though I were in a fishbowl. How stupid could I be? I wasn't going to find anything useful, and I could potentially jeopardize my relationship with the sheriff's department—and Joe—by my willful behavior. I was just about to take Remy and go when I noticed the pile of letters on the floor in front of the mail slot on the front door. I might as well pick them up and put them on the desk to be sorted through tomorrow.

Placing Remy on a down-stay behind the reception desk for practice, I went through the half door that separated the reception counter from the main lobby and crossed over to pick up the letters. Angling them so the light from the lamp at the desk allowed me to read the addresses, I shuffled through the mail. The first few envelopes contained bills from some of the major vendors. As I headed back to the reception desk, the final letter caught my eye. It was a notice from the Board of Veterinary Medicine addressed to Dr. Rachel Cartwright.

Rachel Cartwright?

This had to be Rachel's married name. Perhaps with Michelle's help, I could find out more about Burnham's life before she arrived in Greenbrier.

I stacked the mail on the reception counter and glanced at my watch. Time to go.

A small noise caught my ear, and the hair on my arms lifted when I realized it was the sound of the swinging door from the treatment room. I turned to face the door to the corridor, with my back pressed against the reception desk. In a flash, I peeled off the exam gloves and shoved them in my pocket, my heart pounding like steam engine on the verge of blowing gaskets as I did so.

The door to the waiting area opened, and a tall form stepped out of the dark hallway into the dimly lit waiting area.

It was Montanaro.

Somehow, that didn't steady my heart rate very much.

"How did you get in here?" I didn't care if I sounded abrupt. "The door was locked."

Montanaro walked into the pool of light cast by one of the streetlamps through the front window. His black hair was waved back from his forehead, and a dark shadow lined his jaw. His clothing, which had looked out of place among the jeans and coveralls this morning, now took on an air of deadly sophistication. Lucifer in a three-piece suit, here to make a deal.

Something gold flashed in his hand as he held it up to the light.

"I have a key."

"Shouldn't you have given that to the sheriff?"

Montanaro shrugged his elegant shoulders and pocketed the key. "So, I was less than honest with the hillbilly sheriff. Sue me. I have to oversee my investments."

I don't think my eyebrows could have crawled any higher into my hairline. "I suspect Joe would take a dim view of that."

"Joe is it?" A particularly nasty smile curved on Montanaro's face. "A close, warm, personal friend of the law, are we? Is that why you're here without supervision? Where is your babysitter, by the way?"

"She got called out on an emergency," I said stiffly. "I was just picking up the mail. Shall we go to dinner?"

I wasn't really hungry, but I had a strong desire to be among other people before discussing anything further with Montanaro. Anything to get out of the building, to not feel cornered and trapped. The fact that he'd kept the existence of his key a secret unnerved me. Had he let himself into the clinic the night of Burnham's death? Had she felt the same uneasiness in his presence? Every instinct told me I needed to get out of the building *now*.

"By all means, we can go to dinner if you like." That skin-crawling smile made an appearance again. "But why don't we settle things here where we can keep our discussion private? It's a simple yes or no question, Ginny. Will you join the CVC family or not?"

Up until that moment in time, I would have said I was still undecided. But as soon as he voiced his question, the answer rang in my head as clearly as a church bell on a Sunday morning.

No.

"I've given this a lot of thought." All hesitation fell away. "My answer is no."

"No?" He reared his head back, clearly taken by surprise. "No? You can't be serious. I'm making you a phenomenal offer. It's everything you've ever wanted at a fraction of the cost. Have you crunched the numbers? Do you *know* how much you'll have to spend if you try to start up a practice on your own? Not to mention, CVC is not going away. We're going to be here, whether you sign with us or not. Do you really think there's enough business in this little burg for the two of us?"

"Do you really think you can compete with me?" I folded my arms over my chest, pleased with how calm I sounded. "I'm not without my own resources, as you well know, and I'm not an outsider."

Strong emotions rolled across his face like thunderclouds, and his jaw worked with the effort of holding back his words, presumably something derogatory.

A trickle of unease crept down my spine, reminding me I was alone with a man I didn't trust.

All at once, his expression smoothed out, even as his eyes narrowed. "Are you sure you don't want to rethink your position?"

"Why would I want to do that?" I asked, alarmed by the sense of satisfaction in his voice.

He pretended to examine his nails, which was ridiculous, given the dim lighting. "Just that I have some information that you might prefer to keep private. Something I'm sure you wouldn't want *Joe* to know."

"I can't think of anything that I would choose to keep from the sheriff, particularly if it pertained to Dr. Burnham's murder."

Just saying "murder" out loud reminded me again of my precarious position.

"Oh?" Montanaro was irritatingly arch. "Not even if it had to do with your mother?"

Involuntarily, I took a step toward him with a balled fist. "What do you know about my mother?"

He laughed, seemingly confident he had me hooked now. "The real question is what does the sheriff know? For instance, does he know your mother came to the clinic the night of the murder? That she and Rachel had a loud, nasty confrontation?"

"You're making that up," I said, even as my heart sank. He wouldn't have pulled that story out of thin air. Worse, I knew it was something my mother would have done.

"Your mother came in here Tuesday evening to tell Rachel exactly what she thought of her buying the practice out from under you." Montanaro made finger quotes as he spoke. "She was wearing one of those ridiculous polyester pantsuits that went out of style in the eighties, complete with the little neckerchief, and the teased hairdo. She pinned Rachel down in her office and let her have it with both barrels—figuratively speaking, of course."

His description of my mother was picture perfect. There was always the possibility he'd seen her about town, though.

"If you saw this interaction, why didn't you report it to the sheriff?"

If I had hoped to rattle him, I was disappointed.

"Maybe I knew we might be having this conversation at some point." His teeth gleamed impossibly white in the gloom of the waiting room. "I always like to keep an ace up my sleeve."

"I think you didn't tell Joe about my mother being here because Burnham was alive when she left—and if you'd admitted that, it would have placed you at the crime scene as one of the last people to see Burnham alive. You didn't want anyone to know you were there that night."

The smug urbanity evaporated as Montanaro stepped into the weak light. "You can't prove that."

"No, but I can tell Joe what you told me."

"It's in both our interests for you not to do that." He ground out his words, then checked himself, manufacturing friendliness again. "Let's make a deal. We both keep silent about this, and I'll see that you get a substantial signing bonus with CVC."

"You must be crazy if you think I'd work for you now. After trying to blackmail me?" I shifted my weight to the balls of my feet and clenched my fists. Belatedly, I realized I should have pretended to accept his offer, at least until after I got away from him.

"Why you little—"

With fingers curled like talons he came toward me.

The creak of the swinging half door to the reception area caught my attention. A blur of movement brushed me in passing, and before I knew it, Remy stood on his hind legs with his front paws resting on Montanaro's shoulders. His nose was inches from Montanaro's face, and his tail moved ever so slowly from side to side.

I held my breath in surprise. If you know dogs, you know that is *not* a friendly tail gesture.

Montanaro grunted as he took the full ninety pounds of Shepherd. He had the good sense to freeze in place.

As calmly as possible, I said, "Remy. Off."

Remy held his position just a hair longer. I swear if he'd been a person, he would have done the thing where he made a "V" with his fingers, pointed at his eyes, and then at Montanaro. Instead, with a growl rumbling deep in his chest, he dropped to all fours. He remained between Montanaro and me.

Montanaro cleared his throat to speak. "That's a mighty big dog you have there."

"Yes," I agreed. "He is, isn't he?"

"I think," he began, only to have his voice catch. He cleared his throat again. "I think I'll be leaving now."

"Wait," I commanded. I stepped forward to take Remy by the collar. "Now you can go."

He looked at my face and then down at the dog. Remy leaned into his collar, head and ears up, hackles raised like a Mohawk over his shoulders, his tail flying straight up like a flag and fully bushed out. I could feel the tension in his body beneath my grip on his collar, quivering like an arrow in a cross bow notched for release. Had Montanaro moved before I'd grabbed hold of Remy, the dog would have been on in him in a flash.

Montanaro backed slowly toward the door, but Remy stood like a champion, only emitting another low growl with the movement. As soon as Montanaro left the room, I knelt and hugged Remy fiercely.

I took his muzzle in both hands. "First you broke your stay command. Then you jumped on that mean man. I'm so very glad you're such a bad dog."

He slurped my face with his big ol' tongue, making me laugh.

But now I had to talk to Joe, even if it put my mother back in the suspect's seat again.

Chapter Sixteen

My hand shook as I flicked off the light switch in the treatment area. The confrontation with Montanaro had used up all my available blood sugar. I needed a soda with high-fructose corn syrup in it, or at the very least, a candy bar. Or both. A little voice in my head told me if I had a better diet in the first place, these kinds of glucose plunges could be avoided.

Oh, shut up.

I headed for the back door, with Remy in tow. The air outside might still be humid, but it felt less stifling than the atmosphere inside the clinic. I made sure the door was locked behind us after we exited the building—Montanaro had left it unlocked when he came in. That was another thing I'd have to tell Joe about, the fact that old Monty had lied about not having a key. I wasn't looking forward to that conversation.

The warm night wrapped around me like a damp blanket. Montanaro's car wasn't in the lot, and I hadn't heard him drive off. He must have parked out front on the street. Nerves made me grip Remy's collar as we walked to my car. I had the worst feeling that Montanaro might be lurking somewhere nearby, that he would come rushing out of the shadows swinging a lead pipe or something.

When I heard the squeal of tires coming from the road in front of the clinic, my first thought was that Montanaro had reached his car and was roaring off in a rage, but on the heels of that sound, almost before I could finish my thought, came the shout and the sick thump of a large vehicle hitting living flesh.

I knew that whump of sound all too well. Someone or something had been struck by a car.

I wrenched open the back door of my car and shoved Remy inside, closing him in before I raced to the front of the strip mall.

The light of the streetlamp illuminated what looked to be a pile of clothing in the middle of the road. Up the street, two figures were running in my direction, but I was closest. I dashed out in the road, waving my arms as a car came from the other direction. To my relief, it came to a stop.

But the form on the ground never moved. As I ran up to it, I saw the blood marking the pavement, pooling in a stain the color of India ink in the headlights of the stopped car.

It was Montanaro. He lay like a crumpled marionette, strings cut, legs bent at impossible angles. As I knelt beside him, he opened and closed his mouth several times, but no sound came out.

This was bad. Very bad.

I could see the tire marks on the asphalt leading up to his body, wide swaths of rubber burnt into the pavement. A bit of yellow glass caught the light by my knee. My mind seemed stuck on such minutia, in an effort to avoid the horror of what lay before me. As I stared, Montanaro's lips trembled, and he tried again to speak.

And then my brain, the bit that knew how to act in emergencies, came back online.

"Don't move." I tugged my belt out of my jeans and threaded it around the leg that was bleeding profusely, tightening it in stages. "Help is on the way."

"You there!" I shaded my eyes from the glare of headlights to yell at the driver of the other car. "Call 9-1-1. Don't let anyone else come down the street."

The driver appeared to me as only a shadow behind the bright halogen lights, but I saw him move, and promptly dismissed him from my mind as I went back to assessing Montanaro's injuries.

The wheezing pant behind alerted me to the arrival of the runners on the street, who turned out to be Pastor Harry Boggs and Doc.

"Dear Lord." Pastor Boggs spoke in a voice filled with horror. "That poor man. Is he dead?"

"Not yet," I said grimly. "Pastor, if you could stop traffic behind us, that would be a big help."

"Of course. Yes. Yes. Indeed."

He scurried off; no doubt relieved to have a worthy task that didn't require him to get any closer to the wreck that was Dennis Montanaro.

Beside me, Doc bent over his knees to whoop in air. Then, resting one hand on my shoulder to ease himself down, he squatted alongside. "What can we do?"

"Not much, I'm afraid. He's got compound fractures of both legs. I've slowed down the bleeding a bit, but there's evidence of internal injuries as well. He needs to get to a hospital right away."

I met Doc's eyes there on the dark street and shook my head. Montanaro wasn't going to make it.

Doc pressed his lips together and nodded slowly in understanding. He pulled out a handkerchief with a trembling hand and used it to wipe his mouth.

I felt so helpless. His injuries were too severe to risk moving him. There was little to be done until the paramedics arrived.

"I was in the parking lot behind the clinic. Did you see what happened?" I asked Doc.

Doc continued to mop his face with his handkerchief. "Not really. Harry and I had just come out of the diner. We were too far away to see much. Mr. Montanaro was crossing the street, though I didn't realize it was him at the time. I heard the roar of an engine. Thought it was kids out joyriding, you know? But the car seemed to come out of nowhere, and then there were squealing tires and his shout. When the car struck him, he flew through the air. Just flew." Doc passed a shaky hand over his face. "I'll never forget that sound."

In the harsh glare of the headlights, Doc looked pale and clammy. Like a heart attack waiting to happen.

"I've got this covered." I briefly clasped his hand, conscious of leaving bloodstains on his weathered and abraded skin. In the weird glare cast by the headlights, Montanaro's fresh blood looked like motor oil against the older nicks and cuts on Doc's hand. "Why don't you go over to the curb and sit down. Do you need something to drink? Do you want me to call Hazel?"

"No. No." Doc got to his feet shakily. "I'll probably have to speak to the sheriff. Harry will take me home later."

"Could you make out what kind of car hit him? The color or the license plate, perhaps?"

Doc's smile was weak at best. "I don't see too well at night anymore. I just saw taillights. Might have been a sedan, though."

A crowd gathered. Diners coming out of the restaurants and bars, shoppers struck by tragedy on their way back to their cars. Rubberneckers craning for a better look. Pastor Boggs came trotting back from traffic duty. In the distance, the wail of sirens could be heard.

"I've got the Jeffreys boys re-directing traffic on the south end of Main." Pastor Boggs huffed out his words, clearly shaken by the situation. "From the sound of things, the rescue squad should be here shortly."

For all the good it would do.

Montanaro coughed, his eyes opening wide at the painful effort. I found myself taking his hand. It was already colder than it should be. The contrast between his neatly manicured nails and the wreck that was the rest of his body struck me afresh.

"The ambulance is almost here," I told him, but his eyes were glassy, and I doubted he could hear or understand me. "Pastor, did you see what happened?"

"Oh my," he spluttered, clearly taken aback. "The accident? I'm not sure. Doc and I had just grabbed a sandwich at Sue's. We were headed back to the car when I heard this engine racing. Headlights snapped on, and all of the sudden, this man was pinned in their glare. The truck ran right into him!"

"The lights were off before? You're sure of this?" My head whipped toward him so fast it was a wonder I didn't pull a muscle in my neck. "You think it was a truck? Doc thought it might have been a car."

"Oh no." Pastor Boggs seemed sure at first, and then hesitancy crept into his voice. "Well, maybe not. If Doc thinks it was a car...."

"The leg fractures are mid-thigh. That's suggestive of a small truck at the very least."

"Oh, stop it, Ginny," Doc snapped. "You're a vet, not Jessica Fletcher, you know."

Doc's vehemence stung, but he really looked ill, so I let it pass. Besides, it probably wasn't wise of me to interfere with the memories of the only witnesses. Joe wouldn't thank me for that.

Like magic, the thought of Joe seemed to conjure him out of thin air, for the next thing I knew, he was pushing his way through the crowd. Authority rippled out from him, causing by-standers to step back in his presence.

The relief I felt on seeing him practically melted my bones. Thank God he was here.

"Rescue squad should be here any minute." Joe's voice contained an unaccustomed gravelly burr as he squatted beside me. "How is he?"

I rattled off the worst of the injuries as I saw them, and added, "He needs advanced trauma care."

Joe nodded. The seriousness of Montanaro's injuries were obvious. "They'll stabilize him at General first. They can call a chopper there if needed."

If he makes it that long.

I heard the unspoken words.

"Are you good here?" Joe's quiet words were for me alone. The headlight's glare sharpened the bones of his face and accentuated his five o'clock shadow. It was the face of a fallen angel or a reformed pirate, the bad and the good warring for dominance. He locked eyes with me, and I seemed to feel all he hadn't said and more. "I need to get back to crowd control and make a path for the ambulance. You good?"

I heard his intake of breath and cut him off before he could say anything else. "I'm good. I didn't see anything, but Doc and Harry here were coming out of the diner when they saw him get run down. But I *do* need to talk to you. Montanaro had just been to see me before he got hit."

Joe's frowning gaze should have felt disapproving, but I recognized that he was simply processing what I'd said.

"Right then." He gave my shoulder a squeeze as he stood up. "Come to the station once the paramedics take over. Doc, Pastor Boggs, why don't you head over there now?"

"Come on, Doc." Pastor Boggs helped Doc to his feet. "Why don't we go over to the station and have a nice cup of coffee while we wait?"

"Don't want any coffee," Doc spoke querulously as the preacher led him away. "Keeps me up at night."

A moment later, the EMTs arrived. Joe held back the crowd as they rushed to the scene with back boards and neck stabilizers. It was a relief to turn things over to them. I gave my limited assessment, but they naturally made their own, rattling off findings to each other when they found Montanaro non-responsive.

I stood and tried to take a step back to make room for them, but my legs refused to cooperate, and I stumbled backward, only to have someone catch my arm in a firm grip and hoist me back to my feet.

I wound up practically in my rescuer's arms. Of course, it had to be Joe.

"Do me a favor, Ginge." His warm breath caressed my ear, sending a shiver down to my unsteady legs. "Head over to the station and wait for me there. I'm going to be here a while."

"Okay," I said once I'd recovered my balance. I added as an afterthought, "Don't call me Ginge."

The smile he flashed was one I hadn't seen in a while, full of humor and the sly acknowledgment that he'd pushed one of my buttons. Then it disappeared, weighed down by the need to deal with the immediate crisis.

I left him to it but had only taken a few steps when he called out once more. I held up my hand to shield my eyes from the glare of lights as I turned to see what he wanted.

"Mind letting Toad out for me? She's been in the office for hours."

I made a little air salute with my index finger to indicated I'd both heard and agreed to his request before continuing toward my car. Remy practically crawled in my lap when I got in, and I had to shove him back in order to start the engine. I had to wait for one of the deputies directing traffic to let me out of the parking lot, and then had to take one of the side streets to go to the station.

I sympathized with Lady Macbeth when I stepped into the public restroom at the sheriff's department to wash my hands. Blood is terribly difficult to remove from beneath your nails.

Toad was wild with excitement when I reached Joe's office. Too well-trained to jump on me, she kept doing sailing fly-bys, where she leapt in the air as high as my chest, brushing close without actually touching. She'd pulled some of Joe's things out of an overnight bag and had made a nest out of his clothes. One of his track shoes looked as though it had been nibbled on by rats, but the bulk of the material was still there, so I wasn't particularly worried about anything Toad might have ingested, though I fussed a little as I placed the shoes out of reach.

She became practically hysterical at the sight of Remy when I took her out to the parking lot. There was a ball field behind the station that was mostly fenced, with only an opening for players to go in and out near the dugout. I took the dogs through the gap, letting them run and play. The smaller Toad was built like a cannon ball. She was faster and could corner sharper than Remy as well. When she came at him like a freight train, he'd tuck his shoulder and roll, ducking the collision again and again as she barreled over top of him. I rested against the fence, my fingers curled around the chain links, and watched them play.

Dogs couldn't fix everything wrong in the world, but they certainly made it a better place.

Finally, when their tongues were hanging out and they were more interested in sniffing around than body-slamming each other, I whistled them up and took them back inside.

I picked up Toad's chew bones while they both gulped down water at the bowl in Joe's office. No sense in having them get in a fight over prized possessions. They settled on the floor to wrestle with each other, and I called my mother. When she answered, I filled her in on what had happened.

"Oh dear. That's dreadful." She tsked slightly. "The street is well-lit, and the speed limit is twenty-five. Was he in the crosswalk? I've always said they needed more patrols down there because of the bars and restaurants. Did you see who hit him?"

"No, I was in the lot behind the clinic when it happened." I hurried on before she could comment further on the perfidy of drivers and alcohol. "Look, I need to talk to you about my meeting with Montanaro. When I told him I wasn't going to buy into CVC—"

"You what?" My mother practically screeched. "Virginia Anne Reese, what on earth possessed you to turn down such a wonderful opportunity? You can't be serious! First you let the clinic slip out of your fingers, and then you throw away your chance to get it back again?"

"I turned it down because that's what Dad would have done."

That silenced her.

"Remember when the chain pharmacy wanted to buy him out?" I didn't wait for her response. "He turned them down because he didn't want a faceless corporation telling him what prices to set, upping the cost of a prescription every time it was filled. He didn't want to stock groceries and hair dye because he believed his primary duty was to dispense medication. Well, it's the same for me, Mother. If I'm going to run a clinic, then I want it to be *my* clinic. I don't want to have to answer to some middle manager, meet impossible targets that aren't medically driven, and charge criminally high prices."

Silence, heavy with what felt to me like disapproval, hung between us. Why was it so much easier to talk to her on the phone instead of in person? Why was it easier to find my backbone sitting in Joe's office than it was sitting at her kitchen table?

Joe was right. I needed to move out of her house. I regressed to a teenage girl in her presence.

"I loved your father very much," she said at last. "But Ginny, dear. We could have done a lot better financially than we did if he'd made different decisions. We could have lived anywhere, but he wanted the small-town experience of Greenbrier. We could have been secure in our old age, but he wanted to remain an independent pharmacist."

"Do you remember when Sophie Barton went to get a second mortgage on her house to pay her medical bills?" I asked. At my feet, the dogs pretended to bite each other, their mouths wide open as they swung their jaws from side to side in some sort of choreographed dance.

"Is she the one who discovered her lender hadn't done a complete title search on her house and there was a lien on it in your father's name?"

"Right," I said. "She called her lawyer in a panic because she desperately needed the money, and then came to find the house might not legally be hers anyway. And do you remember what Ethan said?"

My mother sighed. "He asked her if she knew Tom Reese."

"That's right. She didn't. She used the pharmacy in Clearwater. Ethan told her not to worry, that if she knew Tom Reese, she'd know everything would be all right. Can you imagine?" I asked. "A lawyer telling a client not to worry about something like that?"

"We needed that money, Ginny," my mother snapped. "Your father signed over that house to her without a single thought as to how it might affect us."

"Maybe," I conceded, still watching the happy, tired dogs as their play wound down. "But what better legacy can a man leave than that?"

I didn't give her too much time to think about it. "That's neither here nor there right now. Why didn't you tell me you'd gone to see Dr. Burnham at the clinic the night she died?"

"Who told you that?" Shock sucked the breath right out of her.

"Montanaro. He threatened to go to Joe with this information if I didn't sign on with CVC."

"What did you say to him?" Not as breathless this time. More anger.

"I told him I wouldn't be blackmailed."

"Good." Steel crept back into her voice. "Was he there that night? I didn't see him."

"He described you to a T. I doubt he could have done that if he hadn't been there." I hesitated, then soldiered on. "Mom. I have to tell Joe about this."

Chapter Seventeen

STRESS DOES FUNNY THINGS to a person. The events of the last few days should have had me more wired than three cups of espresso, but I was also running seriously short on sleep, so by the time Joe came through the office door bearing white takeout bags from the diner, I was dozing off in my chair.

The enthusiastic greeting of the dogs, combined with the scent of grilled meat, made me bolt upright. I sat, blinking and confused, as the dogs leaped and cavorted around Joe. He held the food above his head as he waded through the mass of canines toward his desk.

"Get off me, you silly mutts." He set a can of soda down in front of me, removed the other from where it had been tucked under his arm, and then placed the bags of food between us. Petting the dogs on the head, he said, "Nice to see you guys, too. But you need to go lie down now. Go. Lie. Down."

He spoke with such authority that Toad dropped to her belly, wagging her little nubbin of a tail as hard as she could. Remy plunked his bottom down, but a thin stream of drool trickled from his mouth, making Joe laugh.

"Sorry, nothing for you guys." He looked over at me, where I was in the process of wiping my face. And my own drool off my shoulder from where I'd been dozing, darn it. He began pulling the food out of the bag, pushing a white Styrofoam container across the desk toward me. "I don't know about you, but I'm starving. Brought you a burger."

My stomach growled loudly in appreciation.

"Oh, thank God," I said, to cover my embarrassment. "I haven't eaten. I was supposed to get dinner with Montanaro. What time is it?"

"About quarter past ten." Joe held up a hand, looking incredibly weary for a moment. "Let's call a moratorium on discussing the case until after we've eaten. Deal?"

"Deal." I opened the takeout box, fully prepared to scrape off everything I hated from my burger, but to my surprise, it was exactly the way I liked it. "You remembered how I like my burgers?"

Joe snorted into his can of soda. His eyes gleamed in amusement. "Ginge, who could forget? You want your burger cooked like a hockey puck, with only a slice of cheese. When I ordered a plain, well-done cheeseburger at Sue's, she knew it was for you right away."

Heat pumped into my face. Hopefully that wouldn't start the rumor mill, but chances were that it already had. I took refuge in biting into the burger, and then moaning my appreciation. "Oh, my God. I've been craving a cheeseburger for weeks. Manna from heaven couldn't taste better."

I chased my mouthful of meat with one of Sue's seasoned steak fries, practically whimpering with delight. Remy came over to my side of the desk and leaned his head heavily against my arm, giving me the puppy eyes big time.

"Oh, no you don't. This is too good for dogs. Go lie down."

He waited a second longer to see if I was really as mean as I sounded, and then with a sigh, withdrew to staring distance. I ignored him and dug into my food. Joe and I ate in silence, rather like hungry wolves.

"That hit the spot," I said when we were done, having eaten a little faster than was comfortable due to the pressure of the watching dogs. If I burped now, I might die of embarrassment. I took one of my remaining fries and broke it in half. "May I?"

"Sure." Joe waved a hand in open permission.

The dogs inhaled their share of the French fry so fast they couldn't have possibly tasted it. When they begged for another, I held up my empty hands and said, "All gone."

They continued to stare at me, as I clearly had more food in my container. Remy shuffled his paws in place as if to remind me he was still there, but I ignored him to drag another fry through the ketchup on Joe's tray. I wasn't a big fan of condiments, but for some reason I wanted the savory, tomato-y taste this time.

"That's new," Joe remarked, pointing at the ketchup. "I can't recall ever seeing you eat that before."

"See, you don't know everything about me." I preened a little, as if eating ketchup made me mysterious and sophisticated. And then laughed because seriously, ketchup?

Joe's grin faded as he chased a French fry around his container. He abandoned it without eating it in the end. "Yeah, about that. I owe you an apology."

"For taking my mother in for questioning?" I kept my voice light. "I should be thanking you. I had some things I needed to do. It was so much easier in her absence."

"You know that's not what I mean." His chair creaked as he leaned back in it. "I was pretty hard on you yesterday. Between the kids dying in the car accident and you finding Rachel dead in her office, I was having a bad day."

"I wasn't exactly having a good day myself." I lifted my hand like a stop sign when he would have continued. "It's okay. I understand."

"No, it's not okay. I'm sorry. I was a sanctimonious jerk." His mouth twisted to one side and the skin around his eyes tightened. "Frankly, you shouldn't let me off the hook so easily. You have every right to be mad at me. I wouldn't blame you if you told me off."

"You want me to talk about my feelings?" I hoped I didn't sound as aghast as I felt.

Joe snorted, brushed his nose with the back of his hand, and cleared his throat. "Nothing so dramatic as that."

Whew. Mentally, I wiped my forehead in relief.

"Fair enough. I *was* mad at you for a while, but I got over it." I pointed at him with a French fry. "Sanctimonious, eh? I see you're getting some use out of that Word-A-Day calendar the office got you for your birthday this year."

That teased a laugh out of him.

"I'm trying to be serious, here." His gaze, intense and earnest, held my own. "I had no call to question how you run your business or to compare your choices to Rachel's. I didn't mean it."

"You say you didn't mean it, but that criticism didn't come out of nowhere." I popped the fry into my mouth. Strangely enough, I'd made peace with his opinion of me. It had happened the moment I'd decided to turn Montanaro down. "You must have given it some thought before."

"It might have come up in a conversation with Rachel. In a general sort of way," he hastened to add, reacting to something in my expression.

"She was talking about the difficulties of changing the clinic's practice philosophy."

"And the difference between running a business and a charity, no doubt," I said dryly.

"It wasn't like that." He scrunched up his face and scratched the back of his neck. "Though you have to admit, if you can't pay your bills, you won't be there to help the next client. Something I'm learning the hard way, trying to budget our department's expenses."

When I said nothing, he scrubbed his face with his hands and continued. "The day you found Rachel, I was just so angry, you know? Two kids dead and one whose life will never be the same again. A new truck, a six pack of beer, and a couple of boys who wanted to show off for a girl."

"We pulled our own stupid stunts, as I recall." The memory of a few such incidents made me shift uncomfortably in my seat, especially the game where we'd dived into the open window of a moving car or slid across the hood, just like on TV cop shows. "It's a wonder any of us survive being a teenager."

"True." Joe gave a tired nod and pushed the food containers to one side. "But I sang the praises of small-town life to Rachel when she was looking to make a change. I more or less convinced her to come to Greenbrier. I can't help but feel responsible for what happened to her."

Curiosity made me ask. "How did you meet her?"

"On a charity run to raise money for one of the D.C. animal shelters." One shoulder lifted in a casual shrug. "Later, she came to see me in the hospital after I'd been shot."

She'd visited him when he needed someone the most—and I hadn't even been aware he'd nearly died.

"I'd already come back here when she called wanting to know more about life in Greenbrier. I swear to you, I had no idea she'd buy the clinic." Regret flashed in those tired hazel eyes, but his next words made me wonder what he was actually regretting. "She should have been safe here."

His decision to return to Greenbrier when his parents no longer lived in the area made more sense now.

I took a deep breath and said, "I saw a letter at the clinic from the Board of Veterinary Medicine addressed to Dr. Rachel Cartwright. Was that why she'd been called out of town? To report to an inquiry?"

He pulled his notepad within reach and picked up a pen to tap on the lined pages. The action drew my eye to his hands, his long, strong fingers marked with the callouses and abrasions that came from being both a carpenter and a horseman. "I suppose you'll find out about this sooner or later, but yes. It doesn't have anything to do with her, though. Not directly. Her husband, Callum Cartwright, ran a big vet practice in Alexandria. He also ran a dogfighting ring."

I said some *highly* uncomplimentary words, in a voice sharp enough to make Remy come over and nose my arm. Right before he tried snagging the food container off the edge of the desk. I pushed the Styrofoam boxes out of reach.

"Dogfighting? And a veterinarian was involved? No wonder she divorced him and changed her name." Poor Rachel. Perhaps I should have been more sympathetic to her when she was alive. "I'm not surprised she wanted to get out of NoVa, either. She must have been desperate to distance herself from the whole situation."

An unwelcome thought crept into my mind. Perhaps the witness protection program wasn't that far-fetched an idea. "Do you think that's why she was killed? I mean, there's money in dogfighting. Some purses can be as high as a hundred thousand dollars, to say nothing of breeding and the sale of dogs. Maybe there were some bad players who didn't want her testifying."

"I can't see how. She was defending her license to the Board of Medicine, not acting as a witness for the prosecution."

Time for a small confession. "I had a friend of mine do a little digging for me. She couldn't find anything about Dr. Burnham's previous life. Granted, I didn't know her married name then, but Michelle said there still should have been some links on the internet. She thought maybe Rachel's profile had been scrubbed."

"Scrubbed?" Joe came to frowning alertness in his seat. "That would take a fair bit of money."

"Money that CVC has," I pointed out. "It might have been worth it to them to polish her image before installing her here in Greenbrier. Montanaro told you about her being a front for his company, right?"

He went back to tapping his pen with narrowed eyes. "You make it sound underhanded. It seemed like a perfectly reasonable business arrangement if you ask me. What with the cost of living going up, the price of real estate skyrocketing, and wages staying nearly the same, I don't know how anyone can start their own business these days."

I probably would have been more understanding had Burnham been upfront about the source of her financing from the get-go, and I told him so. I then went on to explain why I thought many of the practices Burnham had employed—and I'd questioned—were probably in an effort to meet some financial quota from the corporation. Finally, I concluded with why Montanaro wanted to meet with me. "Montanaro made me the same offer."

The pen went still.

"Montanaro wanted you to buy into the clinic? And run it as a CVC associate?" His gaze pierced me where I sat in my chair. After a long moment, he said, "Tell me what happened."

"We met for breakfast this morning. That's when he told me about the clinic being a CVC asset and offered me a similar deal to the one they'd given Dr. Burnham. I told him I'd think about it, and we arranged to meet for dinner tonight to discuss my answer, as well as the management of the clinic as long as there were still animals there."

"You arranged to meet where?" Joe held the pen in his fingers as though about to write down everything I said, but his hand had frozen in mid-air.

I'd already thought about how best to protect Holly's decision to leave me behind to answer the burglary call. "At the clinic once I was done with the patient care this evening. Holly had just left on the call about the break-in. Montanaro caught up with me as I was getting ready to put Remy in my car."

It wasn't *exactly* a lie.

Joe tipped his head slightly, as though he could hear the parts I was leaving out. "Then what happened?"

"I turned him down. He seemed really surprised, and then he got nasty about it."

"What do you mean nasty?" Joe growled.

There was simply no other word for it. His eyes went flinty, his brow furrowed, and his voice dropped into a gravelly register. Both dogs both looked over at him at his change in tone.

In for a penny, in for a pound...

I relayed the incident between me and Montanaro. How he hadn't wanted to take no for an answer. How he'd threatened to go to Joe about the scene he'd witnessed between my mother and Burnham. I described Montanaro's reaction when I refused to be blackmailed, and when I told him reporting my mother would also indict him as well. Joe listened without comment; the only indication he heard what I was saying was the twitch of a muscle in his jaw and the way his fingers tightened on his pen.

I came to the end of my narrative, not sure whether to tell Joe what happened next.

He left me no choice. "Then what?"

"He threatened me. Not in so many words, but he came at me with his hands raised. I remember thinking I was in a bad situation—" I hesitated when I realized I'd almost given the show away by revealing I was inside the clinic and not in the parking lot, as I'd implied. "Er, alone with a potential murderer, and all that. I'd braced myself for a possible assault, when Remy jumped on him and made him stand down."

"Did he now?" A wide grin bloomed on Joe's face and he glanced over at the dogs. "I'd have liked to have seen that. You always said he'd never protect you in a pinch, Remy just looked the part of a guard dog."

"I was wrong." I matched Joe grin for grin. "When he peeled back his lips and bared his teeth, he looked just like a shark. Sure made an impression on Montanaro. He left after that. I was just about to get in my car when I heard the accident."

Technically, still telling the truth here.

The pen began to tap again.

"Witness statements seem to indicate it might not have been an accident. You think Montanaro killed Rachel?"

I shrugged. "He could have. Maybe she had become a liability. Lord knows the clinic was getting terrible reviews. Besides, if Rachel was under pressure to see that her clinic met certain quotas, you can bet as a manager, Montanaro faces the same kind of pressure."

"And he thought he'd kill her and install you in her place?" The way Joe tucked his chin and pulled back indicated he was having none of it. "Seems a little far-fetched to me."

"He certainly gave me the impression he was capable of violence. And he was the last one to see her by his own admission."

"Testimony he might not be able to provide. Mighty convenient if someone wanted us to think he was the killer. Who else would want Montanaro dead?" Joe pinned me in his gaze, as though he knew I'd been holding something back.

Oh dear. I no longer had a choice. I told Joe about finding the positive pregnancy test, as well as seeing someone I thought might be Amber detaining Montanaro as he was leaving the diner this morning.

"When were you planning to share this with me?" Joe's eyebrows bunched in annoyance as he threw his pen down. "This is a murder investigation, for crying out loud."

"I didn't think the pregnancy test had any bearing on the case. It didn't show up in the clinic until after the crime techs had been through." I blew out a sigh. "I only found the test this morning. I'd have said something earlier only I got sidetracked by, you know, the protest and things."

Even to my ears, it sounded like a lame excuse, until I started counting up all the events that had occurred in the last twenty-four hours.

Joe ran both hands through his hair until it stood in messy disarray. "Montanaro's admission to you calls into question some of the statements made by the church ladies, who swore up and down your mother was there all evening. She couldn't have been in two places at once. It does, however, fill in some of the gaps in your mother's accounting of her movements that night. What a mess."

"I don't see what the problem is." If I sounded defensive, I was. "Montanaro saw my mother leave the clinic. Dr. Burnham was still alive them. My mother was speaking in front of the church ladies after that. Her alibi should hold, right?"

"An alibi given by women who already lied about where she was earlier in order to protect her." Joe pinched the bridge of his nose in frustration. "I'm going to have to bring everyone in again for fresh statements and remind them of the penalties for lying to the police."

"Can't you compare the current statements and disregard the ones that are obviously false? Only look at the ones that support each other?"

"A good prosecutor will tear that apart and you know it." Joe shot me a glare. "The DA is looking to make his mark."

"Well, he can jolly well piss on someone else's tree," I groused. Honestly. Some men were as bad as terriers; always picking a fight with someone twice their size and marking their territory wherever they went. I suddenly remembered another strike against Montanaro and snapped my fingers. "Oh, Montanaro had a key to the clinic!"

"How do you know that?" Suspicion deepened Joe's drawl.

"Er, he showed it to me." I floundered a bit and forged on. "Bragging like. He admitted he hadn't told you about it, too."

"Huh." Joe picked up his pen again.

"Come on, Joe." I leaned forward to tap the desk between us for emphasis. "You *know* my mother didn't shoot anyone."

"Yes, but did she leave her gun behind at the crime scene? I'm going to have to bring her back in for questioning, Ginge."

"Don't call me Ginge," I said automatically, my mind somewhere else. I felt like I'd seen or heard something important, but I just couldn't make the connection I needed.

The phone on his desk buzzed. He picked up the receiver. "Sheriff Donegan here."

His eyes met mine over the phone. "I see. Thank you for letting me know."

When he hung up, I asked, "Montanaro?"

"Didn't make it," he said, confirming my suspicions.

I just nodded. I'd known Montanaro's odds for survival were slim the moment I'd laid eyes on him there on the pavement, but I'd hoped this time I was wrong. The silence stretched between us, and I felt compelled to break it at last. "I don't want to tell you how to do your job—"

Joe tossed his pen down once more. It was hard to tell from his expression if he was amused or annoyed. "But you're going to anyway."

"I'm just saying," I went on as though I hadn't been so rudely interrupted. "When you're trying to figure out what's wrong with an animal, you look for a disease process that fits all the symptoms. That doesn't always work. You can have more than one illness going on at the same time. But most of the time, you're looking for one cause for everything."

"You're saying that most likely whoever killed Rachel killed Montanaro too, and probably for the same reasons. Thank you for that most obvious observation, Dr. Watson."

The remark, combined with the slight smirk, tipped the scale on the side of amusement rather than annoyance.

"How come I'm Watson and you're Holmes?"

The sardonic lift of his eyebrow spoke volumes, but then he added salt to the wound by saying, "Elementary, my dear. You're the doctor. I'm the detective. Holmes." He pointed to himself and then to me. "Watson."

I rolled my eyes. "Anyway, you know I'm right. They were both outsiders. And it's not likely we have two killers running around town, is it?"

"No. But there's always the possibility Montanaro's death really was an accident. Or that his death is in retaliation for his killing Rachel."

Pulling his notepad closer, he asked, "Who knew you were meeting with Montanaro this evening? And did they know where?"

I thought about the possibilities. Surely there couldn't be that many. "Well, my mother knew. I mentioned it to her after you released her this afternoon." That didn't look good for her, given what Montanaro knew about her secret meeting with Burnham. "But we made the arrangements at the diner. Anyone could have overheard that."

"Is that where you saw Amber?"

"Inside the diner? No, but it could have been her in the parking lot afterward." Had I mentioned the meeting to Wendy? I didn't think so. "Oh, but I said something to Carolyn Price, the dog groomer. I ran into her outside the station, and she was upset because Montanaro wasn't returning her calls. I told her I'd try to put in a good word for her when I saw him."

"And you had this conversation out on the street? In the middle of the crowd?" The corners of his mouth pulled down as he scowled.

"'Fraid so." Which opened the door wide open to the number of people who could have heard or talked about my plans. "Though I didn't mention where we were meeting that time. Still, it wouldn't have been hard to figure out. Montanaro's yellow car would be easy to follow, and that's assuming he didn't tell anyone either."

"Given the local grapevine, the whole town probably knew you were having a dinner meeting with Montanaro about the clinic. That's not going to help us much." Joe picked up his soda, realized it was empty, and gave the can a sad little shake before putting it back down again. "Logic indicates the two deaths are connected, but I'm darned if I can see a reason for killing them both."

"What about Tony Linkous? Did you ever talk to him?"

"Of course, we did." Joe frowned, and then rubbed the corner of his eye with a finger. "He and a buddy of his are the secret masterminds behind a local podcast. They record it in advance and drop it on Saturday nights." He glanced at his watch. "Tonight, actually. That's when they usually record a new episode."

"Let me guess: *Greenbrier After Dark*."

Joe shot an effortlessly wicked grin in my direction at my sour tone. "You've heard of them?"

"Kim at the diner was raving about them this morning. She said they ran a special episode last night after the murder."

I imagined when the news about Montanaro got out, there'd be another episode tomorrow night as well.

"I listened to a couple of episodes earlier today after she mentioned it. Well, that explains how he knew about pentobarbital."

Joe lifted a questioning eyebrow, and I explained about the podcast's discussion of the best means of a veterinarian committing suicide. "So that means Tony's in the clear?"

"Yes. Not that he had a strong motive for killing his ex-boss anyway."

Joe yawned suddenly, pulling both fists back to stretch his shoulders, and I caught myself measuring the breadth of them with his action.

"Sorry," he added, yawning again. "Long couple of days."

"Can I ask you a question?"

Instantly the shutters went down.

"Not if it has to do with the investigation," he said with cool deliberation.

"Nothing like that." I indicated the carryall on the floor. "I couldn't help but notice you have an overnight bag here. Toad had pulled some of your stuff out. Are you sleeping at the station again?"

"Guilty as charged." His grin was self-deprecating, and he rubbed the back of his neck once more. "I'm beginning to think I made a big mistake."

"What?" My heart sank like a lead weight to the bottom of my stomach. What was he saying? Did he regret coming back to Greenbrier? Was he planning to leave again? "What kind of mistake?"

"Buying the property out by Potter's Mountain. Thinking I could build the perfect house with my own hands, all while being the sheriff here. The RV is like an oven in the summer and an ice box in the winter. Half the time I'm too tired to lift a hammer when I get home at night, providing there's any daylight left. And that's when I don't get called back out again." He paused to look at me curiously. "What did you think I meant?"

"Nothing. Nothing." I hurried on. "It's a shame, though. You love that land."

"I do. It's gorgeous. I feel a great sense of peace when I'm out there. But as long as I'm sheriff, it's probably not the right place for me." Regret roughened his voice. "I should sell it and look for something closer to town."

"In the meantime, you're bunking down here? On the couch in the break room?" I pulled out my key ring. "That's ridiculous. You can't possibly be getting a good night's sleep in the station."

"What are you doing?" He eyed me suspiciously.

I freed a key from my ring and held it out. "Here. It's the key to Amanda's house. I want you to take it. The place has been cleaned. All her personal stuff is gone. Last time I checked the spare rooms had fresh linens. Not much there in the way of food, but you can pick up some tomorrow."

"If you aren't staying there, why should I?"

I lifted an eyebrow.

"You know what I mean." He pulled a face. "You're not staying there because the probate hasn't gone through. So how is it right for me to be there?"

"I don't think anyone is going to report you to the authorities." I waggled the key. "Come on, you'll be doing me a big favor if you go there tonight. You can feed the animals for me. Hey, you can even go for a swim."

He just stared at me with a mulish expression. I knew he was going to martyr himself, so I played my trump card. I added, in a sing-song voice, "There's a jacuzzi in the master bathroom."

I could tell the word "jacuzzi" worked its magic on him by the way his ramrod posture eased. He seemed posed to argue the point further, but instead accepted the key. I felt as though I'd just hit an impossible target at the county fair, but I kept my reaction to myself. No need to be smug about it.

He acted like he was making a big concession. "Okay. But just for tonight and only because you need help feeding the horses."

"And the barn cats."

"And the barn cats. You could join me for that swim, you know." His trademark crooked smile made an appearance. "How about it, Ginge? You and me in a midnight dip? For old times' sake?"

I could suddenly picture it. The pool would be lit from within, a cool blue glow that would highlight Joe's smooth, sleek form as he cut through the water with strong strokes. He'd break through the surface and make his way to the edge, flipping his hair back as water poured off his gleaming shoulders. That smile would be there, the one that felt like the devil had created it for me alone. All I'd have to do is step into the water...

That would be one way of creating new memories at Amanda's to replace the bad ones.

I looked up to see Joe smiling at me with the exact wicked expression I'd just envisioned.

Oh no. No. No. No.

I'd already been down this path before, and as much I remembered how wonderful it felt to be held in Joe's arms, the rational part of my brain gave me a dope slap. I was as much to blame as Joe was here, sending out mixed signals and missing him when he hadn't been around, but resurrecting a relationship that had failed the first time was stupid.

But it would be fun while it lasted.

A fit of coughing overtook me, and I hastily drank the now-warm, mostly flat dregs of my soda. "Maybe some other time. I have to go home and have a little talk with my mother."

Chapter Eighteen

Before I left the station, Joe informed me that he'd had Brian from the hardware store install a padlock on the back door of the clinic.

"As far as I know," Joe said as he walked Remy and me to the door, Toad glued to his heel, "there shouldn't be any other keys unaccounted for. The locks were changed after Wendy was fired, and she turned in her key anyway. So did Tony when he quit. Rachel's key was on her ring. We collected keys from you, Erin, and Amber, and now we have Montanaro's as well."

He paused at the door and said, "I know that look. What?"

I grimaced. "It's just that my old key worked in the new lock. Granted, I think the lock was broken, but clearly it didn't take much to get the door open. Someone could have jammed a screwdriver in it or something."

"Ginny..."

Uh-oh. No nickname and in a warning tone.

"I'm just saying—"

"Leave it to the pros, would you? It won't matter much longer, anyway. Word is the clinic will be released by the crime techs by Monday. Maybe even tomorrow." He leaned against the door jamb, crossing his arms over his chest. "Thanks for letting me sleep at your place tonight."

I opened my mouth to correct him, but snapped my lips shut. He was right. Time I started thinking of it as mine or list it with a realtor.

"No problem."

Remy didn't want to leave Toad, and I had to haul him away by the collar, which marred the impression of the indifferent, consummate professional I'd tried to cultivate on leaving. I smothered a grin as Toad tried to follow us, and Joe was forced to leap from his casual pose in the doorway and prevent her from coming with us.

Dogs prevent you from taking yourself too seriously.

As expected, my mother was waiting to pounce on me when I got home. She wasn't the only one. Ming meowed in that raucous voice only a Siamese can produce until I gave him a small amount of kibble. Then I gave Remy a crunchy bone, even though he deserved filet mignon. He accepted it eagerly, and then crashed on the couch. A tired dog was a good dog.

Mother wanted to rehash the entire events of the day and was impatient with my delays.

"Well?" She folded her arms and tapped her foot like the schoolteacher she'd been. "What happened?"

I caught her up on events, including Montanaro's death. Relief at the news of his death flickered in her eyes for a moment but snuffed out when I told her Joe knew about her meeting with Burnham and would be seeking another interview.

"Why did you tell Joe I saw Burnham that night?" She fumed as I poured myself a glass of cold lemonade and took a seat at the table. "He didn't need to know that. With Montanaro dying, no one would have ever known!"

She pushed a coaster toward me so my glass wouldn't leave a ring on the polished oak table.

I looked at her over the brim for a long moment. "He may have been a low-life, but Montanaro was a human being who died in a brutal manner this evening. Think for a moment how you sound."

"That's precisely my point!" She sat down across from me and spread her hands. "He's dead. Had you said nothing to Joe, no one would have ever known. You're not a teenager anymore. You don't have to share all your secrets with that boy."

I stared at her, sitting there in her still-crisp pantsuit, with not one strand of her Nancy Reagan hair out of place as she radiated disappointment and disapproval. I'd been on the receiving end of such glares my entire life.

"I didn't share my secrets, as you put it, with Joe because he was once my boyfriend." I set my glass down a little harder than necessary and leaned forward to make my point. "I did it because it was the right thing to do. This is murder. Maybe even more than one."

My mother stiffened and rocked back in her seat. "More than one? What do you mean?"

"I mean that Montanaro's hit-and-run was probably deliberate. And it looks like you have a pretty good motive for both murders."

"You can't possibly think—" she spluttered.

"No, of course not." I left out the part where the manner of the killings wouldn't be her style. "But it doesn't look good. Why on earth did you go see Burnham? Especially when I asked you to leave it alone."

Instead of responding right away, she began fiddling with the remaining coasters.

"I thought Burnham should know she didn't have a snowball's chance in Hades of making a go of the clinic. Not with the prices she was charging, or the fact everyone knew you'd been planning to buy the place." She abruptly pushed aside the coasters and looked up at me. "Not when she was clearly an outsider."

I rubbed my temples, trying to make sense of her actions. "What possible result could have made such a confrontation worthwhile?"

Unlike my own fair skin, which betrayed my every reaction, my mother's sallow complexion rarely revealed her emotions. But this time, I could detect the heightened flush on her cheeks. "I offered her money to leave."

"You did *what*?" I gasped.

"You heard me." She lifted her head with stubborn pride. "I offered to buy her out."

I pinched the bridge of my nose and took several deep breaths. "Okay, aside from the fact that you didn't run this by me first, where were you planning to get the money for grand scheme of yours?"

"I don't need this big house all to myself." She sniffed as though selling her home of fifty odd years was no big deal. "I'd be fine with a little apartment in town."

An appalled curiosity overcame my better judgement. "What did Burnham say?"

"Well, that's just it." My mother frowned. "I think she was tempted. I even got so far as to pull out my checkbook. To write her an advance, you know. She said she'd have to think about it."

Oh-ho! I bet Montanaro hadn't liked that. It was weird to think my mother's crazy scheme might have worked.

There was still the matter of the gun, though.

"I need to know, Mother. Did you or did you not go into the clinic brandishing your gun and threatening Dr. Burnham?"

"I should say not!" She clasped her fingers on the table in front of her. "That is to say, I didn't threaten her. Not in so many words. And I think 'brandishing' makes me sound like a hooligan. I merely laid the gun on the desk. I had to take it out of my purse to get my checkbook."

Tempted as I was to gently thump my head against the tabletop, my mother's soft exclamation stopped me. I looked up at her. "What?"

"As I said, she seemed tempted, but then she got quite rude and demanded I leave." My mother had the grace to look shamefaced. "I must have left my gun behind by mistake."

I could picture the scene. Rachel Burnham might well have been inclined to listen to my mother, particularly if she'd been regretting her decision to buy the clinic and feeling trapped by her deal with Montanaro. But then my mother had to go and pull her gun out of her purse. If I'd been Rachel, that would have made me uncomfortable too. She probably changed her mind and wanted my mother out of the clinic. I could see my mother getting flustered and neglecting to put her gun back in her purse, especially if she'd emptied the contents to retrieve her wallet.

I could also imagine that Rachel wouldn't have been in any hurry to call my mother's attention to her lethal weapon. She probably thought the wiser course of action would be to not return the gun to my mother. No doubt she'd planned to lock it up and give it to me. She might have even planned to turn it in to the station. "Well, now we know how your gun got into Burnham's office. You'll have to tell Joe this tomorrow."

Her expression turned mulish again but before she could protest, I said, "Whatever possessed you to make such an offer in the first place? Without even talking to me. Seriously, Mom. What's up with that?"

She began to twist her engagement ring, a small diamond solitaire, around her finger. The overhead light caught the stone as it moved in a flare of tiny prisms, like a miniature lighthouse. With a sigh, she appeared to notice her actions and placed her hands flat on the table.

"You were always my smartest child," she said unexpectedly, catching me completely off-guard. "The prettiest and brightest of my girls. Oh, yes, Eliza Jane was quite the charmer, and she never had to worry about making friends or fitting in, but there was something special about you."

"Hold up here." I couldn't believe what I was hearing. "Liz is the one who's done everything you wanted her to do. Married a great guy, had two kids, bought a nice house, and makes a respectable amount of money. I'm the failure."

"No! Wherever would you get that idea?" My mother seemed truly shocked.

"Where would I get that idea?" I spoke each word with careful deliberation. "Oh, I don't know. Maybe it's because my entire life, I've never heard you say one positive thing about me. You think I'm pretty? All I ever heard was what a hulking Amazon I was. When I got braces, you told me I would have to work extra-hard to make friends. Or how about the fact you kept drilling into me that I'd better learn how to take care of myself because no one else would want me? Liz was the pretty one. The graceful one. The talented one. Liz was the one you took to piano recitals and ballet classes. She was the one who prepped as a debutante."

Mother looked at me with utter confusion. "But you didn't want to do those things."

"I was asked to drop out of those things." I still remembered the shame of being told by my instructors I didn't have the right physique or ability to take the kinds of lessons my sister excelled at performing. "I wasn't good enough."

"You were sick a lot as a child. You couldn't keep up with the lessons. That's why you were asked to drop out. And when you were better, you insisted on horseback riding lessons instead."

Huh. That's not the way I remembered it at all.

"As a matter of fact, I tried to move you into something else." She folded her arms and glared at me. "When you were eleven or twelve. You came to me and said you'd outgrown your riding gear—jackets, boots, hard hat, and so on—you called it a riding habit. Do you remember that?"

I shook my head. Where was she going with this?

"I said I wished you'd outgrow your horse habit because it was terribly expensive. And *you* said—"

The memory resurfaced suddenly.

"I said it couldn't be any more expensive than a cocaine habit." I smothered a grin at her expression. "And you took me straight to the tack store."

Sometimes being a smart-aleck kid paid off.

The urge to smile faded. Wanting to hold onto what felt like deserved outrage, I pointed out, "You only came to one horse show. You left partway through the competition and never came again."

"My dear child." My mother lifted both eyebrows. "Yes, your father and I came to one competition. In the pouring rain. You raced around the arena on a green-broke pony jumping fences when other horses were slipping and falling. It was the most insane display I'd ever seen. The little demon pony you rode bucked like a fiend, and we watched with our hearts in our mouths to see if you'd come off and be trampled to death."

"I stayed on because I didn't want to get caked with mud." I snorted at the memory. It *had* been a terrible decision to compete that day. The show should have been cancelled due to the weather. At the very least, my instructor should have pulled our entries. But we were determined to go, and twelve-year-old girls shouldn't be the ones making such calls. "That was one show, however. You never came to another one again."

"We couldn't." My mother shook her head. "If we'd continued to come to your events, we would have put a stop to it. I couldn't watch you risk your life like that."

"They weren't all like that one."

Her eyebrows shot up her brow in patent disbelief.

Slowly, the sacrifice she'd made began to dawn on me. "But you didn't forbid me to go."

"You were utterly, brilliantly fearless." She locked eyes with me. "How could I destroy that?"

Her words shook me to the core. Knocked hard against my belief that I'd never been good enough for her. And then I remembered. "You didn't come to my high school graduation. Neither you nor Dad. You said, 'If you've been to one high-school graduation, you've been to them all.'"

"Well, that was an unfortunate turn of phrase." She spoke with brisk matter-of-factness. "And you have to admit, it *is* true. There is a distressing sameness to those kinds of interminable events. Your father and I were busy people. Besides, it was your time to say goodbye to your friends. Most of whom you'd never see again. I should like to mention that you didn't attend your own college graduation."

"I didn't see the point." I wrinkled my nose at the notion of sitting for hours under the broiling sun in a football stadium with hundreds of other graduates and their families. "You taught me that nothing short of an extraordinary achievement was noteworthy enough for celebration, and that nothing I did was remarkable enough to note."

Her mouth fell open at that.

"I'm sorry I ever gave you that impression." She pressed her fingers to her lips momentarily, but then seemed to pull herself together. When she spoke again, there was steel in her voice once more. "You are an accomplished professional. If I pushed you hard as a child, it's because I wanted more for you than a life in Greenbrier, marrying your high-school sweetheart and having babies before you were an adult yourself."

Surely, she didn't know how close I'd come to doing just that. Did she?

"Like you."

"Like me," she agreed. She then tapped the table between us. "Don't you ever call yourself a failure. You got out of this town and made something of yourself."

I skated over the implication that raising two kids and teaching school all those years here in town didn't seem to count as accomplishments in her book. Instead, I said, "But I came back."

"You did. And that was your choice. Your father needed you and you decided to come home. It was the right thing to do."

Note how it was my *father* who needed me, not her.

My reaction to that statement apparently went unnoticed by her, for she continued, "Which is why I went to see Burnham." She leaned back in her seat with a look of supreme satisfaction. "If you have to live in a small hive, you might as well be the Queen Bee."

I covered my face with my hands for a moment, rubbing my forehead. There was so much wrong with our relationship, I didn't even know where to begin. Finally, I lifted my head and said, "Look, Mom. I appreciate you looking out for me all these years. I know you wanted to teach me to be an independent woman, and for that I'm very grateful. But I *am* an adult now, and I'm capable of making my own choices. I don't need you going to bat for me against the competition or selling your house to pay for my business. I don't want you deciding for me what I should be doing or who I should be seeing—"

She interrupted. "If this is about you and Joe going your separate ways after high school, you should thank me for that."

Count to ten. Count to ten. Count to ...

"I should thank you." I leaned my elbows on the table and laced my fingers. "How so?"

"High school romances never last. You would have torpedoed your life, your plans, to do what? Follow him to the city? Live in some dumpy apartment on his measly paycheck while you looked for unskilled work?" The previous softness was gone now. She was all sinew, bone, and talons again.

"You and Dad worked out just fine."

"Your father was different," she snapped. "Even so, I soon realized I had to make a life outside of being his wife and the mother of his children, so I went back to school and got my degree in education."

"And made a difference in the lives of hundreds of children over the years. Was it really such a bad life here in Greenbrier?"

"No, but I wanted more for you." She sat, rigid and unyielding, in her chair. "You deserved more."

I'd spent a lifetime dancing around her mercurial temper. Squashing any smoldering resentment over her interference in my life was second nature by this point. She wasn't going to change. If I expected the dynamics of our relationship to be different moving forward, the change would have to come from me.

I needed to put some distance between the two of us first. I scarcely knew what to think about the revelations that had just taken place.

I took my glass over to the sink to rinse it. Standing with my back to her, I looked out the kitchen window at the fireflies winking on and off in the dark yard beyond. "I'm going to talk to Mr. Carter about moving into Amanda's place before the probate goes through."

Instead of protesting that it was ridiculous for me to move out when there was plenty of room here at her house, she surprised me by saying, "So, you're keeping the property, then?"

Until just then, I hadn't decided, but when I spoke, the answer came to me. "For the time being. It will be fall before the probate goes through. Best to wait until spring to move the horses if I intend to sell. Who knows? By then it might feel like home. But this running back and forth to take care of the animals out there is wearing me down."

"I thought you might leave the area. You don't have to stay, you know."

I turned to face her. "Was that what this was all about? You making an offer to Burnham because you didn't want me to leave Greenbrier again?"

"Don't be ridiculous. I just said you didn't have to stay."

Her hands lay folded in front of her on the table. She'd always been a little vain about her hands, but I could see now the thickening of her knuckles and the thinning of her skin. The manner in which she tightened her fingers belied the calmness of her dismissive statement.

No, I didn't have to stay, but now that I was financially independent, there'd been no guarantee that I *would* stay. Not once the deal on the clinic fell through. Her buying Rachel out would have made it virtually impossible for me to move away and start life over in a new town. I digested this in silence. There was no point in making a big deal of it. Mother would just deny it anyway and calling her out would only back her into a corner where she'd double down with volcanic fury.

If Liz had been there, she would have chided me for not standing up to Mother. She might have been the favorite daughter, but I'd been witness to plenty of blow-out arguments that had ended with Liz storming out. When Liz had moved in with her future husband, Dave, without a wedding or engagement ring, my mother didn't speak to Liz for over a year. It was as though she hadn't existed. It wasn't until Liz had set a wedding date that my parents had suddenly remembered they had another daughter. The disownment disappeared as though it had never happened.

I'd decided a long time ago if I couldn't be the best daughter, at least I'd be the *good* one. There was a reason I was the one who came back to Greenbrier and not Liz. I was the only one who could deal with our mother.

Possibly because I didn't really deal with her at all. I just absorbed whatever she threw at me and pretended nothing was wrong.

I set the rinsed glass on the sideboard. "Depending on what Mr. Carter has to say, I'll move out this weekend."

"I see." She stacked the coasters neatly and placed them in the center of the table. "Did you by any chance buy any cookies while you were at the store today?"

I took the change of subject for what it was: a peace offering.

"Yes," I said. "Vanilla wafers."

Her favorite.

"Well, since you're up," she said with her usual bite, "I'll have two."

I pulled the box out of the cabinet, set it down on the table in front of her, and left the room.

Chapter Nineteen

Suggesting that Joe sleep at Amanda's hadn't been an entirely altruistic move on my part. Having him temporarily take over the feeding of the animals there meant not only was I able to skip driving out to the property after an utterly exhausting day, but that I also got to sleep in the following morning.

Well, as much as I ever sleep in. When you get up most days around six a.m., even an extra half-hour of sleep feels like winning the lottery. Animals don't understand the concept of *sleeping in*.

Especially cranky old Siamese cats.

My mother was at the kitchen table when I went downstairs, with her war paint in place and in the center of a citrusy cloud of Jean Naté scent so strong it made Remy sneeze.

"There's oatmeal on the stove," she said, wrapping her hands around her coffee cup.

As I expected, it was as if the conversation of the night before had never taken place.

I took a quick glance at the congealing, half-burned mass in the pot. "Thanks. I'm not really hungry. You look nice. Are you heading into town?"

"I'm going down to the sheriff's station." She took a sip of coffee. "I thought I'd get my statement over with."

"Um." I glanced at my watch. It was only quarter after seven. "Are you sure you don't want to wait until Mr. Sampson can be there with you?"

"I fired him, remember?" She arched a fine eyebrow in my direction.

"Seeing as I was the one who had to negotiate for the return of our retainer, yes, I do." Chances were good Sampson would tell me to go fly a kite if I called saying we'd changed our minds, too. "But that was before

I knew about your meeting at the clinic with Burnham, or that you left your gun there. We might want to re-think having a lawyer present when Joe questions you."

"Let me ask you one question." She placed her cup on her saucer with a clatter. "Do you trust Joe Donegan or not?"

"Trust him? Well, of course I trust him." I shook my head at her just the same as I filled Remy's and Ming's dishes with food. "These things aren't always up to Joe, though. He told me the D.A. is pressuring him to close the case, and it sounds like he's more concerned with making his mark than finding out who killed Dr. Burnham. Having a lawyer present only makes sense."

"I'm not going to sit around all day waiting for some overpriced lawyer to listen to me come clean to Joe. I have a hair appointment at nine."

"I'm not sure what time Joe gets in."

"If he's doing his job, he should be there already. If not, someone else can take my statement, can't they?" Her brows lowered in frowning disapproval. "Surely, *someone* will be there at the station."

Right. Well, I tried.

"I'm sure there'll be someone to take your statement." There's a fine line between being soothing and sounding patronizing, and with my mother, the line was always in flux. I poured coffee into a travel mug and capped it. "I've got to run. I'm meeting Holly at the clinic. See you later."

Because I didn't have to dash over to Amanda's to feed critters, I had plenty of time to stop by Brenda's Bakery for one of her delicious blueberry scones. I was pleasantly surprised to see she hadn't run out yet and bought a box of six to take with me.

My next pleasant surprise came when Holly met me in the clinic parking lot.

"The techs cleared the scene." She held out a set of keys. "You won't need me to babysit you anymore."

"Aw. I'm going to miss your help." The keys looked so new and freshly cut, the edges could have sliced paper. "I'm guessing you'll be glad to be released from poop duty, though."

"I live to serve," Holly quipped gravely, and then smiled. "Say, about last night. I appreciate you not ratting me out to the boss about leaving you at the clinic."

"Under the circumstances, I think Joe would have understood, but I was happy to omit the details. Scone?" I held open the box.

"Oooh, thank you." She reached in, selected a scone, and took a blissful bite. Still chewing, she added, "Don't get me wrong. Joe's a good sheriff and a good man to work for. Pete Linkous should have retired long ago. We were lucky to get someone experienced like Joe elected. Joe doesn't treat me as a second-class citizen whose only purpose is to make coffee and go on a bakery run." She emphasized her point with a little wave of her scone. "But he's pretty strict about the rules. Bend them too far, and your ass is grass and he's the lawnmower."

I laughed at that. "He's been known to bend a few rules in his day."

Holly nodded in perfect seriousness. "That I don't doubt. He's not fussed about the little stuff like the uniform code or eating in the car. He hates paperwork himself, so he'll even cut you some slack on that too. But woe be unto you if you fail to log evidence properly or follow procedure. Anyway, thanks for not letting the cat out of the bag."

"You know me. Cats belong in carriers until you're ready to vaccinate them," I said, trying out the keys until I found the one that fit the shiny new padlock. "Hey, does that mean the staff can come by and pick up anything they might have left behind? I probably won't be able to get in touch with CVC headquarters until Monday, and there's no telling when the clinic will be open for business again. Or if they'll still have jobs."

"Sure." Holly shrugged, still munching on her scone while Remy looked up at her hopefully. "I don't see why not."

"Great. I'll contact them."

I waved goodbye and sent Remy into the building ahead of me, following behind with my thermos and the rest of the scones.

Even though there were only the boarders left in the clinic, it took a lot longer to clean and feed the animals without Holly's help. Around 9 a.m., I figured most of the staff would be awake, so I took a break to make phone calls. Amber's phone rolled over to voice mail. I thought it unlikely she'd listen to her messages from an unknown number, so I texted her, telling her to arrange to pick up any belongings she may have left behind either this morning, or when I came back to do one of the later rounds. I left the same message for Erin.

There was no answer from Amber, but Erin immediately texted back. She didn't think she'd left anything behind but would be down to check before I left this morning.

Belatedly, I remembered Wendy's request that I look for her belongings. I hadn't run across her raincoat or scarf, but since I still had her number from when we both worked together at the clinic, I sent her a text saying when I'd be in the building if she wanted to stop by and look for her things.

There was no point in trying to get hold of Tony. No doubt he'd cleared his stuff out the night he'd quit. Carolyn, however, would be delighted to hear from me.

She picked up on the third ring.

"Carolyn, it's me, Ginny Reese. Listen, the clinic has been released as a crime scene. I'm here taking care of the boarders. Do you want to swing by and pick up your grooming equipment?"

"Really?" The surprised relief in her voice came through loud and clear. "How did you manage to talk Mr. Montanaro into releasing it?"

"I'm guessing you haven't heard. He was killed last night in a hit-and-run."

"Shut the door," she exclaimed. "Are you *serious*?"

"As a heart attack. I didn't see it happen, but I heard it and was there when they took him to the hospital."

"That's terrible." She paused, and I could picture her shaking her head, her little beaded braids clicking together. "Granted, I didn't like the man one iota, but what a horrible way to die. Did you say hit-and-run?"

"Yes." I hesitated. Joe had shared his thoughts with me during our little brainstorming session but that didn't mean his speculations were for public consumption. Best not to say anything about indications the incident wasn't an accident. "Right out in front of the clinic."

"Well, Lucky's Bar is just up the street. Still, I can't believe it." It was her turn to hesitate now. "You're sure you won't get in trouble letting me take my supplies?"

"Better to ask forgiveness than permission, I always say. Deputy Walsh said the building had been cleared and staff could pick up personal belongings." That was my story, and I was sticking to it. "I haven't called CVC headquarters yet. As far as I'm concerned, you have the clearance to grab your stuff, but I can't answer to what the company will say come Monday. Can you pick up your things today?"

"That's wonderful—I've been so worried about this." Another pause, and then she said, "I'd come down right now, only Seth took the truck to go pick up some lumber. He's not going to be back for a while. I'm afraid the grooming table won't fit in my car. I don't want to hold you up, though."

"Not to worry." I checked my watch. "I haven't heard back from the rest of the staffers, and I have to return later this afternoon to take care of the boarders again anyway. Why don't you call or text when Seth gets back? We can set up a pickup time this afternoon."

"You're an angel. I'll do that. I can't tell you what a relief this is to me."

She rang off, and I went back to hosing down the runs.

When I was finished, I went up front to make some phone calls where I could sit at a desk and make notes on the records. I might as well catch up with my own workload while waiting for Erin, and I needed to check in on the patients I'd discharged yesterday. The reception area had an abandoned feel as I entered the waiting room. Dust motes tumbled lazily in the beams of sunlight that came in though the main window. I pulled the blinds. No point in letting anyone think we were open for business.

A creepy sense of déjà vu came over me. What had Rachel's last actions been before she was shot? The killer must have seen my mother's gun there on Rachel's desk, making it more likely her death had been a spur-of-the-moment decision. I tried to picture the scene the way they depicted it in all the crime shows: plucky heroine standing in the center of the room while the shadowy figures of the victim and the killer performed their macabre dance around her.

Yeah, right. Burnham hadn't even been killed in the reception area.

Curiosity drew me down the hallway. The door to Burnham's office was closed, but the yellow crime scene tape had been removed. I'd placed a hand on the knob and had begun turning it when something brushed against my leg.

I squawked and leapt into the air, only to realize it was Remy.

"You scared the crap out of me," I scolded, smoothing his ears at the same time.

His tongue lolled out of his mouth as he wagged his tail.

Taking hold of his collar, I opened the door for a peek inside. The interior of the room was a wreck. Fingerprint powder coated everything in a fine silver dust. A large piece of carpet next to the desk, which I recalled being soaked in blood, had been cut out and removed. The electronics were gone, as were all visible correspondence and files. The chair in which she'd been seated had been pushed back against the wall, but the surface of the desk was still stained, and a couple of blue bottle flies buzzed over it.

I needed to call the main CVC office to let them know about Montanaro and ask what to do about the clinic. My contract with Burnham technically ended today, tomorrow morning at the latest, and I had no idea if I was going to be paid for continuing to take care of the boarders. CVC needed to get professional cleaners in as well.

Too spooked to work at the front desk, I grabbed a chair and wheeled it back to treatment room. Normally, there wasn't any time to sit down in the work area, hence no chairs, but the gloomy atmosphere of the rest of the clinic was getting to me. I preferred to make my calls in the well-lit treatment room.

Tiffany's people didn't answer, so I left a message. Mrs. Oberstein was so pleased to hear from me that I nearly had to fake an emergency call to get her off the line. As relieved as I was to hear Pirate was doing well, I made a mental note to stop by to visit Fran sometime next week when I got the chance, to check on her as well as the cat. I'd just ended the call with her when Remy sat up alertly, ears pricked, and got to his feet.

I followed him down the hall. Someone was knocking at the back door.

I'd turned the catch on the doorknob when I'd come in. There was no peephole. Perhaps no one had needed a key to get into the clinic the night Burnham was killed. Would she have opened the door to someone pounding on it? Maybe, if she thought it was someone with a sick pet. Especially if that person had called and said they were on the way with an injured animal. I had no way of knowing.

I held Remy back by the collar as I unlocked and opened the door.

Erin stood on the other side of the door, smiling at me. "I think I might have left one of my schoolbooks here."

"Come on in." I stepped back to let her enter the building and shut the door behind her. "Were you assigned a place to store your things while you were working?"

"Not really. But there was a cabinet where we could leave stuff. Did you get hold of the others?" Erin pushed the swinging door open into the treatment area and held it open for Remy and me.

"Mostly. I had to leave a message for Amber." I took my seat in the chair stolen from reception and watched as she went to a storage cupboard and began searching it. "You haven't heard from her, have you? I'm a bit worried about her."

Erin let out a little cry of satisfaction and pulled out a textbook. Tucking it in her bag, she gave a little shrug. "Not today. But that's not unusual for a Saturday. It's still kind of early. Why are you worried?"

I'd spent a good bit of the morning while cleaning cages planning how best to pose this question without ruffling feathers. I hadn't come up with anything. "Well, it's like this. I found a home pregnancy test in the kennel trash can yesterday. It was positive."

Erin's dark eyes went wide at my words. "Oh wow. You weren't supposed to see that."

It was my turn to shrug. "I was emptying a litter box and everything in the can shifted. It wasn't yours, was it?"

"No way." Erin took a step back. "I swear to you."

"I didn't think so. Relax." I held up a hand in a gesture of peace. "I'm not planning to tell anyone. I'm just concerned, that's all. I saw Amber talking with Montanaro outside the diner yesterday morning. Pretty early so it must have been something important. Especially since it was clear she didn't like him. So that combined with finding the pregnancy test, got me to thinking..."

Erin began to twist the handle of her bag. If she wasn't careful, she'd wind up tearing it. "Look, it isn't my story to tell."

"But there *is* a story here."

"You should talk to Amber." There was a defiant tilt to her chin now.

One of the things I'd debated while cleaning cages was how much to reveal to Erin when I spoke with her. I knew anything I said she'd take straight to Amber, but the longer it took me to track down the other girl, the less likely I'd have the element of surprise anyway. Unless Amber was still asleep, she'd be running into the town gossip mill soon enough.

"That's cool. I'll talk to her when I catch up with her. It's just—" I hesitated for effect. "—you know about Montanaro, right? Someone ran him down with a car last night. He's dead."

"He's *what*?" Erin gawked at me for a moment before slapping her hand over her mouth.

"Yep." I nodded. "Dead as a doornail. Hit-and-run."

"You don't think *Amber* had anything to do—" The way Erin suddenly broke off made me think she'd recalled something to give her pause about defending Amber to me. She began sidling toward the exit.

"I know the sheriff wants to speak with her." I followed her as she edged out the door. "Do me a favor, okay? Tell her to contact Sheriff Donegan if she gets in touch with you."

I walked her to the exit and locked the door behind her. Remy was suspiciously absent from the hallway when I turned away from the door. Normally, he'd have followed me, which made me wonder what he was up to now. A text alert went off as I walked along the dimly lit corridor to the treatment area.

It was Amber, wanting to know when she could come and pick up her things. I glanced at the time and texted back.

If you get here in the next ten minutes, I'll wait, otherwise I can meet you later.

After a pause, she responded.

See you when you come back to walk dogs this afternoon.

I had mixed feelings when I read her text. It gave me more time to think about what I'd say to her, but also made it more likely she'd find out about Montanaro, and I'd wanted to witness her reaction when she found out. Given the likelihood Erin had already texted her with the news, however, the point was probably moot.

Snorting at my own foolishness, I began walking toward the treatment room again. Another text came through just as I was about to open the door. This time it was Carolyn, saying she could bring the truck over around one p.m. if I was still willing to meet her. I texted "yes" as I walked through the swinging door.

There I found Remy, dancing with excitement as though I'd been gone for hours.

I also found the bakery box on the floor, empty of my scones, and the waxed paper licked spotless.

"You rotten beast." I picked up the box with the vain hope there would still be a scone hiding within. "That was my breakfast for the following week!"

Remy was decidedly unrepentant. His tongue hung out of his mouth as his tail swept from side to side. There were crumbs on his nose.

Oh well, he deserved a nice treat after protecting me from Montanaro.

Chapter Twenty

To my surprise, when I'd called the CVC headquarters number, someone answered. I guess when you run a bunch of animal clinics across the country, you have to have a team trained to put out fires at all hours of the day or night, including weekends. The employee I got on the phone sounded suitably shocked when I informed her about Montanaro's death, which was gratifying in a weird way, and said she'd have someone get in touch with me first thing on Monday regarding the management of the clinic. We agreed that in the meantime, I would continue taking care of the boarders through the weekend. She would take over trying to locate their owners and getting them discharged as soon as possible. She also said she'd handle hiring a clean-up crew, and that she would put them in touch with the sheriff's department about gaining access to the building.

For a moment after I ended the call, I fantasized about the cleaning crew finding a crucial piece of evidence in my presence that would allow me to solve the case. There was at least one television show out there based on that premise. I gave it up as a lost cause, though. First, that sort of thing never happened, and second, I could trust Joe to deal with this on his own. My interference was neither necessary nor desired.

That didn't stop me from sitting down with a calculator and going over the controlled drug logbook. What few math errors I detected had been noted, corrected, and initialed by Rachel when she'd taken over the practice. There were no serious anomalies.

If only I could shake the feeling I'd heard or seen something important.

For the next couple of hours, I busied myself with my own neglected practice. I scheduled appointments as best I could, given that the fate of the clinic was still up in the air. Since the scene had been cleared, it was quite likely CVC would decide they no longer needed my services to care for the boarders, and they would probably pay one of the girls to continuing feeding and cleaning. Until then, however, I had to assume I would be at the clinic three times a day.

Feeling the need for some green stuff in my diet, I left Remy in one of the empty runs, had a salad at *Calliope's* for lunch, and returned to the clinic for the afternoon animal care.

Carolyn arrived shortly thereafter. She brought Seth with her, and after introductions, I helped them take her belongings out to her truck. It was a big blue Silverado that, judging from the scratches and dings, was clearly a work vehicle. Between the three of us, it took very little time to stow Carolyn's gear. Seth tucked the table under one arm as though it were as Shih Tzu, and I held the doors open for him as he took it out.

"I can't tell you how much I appreciate this," Carolyn repeated for the second or third time as she put the large pet dryer in the bed of the pickup.

"Like I said, it's your stuff. The corporation is likely to take over things again Monday, so I was only happy to help." I set a carry-all filled with various medicated dog shampoos and conditioners in the backseat of the truck. "If you decide you're going to work out of another clinic again, though, you might want to put your name on your equipment."

"I've got an engraver." Seth slammed the tailgate shut. "I'm going to label all of her things this afternoon."

"Good idea." An engraving was harder to remove than a simple nametag. "I'd photograph everything as a digital record as well. Include serial numbers if they are present. I had a house fire recently, and I had the dickens of a time proving what I lost."

"I never thought of that, but it's a good suggestion." Carolyn glanced back at the clinic with a twist of her lips. "Though I'm not sure what I'll do in the future."

"Things will work out, I'm sure."

She gave me a tired smile. "Maybe. I hope so."

I watched them leave, glad I could at least make sure she got back the tools she needed to stay in operation, no matter what form it took.

As I watched them pull out of the parking lot, it occurred to me that Carolyn had one of the better reasons for wanting both Burnham and Montanaro dead. There was a good chance Rachel's death would release Carolyn from a ferocious non-compete clause, one that would essentially prevent her from working anywhere in the nearby area. Could I really picture her killing Montanaro over the refusal to return her equipment?

His death did allow her to get her supplies back. But that would have happened anyway, right?

Honestly, my mother was the strongest suspect. She'd been onsite the night Rachel was killed. She'd been heard to threaten Rachel and she was known for her temper. Heck, she'd brought her own gun to the meeting, and it was the murder weapon! Montanaro had been about to expose her to Joe, although my mother hadn't known that. A good prosecutor would have no problem convincing a jury she *had* known, however.

Which is why I needed to come up with another strong suspect as soon as possible.

I glanced at my watch. Amber should be arriving at the clinic any minute now. If I was any sort of amateur detective—and I wasn't saying I was—I would have already earned my stripes by poking through Amber's things as soon as I knew in which cabinet the staff stored their personal belongings. Giving myself a mental dope slap, I hurried over to the cabinet where I'd seen Erin retrieve her book.

Behind the door was the usual catch-all of most places where'd I'd worked: a gray sweater liberally covered in cat hair, a packet of ponytail holders, a single mitten left over from the winter, a half-empty container of cat treats, a stack of outdated brochures provided by a sales rep, and an empty eye-glass container that I suspected might belong to Wendy. A blue raincoat was there as well, balled up and stuffed in the back. No sign of the scarf Wendy had mentioned.

There was also a small canvas bag.

Jackpot.

Inside the bag, I found a set of crumpled plum-colored scrubs with the ubiquitous animal-print border, this time in leopard spots. There was also a pair of sneakers, as well as an extensive makeup bag, including an empty container for false eyelashes, a pocket-sized curling iron, and three different shades of long-lasting lipstick. I strongly suspected the bag had held a change of clothing for a night out on the town, and by that, I meant the bright lights of Birchwood Springs.

But nothing incriminating. Not even anything suspicious, which was disappointing. I was certain Amber had been up to something untoward at the clinic, given her squirrely behavior the day of the murder. But my "jackpot" was more coming up cherries at the nickel slots than it was a winning lottery ticket.

Only, would Amber keep anything important in the community cupboard where anyone could come across it?

No.

If I were going to hide something at the clinic, it would have to be in a place no one would think of looking, but also easily accessible. That eliminated an astonishing number of potential hiding places. Anything in a drawer or cabinet was likely to be seen by someone else. Dr. Burnham's office was off-limits, as there would be few legitimate reasons for entering a private area. The storage room was within easy reach, but the very public nature of the room meant anyone going in to retrieve bandaging material or cleaning supplies might stumble upon Amber's secret.

Always assuming that Amber had anything to hide, and if she did, that she'd hidden it at the clinic.

I couldn't shake the feeling that there was something important she didn't want found, however. Her obvious discomfort when we were discussing the processing of the crime scene, as well as her willingness to come back to take care of the boarders, was suspicious in my book. Which is why I went as far as to climb up on the exam table and push up the ceiling tiles to shine my cell's flashlight into the space above the tiles. The fact I found nothing but insulation and cobwebs didn't surprise me, but it disappointed just the same.

I jumped down off the exam table, wincing when my knees complained at my impact with the hard floor. If Amber planned to show up, she'd be here soon. What was it she was so eager to get her hands on? And where would she have put it?

I suddenly recalled my first Christmas back in Greenbrier. My mother, never keen on gift-giving at the best of times, preferred to give practical gifts rather than something from the heart. That year, along with a multi-tool that allowed you to cut your seatbelt and break your window in the event your car became submerged in a raging river, she'd also given me one of those fake rocks to hide a key inside. I'd laughed it off, saying a better deterrent would have been a pile of fake dog poop instead.

Guess what I got for my birthday? You got it. A fake dog poop Hide-A-Key.

That said, there was something in the idea that there were certain things most people left alone. The pregnancy test had been dropped in a dirty trash can. What if Amber's devious mind ran along similar lines when it came to other hiding places?

I marched into the room reserved for the hospitalized cats and went straight to the large bin that contained cat litter. For ease of use, the litter was stored in a plastic trunk, and staffers used a scoop to fill clean trays. Surely the police had checked the bin. Still, it was a lot of litter. If they hadn't sifted through it, they could have missed something small. I ignored the stack of trays and began digging into the bin with the scoop, working my arm into the heavy litter until I hit the bottom of the container. Sandy litter clung to my skin as I dug around. I'd have fun cleaning that off later. But any distaste I might have felt vaporized the second I felt the scoop hit something.

Paydirt!

Using the scoop to pry up the edge of the whatever object lay buried within, I managed to turn the item on its side and grab it. The sand pulled at my arm as I withdrew my hand, clutching a small notebook in a plastic baggie. The notebook wasn't even as big as a pack of cards, and not nearly as thick. I brushed off the litter as best I could back into the bin and opened the baggie.

The tiny notebook inside the bag was held closed with an elastic band. Not really Amber's style. In retrospect, I would have thought her more likely to keep anything important on her phone. The lined pages were filled with cramped notations, along with numbers and dates. At first, the references seemed meaningless, as the notes were full of abbreviations known only to the author. But you know how if you let your eyes go out of focus you can suddenly see the hidden image of leaping dolphins or howling wolves in one of those Magic Eye pictures? That's sort of what happened next. One movement I stared in blank confusion at the notes; the next the abbreviations made sense. And once the abbreviations made sense, the rest fell into place.

The abbreviations were a list of the vendors used by the clinic, ordered by date. The first set of numbers probably showed the purchase price of each item. The second set itemized the sale price for each item with the final column indicated the percent markup. It wasn't just supplies, either. There was an entire section for services, reflecting the large change in fees that corresponded with Rachel buying the practice. The last entry was a few weeks ago. If I had to guess, someone was tracking the massive markup Rachel had made on almost everything Greenbrier provided since her purchase of the practice.

Nothing in the notebook indicated fraudulent activity. But there in black and white, the pattern of excessive markup was damning. Given that Rachel and Montanaro were still maintaining the fiction that the clinic was independently owned, there was probably a lot in the notebook that CVC would have preferred remained hidden.

I pushed open the swinging door to the treatment room with my elbow, still flipping through the notebook, when I was stopped by a soft exclamation.

I looked up to see Wendy standing in the middle of the room, blue raincoat in her hand.

"How did you get in?" I didn't intend to snap, but seeing her there like that was unsettling, to say the least.

"You texted me. The door was unlocked." She spoke in a flat manner, as unfriendly as I'd been myself. "What are you doing with my notebook?"

Chapter Twenty-One

"*YOUR* NOTEBOOK?"

That was the last thing I'd expected her to say.

Wendy was dressed for another shift at the grocery, wearing the Bucky's uniform that was miles too big for her. She shifted uncomfortably, twisting her hands around the blue raincoat as though she were strangling a chicken. Then she lifted her chin defiantly. "Yeah. Mine."

"Hidden in the cat litter?" I asked, holding the slightly dusty notebook up.

"I didn't want anyone to find it. I wasn't able to grab it before I was fired."

I rotated the slim volume in my hands. "Ah. So this is what you wanted to retrieve. Huh. I thought it was Amber's."

"Amber's? Why on earth would you think that?" Wendy's unease shifted to frowning intensity.

I shrugged. "Something about the cagey way Amber wanted to get back into the building before the crime techs had released it. When I found this in the bottom of the cat litter bin, I assumed it was hers. But it's not really her style, is it? If she'd been spying on Dr. Burnham, she'd have scanned invoices into her phone or something."

"I wasn't spying."

Wendy took an angry step forward, and I realized that not only had I left the door unlocked after I came back from lunch, but Remy was still confined to the kennels. He'd stepped up to the plate when Montanaro had threatened me, but would he intervene with someone he knew and liked? I wasn't sure. The hair on the back of my neck prickled.

"I wasn't," Wendy insisted, as though I'd spoken. "Okay, maybe technically I was spying but I hadn't done anything with the information. I was just keeping track."

"Of the inventory costs compared to the markups." I held the notebook up between my fingers like a playing card.

"If you know that much, then you know how outrageous the price differences were. It wasn't just on inventory though. She increased the price on services by two hundred percent. Two hundred." Wendy stabbed the air for emphasis. "Oh, not at first. But after a few weeks, the fees skyrocketed."

"Well, that couldn't have been a secret," I said as reasonably as possible. "There were plenty of complaints about the increased costs on social media. Still, she had a lot of upgrading to do. Replacing the lab equipment, installing a computer network—"

"And yet there weren't any invoices for those big-ticket items. New stuff just appeared without any indication she'd paid for it."

Oh dear. A lot of this outrage on Wendy's part could have been solved had Rachel been upfront about her financing from the beginning. I honestly didn't know how much to say. The truth about Rachel's relationship with Montanaro wasn't likely to be a secret for much longer, but it wasn't my secret to share. At the same time, I really wanted to see Wendy's reaction to the news.

"I'm sure there's an explanation for all of this." I tried for soothing, but it backfired on me.

"Don't tell me you're on *her* side," Wendy snapped. "You of all people."

"Dr. Burnham is dead. I don't think she has a side anymore." I tipped an open palm outward. "There's more to her story than you realize."

"I can't believe what I'm hearing. You're defending her." Wendy huffed in annoyance.

"I'm just saying there was more going on than either you or I knew. I don't think it was all under Dr. Burnham's control."

"That's one of the things I like about you, Ginny." The look Wendy gave me was *not* one of admiration. "Your willingness to see the other side of the story. But it's also a weakness. You should have sued Doc for breach of contract, you know."

The idea of suing Doc for selling the practice to Rachel Burnham took my breath away. "I couldn't do that."

"I know." Wendy tightened her lips and held out her hand. "My notebook, please."

Without warning, the swinging door to the hallway opened and Amber walked in. She stopped in her tracks on seeing Wendy and me. With a lift of her eyebrow and an unpleasant archness to her tone, she asked, "Am I interrupting?"

Wendy shot her a venomous glance. "No. I was just leaving."

But she remained in place with her hand extended.

"So you found it," Amber said with a purring satisfaction. "I wondered where Wendy had stashed it."

I'd been about to hand the notebook over when my hand froze mid-air. "You knew about the notebook?"

"Hard to miss." Amber popped her chewing gum a few times. "If you're going to be a corporate spy, you should be more subtle about it, Wendy."

"Corporate—" Wendy said the word as though it were part of a foreign language, and I could see the wheels starting to turn in her head with the association. Another moment or two, and she'd probably guess who Rachel's backers were.

"What were you planning to do with the notebook when you found it, Amber?" I tipped my head to one side. "You'd already gotten Wendy fired, hadn't you? Why did you want the notebook?"

The hiss of Wendy's sharp intake of breath caused me to glance at her, but it was Amber's slow clap that held my attention. "Oh, congrats. I guess you really are like that old *Murder She Wrote* bag."

For the first time, I realized that Amber's eyes were red and swollen, and her mascara slightly smeared.

"You were the one who removed the name tags on the cats." Wendy's voice shook with fury. "You were lucky nothing horrible happened to Snowball!"

"Oh relax. It's not like someone accidentally spayed her or something." Amber rolled her eyes. "Besides, I thought the Gardeners would have realized they had the wrong cat before they took her home."

"Needless to say, it was reckless and cruel of you to do something like that." I was pissed and wasn't above letting it show. "Why *did* you do it?"

Amber gave a heavy sigh. "Because Wendy was spying on Dr. Burnham. I told Dennis she was up to something, and he said she had to go before she let the cat out of the bag."

It said something that Amber never even picked up on the unintended pun she'd just made.

"By the cat, you mean that the clinic was really being run by CVC."

Wendy gasped and covered her mouth with one hand. "Oh, my God. That explains so much."

"Well, duh," Amber said with another roll of her eyes at Wendy. "It's your own fault you got fired, you know. They would have gone public with the news eventually, but you threatened the timeline. It didn't help that you kept harping about how things used to be done. Nobody wanted to hear about prehistoric times."

"If everyone had been upfront about CVC's involvement in the first place, it wouldn't have mattered." Wendy wheeled on Amber. "I guess your job was safe, given you were sleeping with the business manager. Though you probably didn't count on getting knocked up by him. How's that working out for you?"

I winced at that. Wendy only knew about the pregnancy test because I'd mentioned it to her.

"You shut up." Amber looked as though she might leap forward to claw Wendy's eyes out. "You shut your mouth."

Amber then turned her anger on me. "You just had to go around telling everyone about that test, didn't you?"

I opened my mouth, but didn't know what to say, and closed it helplessly.

"You've got nothing on me. I made notes on the practice. Big deal. For all you know, I was just doing my job as the person in charge of inventory." Wendy fired off another scathing glance at Amber. "What goes around comes around, I always say. You got me fired, but now you're out of a job too. Karma came back to bite you."

Before I could react, she snatched the notebook out of my hand and brushed past Amber without another word.

Leaving me alone with a red-eyed, red-faced furious woman.

"You just couldn't keep your nose out of it, could you?"

"I'm sorry, Amber. I know you don't believe me, but I was trying to help."

"Right." She curled a lip in disdain. "You were being nosy, that's what you were. Want to be the one who solved the murder, didn't you?"

"Hold up there." I made my hand into a stop sign. "I'm not doing this for fun. My mother is a suspect."

"I wonder why that is?" Amber's voice became shrill. "Where was she last night, huh? Where was she when Dennis got run over?"

Unexpectedly, she burst into tears and covered her hands.

"Oh dear." I wheeled the chair over to her. "Please. Sit down."

To my surprise, she took the seat. Scrubbing her face with the heel of her hand, she said, "I don't know why I'm crying. I didn't even like him all that much."

"Yeah, I kind of got that impression the other day from you and Erin. You want to tell me what happened between you two?"

She sniffed and wiped her nose with the back of her hand. I peeled a couple of tissues out of a nearby box on the counter and handed them to her.

"Not much to tell. We went out a few times. One thing led to another." She looked up from her tissues, her eyes hard and angry. "He lost interest in me after that. When I told him I was late, he had the nerve to say the baby could be anyone's. I told him I'd slap him with a court order for a paternity test. The baby was his and he was going to take care of me."

"But you helped him get rid of Wendy?" I couldn't hide my confusion.

"He still needed me. I wanted to show him I could be useful. I knew that notebook was probably still in the building. Dennis wanted to make sure Wendy didn't have it." She gave me a rather assessing glance. "I looked everywhere. Where'd you find it anyway?"

"In the clean cat litter bin."

Appreciation for Wendy's cleverness dawned in her eyes. "Huh. Smart."

"Sheriff Donegan wants to talk to you, you know."

Her expression soured. "I don't see why. It's none of his business."

I had to be careful how I phrased things. "You never know what's important in these kinds of investigations. You might be able to help give a timeline as to where Mr. Montanaro was the night Dr. Burnham was murdered. Some new evidence has come to light that indicates he was at the clinic that night."

Amber heaped scorn on me with a single glance. "Dennis didn't need to kill Dr. Burnham. He held all the cards. If he wanted her gone, he could have had her transferred to another CVC clinic like that."

She snapped her fingers for good measure.

I digested that for a moment. "I'm guessing then if Dr. Burnham had wanted out, she could have put in a request for a relocation?"

Amber's shrug suggested she didn't really care. "I dunno. Maybe? I don't think there was much flexibility on her end. Dennis said she bought into the franchise, not the other way around."

Dennis seemed to have said a lot.

"Do you think someone wanted to kill Dennis too?" Amber's anger and defiance seemed to melt away. Once again, I was reminded of how young she was.

"It's possible," I said cautiously.

"Well, it wasn't me." In a blink of an eye, her vulnerability retreated behind a hard shield. "I'm in a fine mess. I needed him alive."

Once Amber left the clinic, I found myself with nothing to do for the afternoon until I needed to return to take care of the boarders again.

I collected Remy from the kennel area and sat in my broiling car while I decided what to do with the unaccustomed block of time. I felt like a miser staring at a pot of gold. I could think of so many things I needed to do. But only one thing I wanted to do.

I drove out to Amanda's place.

As I came through the entrance to the property, I saw the place with new eyes. The horses grazed peacefully out in the far field. Flowers nodded their heads in the breeze as I swept up the driveway to the house. Blackjack, one of the feral cats, lay snoozing in the sun in one of the flowerbeds. As I got out of the car with Remy, the sonorous murmur of wind chimes greeted me.

This could be home if I let it happen.

Joe's SUV wasn't in the drive. I hadn't expected him to be there but felt a little jab of disappointment just the same. That was replaced by a small sense of satisfaction when I discovered his shaving kit still in the guest bathroom. I didn't know what the future held for the two of us, but it pleased me to see he intended to return this evening. After all, it was a big house. The future would sort itself out.

In the meantime, I took my dog for a swim.

It was one of the nicest afternoons I could remember.

Remy and I cooled off in the water, and then I read under one of the large umbrellas shading the chaise lounges by pool while Remy chewed on a tug toy. The dark memories of finding Amanda's body on that frigid March morning and confronting her killer in the house a few days later faded in the brilliant sunlight. We stayed outside until my stomach began to growl, and as I got dressed and ran my fingers through my damp hair to fluff it up, I found myself thinking I could get used to spending my evenings after work in such a peaceful manner. In my mind, I installed Ming back in the house where he belonged. I saw myself in a white cotton blouse and loose, flowing pants elegantly serving an assortment of fruits and cheese to imaginary friends. When I poured out a round of Merlot, the friends disappeared and left only one person behind. Joe. Who accepted the wine and gave me that crooked smile as he took a sip.

Hmmm. Or maybe not.

My little fantasy of Joe and I staying together at Amanda's—no, *my* house—was just that. A fantasy. There's no way the two of us could share the house without tongues wagging. But it made sense on many levels. His horse was already here. Toad and Remy could burn the energy off each other in the evenings, which would benefit both of us. There was the pool, and the closer proximity to town than his place out on Potter's Mountain.

Oh, who was I kidding? If I ever decided to give up this vet business, I might have a career as a scriptwriter for Hallmark. In the real world, the fact that I even fantasized about Joe and I living together under the same roof was a bad sign.

It could never happen.

On that note, I changed clothes, whistled up Remy, and headed back into town.

If I took care of the boarders first, I could swing through a drive-through on the way back to my mother's house. The next day would be a repeat in terms of taking care of the clinic, but on Monday, I'd call Mr. Carter and see about moving. He'd indicated before without anyone to contest the will, I had every right under the circumstances to take possession of the house early.

It was past time for me to exercise my rights.

I found myself looking forward to Monday, when CVC would take over the clinic again. Yes, if it had been my clinic, I would still have a lot of responsibilities, but I could hire people to do the extra work. Maybe opening my own place *was* the way to go. Wendy would make a terrific office manager. Carolyn would love not having to go back to the chain store. I could hire a vet to do the surgeries, and make sure I still offered some house-call services to my current client base for the time being. Maybe my mother was right: if Greenbrier couldn't support two vet clinics, then at least I'd have the home ground advantage over the next person CVC brought in. Perhaps my chat with Mr. Carter on Monday should include looking at my future assets and getting a recommendation for a financial advisor—something else I'd been putting off doing. I should contact a realtor as well.

These engrossing thoughts kept my mind busy as I greeted the boarders and began moving dogs so I could hose out runs. There's something about doing mindless physical work that frees the brain to sort through all kinds of information. I believe it was Agatha Christie who claimed she got the best ideas for her mysteries when doing the dishes. In this sort of freestanding brainstorming, I neglected to pay enough attention to Jaeger as I transferred him from one run to another. He pulled on the leash so hard as I opened the door to his new run that he jerked me forward into the chain link fencing. The latch came down on my hand, causing me to swear when the metal catch pinched the tender flesh between my thumb and forefinger.

I retrieved the leash from the bouncy Labrador, shut him safely within, and inspected my hand. The skin was torn slightly, and I was already developing a nice blood blister.

But it wasn't the sight of the minor injury that left me frozen in the kennels, staring at my hand.

It was the realization that my wound was in the same location where a slide bite would occur from mishandling a semi-automatic gun. Joe had said there was latex caught in the slide of the murder weapon. That could only have come from the murderer holding the gun incorrectly when firing it, crossing the top of the gun hand with the thumb of the other to hold it in a two-handed grip. When the trigger was pulled, the slide snapped back, rolling over the hand in a painful manner.

It was the memory of where I'd seen such an injury and on whom.

I stood for a full minute, ignoring the barking dogs while I tried to process the information that had just flooded into my brain. All the pieces clicked into place.

No. Just no.

But at the same time, *yes*.

With shaking hands, I pulled my phone out of my back pocket and scrolled through my contacts to find Joe's number. I came through the door to the treatment area still wondering how to phrase my sudden moment of discovery when I came to an abrupt halt.

The person I'd been thinking about was seated in the rolling chair by the exam table, fondling Remy's ears. Remy wriggled happily under his touch, oblivious to the old, long-barreled Colt Diamondback lying on the table beside them.

"Hello, Doc," I said.

Chapter Twenty-Two

"HELLO, GINNY. YOU DON'T seem surprised to see me." Though he continued to pat Remy, he rested his right hand on the exam table next to the gun.

I might have tried for cheerful obliviousness except for the chilling presence of the weapon.

"It was the wound on your hand." As I pointed, he looked down at nicked skin, now scabbed over, on the web between his thumb and forefinger on his left hand.

"Ah." He sighed as he rubbed the injury. "Trust you to notice that little thing. You're making this very hard on me."

I might have been staring at a stranger. The man before me bore little resemblance to the jovial and compassionate mentor I'd grown up wanting to emulate. He seemed to have aged in the last few weeks: both his clothes and his skin hung off him in folds, as though he'd lost weight. The ruddy color from days in spent in the sun was gone as well, leaving him looking gray and older than his years.

"Are you ill?" I blurted out.

He gave a soft little laugh at that. "Not in the way you're thinking. The last few months have been tough, however."

His index finger seemed to tap restlessly on the silver metal table. I realized it was an uncontrollable tremor instead.

Without looking at my phone, I slid a finger across where I thought the numbers were on the keypad. I had no hope of sending a coherent message, but perhaps an incoherent one would alert Joe to my situation. It was a longshot, but I didn't see what else I could do.

Ice ran through Doc's voice as he spoke. "Put the phone down, Ginny."

I tapped where I hoped the "send" button might be and tossed the phone on the nearest counter, where it landed with a clatter. Remy glanced my way at the sound but didn't leave his place of worship at Doc's feet. His tail swept gently from side to side as he nudged Doc's arm with his nose.

"I don't understand. Please explain this to me."

If I'd hoped to remind Doc of our relationship, to soothe him into the role of lecturer, my attempt failed miserably.

"Explain? What's there to explain?" Red spots appeared on Doc's cheeks, as though he had a fever. "Worse decision of my life, selling the practice to that woman. I should have known better. No one that young could have that kind of money unless she came from a wealthy family. I thought she did."

Remy's ears dropped to half-mast at the anger simmering behind Doc's words, and he rested his head on Doc's knee with a sigh so hard it fluttered his lips. Doc ignored him to rage on. "And you were no help at all."

"Me?" I might have been able to keep the indignation out of my voice, but not the surprise. "How is this my fault?"

"You dragged your feet about buying the practice. Don't think I don't know you had your doubts." Doc's scolding might have seemed parental, except for the gun by his hand. "You could have gotten a loan with your proposed inheritance as collateral. The bank would have snapped it up. If you'd only committed to the purchase, none of this would have happened."

Making this my fault was a bad sign. At the very least, I had to attempt to get him to see reason.

"If I'd known about Dr. Burnham's interest, I would have done exactly that."

He shook his head, though whether at my words or the situation, I had no idea.

"The sale had already been completed before I found out about it. I'm not sure what you expected me to do."

"I'll tell you what I didn't expect you to do!" Doc slammed his hand down on the exam table hard enough to make the gun jump a little. Remy lifted his head and retreated a step. "I didn't expect you to go down the same path as that Burnham woman."

I couldn't help it this time. "What on earth are you talking about?"

"You know exactly what I'm talking about." A little fleck of foam appeared at the corner of his mouth as he spat his words. "That woman came in here with her ill-gotten money and sold my clinic up the river into corporate greed. *My* clinic. The one I built from the ground up. The one I slaved over for nearly fifty years. The nights I spent here taking care of patients—there were no emergency clinics in my day—seeing clients all morning, doing surgery all afternoon. Eating my lunch while watching a dog or cat recover from anesthesia. Skipping the children's plays and ballgames because I was needed here. I almost missed my daughter's wedding because the mayor's dog got hit by a car that afternoon. I gave my heart and soul to this place, and to this community. And what does she do? Sweeps in here and destroys it all—my lifelong reputation—within a matter of weeks."

I *knew* keeping the corporate involvement a secret had been a bad idea.

"No one who knows you blames you for the changes Dr. Burnham made." Aiming for diplomacy, I continued. "People were angry with her, not you."

"That's what you think." He pointed a gnarled index finger at me that shook slightly. "Not a day went by when someone wouldn't stop me after church or at the diner to tell me about what horrible experience they'd had at the clinic. Whether it was the outrageous fees, or the change in staff, or something that was said or done. It was so bad, Hazel and I talked of moving."

Mentally I winced. I opened my mouth to speak, but he cut me off.

"She had to go. You can see that, can't you? I saw the lights on when I went to pick up Hazel from the church meeting that night. That business manager of hers had just left in his fancy car. It seemed like a sign, you know?" He worked his jaw from side to side as though struggling to get the words out. "My old key still worked. Cheap lock. Broke when I turned the key. I came in quietly. Wanted to give her a bit of a scare. Thought it might convince her not to be such a miser with her maintenance and repairs. It wasn't like she didn't have the money."

Eyeing the distance between me and the gun, it was unlikely I could dive on the weapon before he reached it. The wheels on the heavy steel table were locked in place. There was no way I could shove it aside. There'd been no response from Joe. Either he hadn't noticed the text, or he assumed it was a mistake on my part. I was on my own.

Doc rubbed the scab on his hand and continued speaking, almost as if to himself.

"She was in the office. She'd just gotten off the phone with someone when she looked up and saw me." A tight smile stretched his lips. "She wasn't happy about that. No siree. Wanted to know what I was doing in her clinic. *Her* clinic."

His face had grown red again. "Like I hadn't been there day in and day out, rain or shine, for the last fifty years. I said as much, and that's when she told me about the clinic really belonging to CVC. She said the corporation was planning to move the whole practice into a brand-new building, designed to her specifications, with a huge hospital and boarding facility. She couldn't wait. She said if she'd had her druthers, she'd set fire to the building as soon as it was cleared and collect the insurance money."

His expression became eerily calm. "She ordered me out. That's when I saw it. The gun lying on the edge of the desk, partially covered by a file. The phone rang again, and when she answered it, I did as she asked. I left. Only I came in here and got a pair of exam gloves."

"You went back and shot her." I'm surprised my voice didn't shake. "And then staged it to look like a suicide."

"I didn't realize it was your mother's gun." Doc made a little depreciating shrug and then nodded at his weapon. "I thought it belonged to Dr. Burnham. Doesn't your mother have a revolver, like mine? Wasn't used to the slide action. Hurt like the devil when it caught my hand."

"You'd have let my mother go to jail for a murder she didn't commit?" Indignation crept into my voice despite my efforts to remain calm.

"Hazel was mad about that too." Doc seemed suddenly rueful. "That's why she was so adamant about giving your mother an alibi for that evening. I told her it would all work out in the end, but Hazel was dead set against it. Said we had to fix things."

Any softening toward me he might have been experiencing evaporated with his next words. "But then you got all chummy with that business manager. Whatsisname. Montana."

"Montanaro."

"Montanaro." Doc's upper lip curled. "That's the fellow. There you were having breakfast with him at the diner, looking over the brochures, planning to pick up where that Burnham woman left off. Destroying my legacy."

"Hold up there." I raised a cautious hand. I hadn't noticed Doc at the diner yesterday morning, but that didn't mean anything. Anyone could have overheard my conversation with Montanaro. "He sprang all that on me at breakfast. I had no idea."

"But you weren't going to say no, were you? It was the only way you could take charge of the practice you wanted." He picked up the gun. "It was never going to end until CVC and their representatives were gone. Burnham was dead. Montanaro had to die. I'm sorry, Ginny, but you must go too. You made a deal with the devil."

"I did not," I said sharply as he pointed the weapon in my direction. Remy whined unhappily but did not move from his place near Doc's chair.

The vintage Diamondback wavered in Doc's grip and he brought his other hand up to steady his aim. With his thumb, he cocked the hammer. "You met with him that night in the clinic. I saw you."

"I did meet with him. He pulled the same trick you did—coming in the building without warning even though the door was locked. I told him no. I couldn't work with a man like him or a corporation like CVC."

"You're lying," Doc said, but he lowered the gun slightly.

"I'm not. You know me, Doc. I wouldn't lie to you about this." I hesitated, then added, "It was Hazel who ran Montanaro down last night, wasn't it? You made sure you had a solid alibi—dinner with the preacher—while she drove the truck. Placing you in the perfect position to confuse any witness statements as well."

She'd been there in the crowd when I told Carolyn I was meeting Montanaro last night.

"She was so mad about me using your mother's gun. Said I shouldn't have tried to make it look like a suicide. I hadn't counted on Joe figuring it out. Pete Linkous wouldn't have, that's for sure. As soon as it became apparent it was murder, what with you nosing around and all, Hazel was sure you'd put it all together. Then she pointed out that as long as CVC had a presence in the town, my legacy would never be safe." Doc rubbed a watery eye with the end of his finger. "I wanted to buy the practice back, but she wouldn't hear of it."

I bet she wouldn't. Somehow, she'd convinced Doc to compound his first crime by committing two more. All to protect her new-found wealth.

My cell phone chimed with the notification alert I'd assigned to Joe. Remy turned his head and swiveled his ears toward the sound. Doc brought the gun back up to full height again. "Don't answer that."

"I don't have to. That's Joe. He knows about all of this. It's no good, Doc. It's over."

The odds of Joe understanding my gibberish text message enough to affect a rescue, always assuming he could also guess where I might be located, were slim to none. If I made it out of this alive, I'd have to take up poker.

"No." Doc shook his head angrily, like an old bear being swarmed by bees. "He's got nothing on me. He's got no reason to even think it could be me. Hazel saw to that when she took care of Montanaro."

"You mean, when she ran him over with a pickup truck."

He grimaced and closed his eyes briefly.

"That was a lot harder to see than just pulling a trigger, wasn't it?" I nodded as if in commiseration. "What was it you said that night? You'd never forget that sound."

Doc wiped a hand over his mouth and returned it to his grip on the gun. When he spoke, gravel ground in his voice. "That's enough of that, young lady."

Remy whined again and scooted forward to lay his head in Doc's lap. My breath caught my heart and held it captive in my throat for several long seconds as Doc looked down at the big Shepherd eyes gazing up at him. A pained sound escaped Doc's lips, and he took one hand off the gun's grip to stroke Remy's head.

When my heart began beating again in triple-time, I knew I had to take the chance.

"It's not just me you'll have to shoot, you know."

Doc met my steady gaze with startled eyes.

"You'll have to shoot Remy, too."

"No." He barely whispered the word.

"Yes." I stood perfectly still, not wanting to make any sudden moves. "Montanaro got ugly with me last night, and Remy came to my defense. Joe knows about that, too. If you shoot me but leave Remy unharmed, it will be obvious Remy knew my killer. Can you do that, Doc? Is that the legacy you want to leave behind? After a lifetime of saving animals, do you really want to kill a healthy dog for no other reason than to protect yourself?"

As if he understood my words, Remy got to his feet and wormed his way under Doc's raised arms, shoving his head further against Doc's chest, sweeping his plumy tail from side to side.

Doc uncocked the hammer and laid the gun down on the exam table to take Remy's big goofy face in both hands. "No. I couldn't do that."

The rear door to the treatment room swung open, and Hazel marched in, clutching a tire iron in one fist.

"I thought as much." She fixed her gaze upon me in a stare so cold it should have given me frostbite. I never knew so much hate could exist in one person. She wheeled on Doc with icy fury. "I knew you'd be squeamish about killing Ginny. Ginny this and Ginny that. You've been singing her praises for years. You think more of her than you do your own children. Your children! But to jeopardize everything we've worked so hard for our entire lives over a *dog*? Amos Hamilton Smith, you take the cake."

She stormed forward, reaching for the gun.

"No!" Doc shouted, grabbing for the weapon at the same time.

Hazel raised the tire iron over her head, her face contorted into a horrible grimace of rage. I stood frozen in shock, but Remy let out a happy bark and leapt at Hazel with his feet extended, snapping at the metal rod out of his reach. His paws collided with her shoulders and she screeched as she fell backward. The tire iron flew out of her hand as her arms pinwheeled for balance. She crashed to the floor with Remy on top of her. The metallic ring of the tire iron as it slammed into the cabinets caused Remy to jump away, his ears and tail tucked at the loud sound.

Hazel lifted her head briefly, then allowed it to fall back to the floor with a groan.

I plucked the gun out of Doc's hands while he laughed until tears coursed down his face.

Chapter Twenty-Three

It was very late when I stumbled through the door of my new home with a load of groceries in my arms. Remy raced down the hallway ahead of me, looking for Ming, no doubt. There would be time enough tomorrow to bring the elderly Siamese back to the house he'd lived in for so many years. I'd updated my mother on everything that had happened and persuaded her to open a smelly can of food for Ming. I'd be back in the morning to take care of him and pack my things.

One way or another, tomorrow I was moving into the house Amanda left me.

I never did get dinner.

After I'd taken the gun away from Doc, I'd called Joe. He hadn't understood my garbled message; he'd assumed it was a butt dial and had only returned my text to tease me about it. Once I filled him in, he'd come flying out to the clinic guns a blazing, with the rescue squad in tow. Hazel had been taken to the hospital under armed guard. Doc had confessed to everything in the meantime, including Hazel's involvement in Montanaro's death.

When recounting the events, I'd held it together fairly well until I got to the point where I described Doc's indecision about shooting Remy, whereupon I dissolved into a weepy mess. Joe had left the interview room then, only to return minutes later with a candy bar from the vending machine.

"I know this mode of yours," he said with his devilish smile. "You passed hangry hours ago, and now you're in the low-blood-sugar crying zone."

I wiped my eyes and accepted the stale candy bar without comment. A few minutes later, I finished telling my story.

Despite having a confession on the spot, so to speak, it took longer to wrap up things than I expected. It was well after eight p.m. when I was released from the sheriff's station, and by the time I'd stopped by Bucky's for supplies, it was almost nine.

First things first. I turned off the alarm and staggered along the hallway toward the kitchen because heaven forbid I make more than one trip to bring in all the food I'd bought. After I peeled the plastic grocery bags out of the death grip I had on the handles, I ferreted through them to locate a bottle of Merlot. Odds were Amanda had some higher quality wine stashed someplace I'd yet to find, but I wasn't taking any chances. I poured myself a nice, generous amount into a stemless glass and left it to breathe on the counter while I put the food away.

Remy leapt and cavorted until I took out the small bag of kibble I'd purchased and poured some into a bowl that was undoubtedly too nice to use for dog food.

I'd just collapsed into a chair at the kitchen table and taken a first, appreciative sip of wine when the doorbell rang. Barking, Remy galloped down the hallway to the front door. I followed him, clutching my glass of wine like the lifeline it was.

Somehow, I wasn't surprised to see Joe when I opened the door.

"Hey." He pressed a shoulder into the jamb and leaned against the frame in the manner he'd been doing as long as I'd known him. Honestly, there were days when I wondered if he'd been filleted, he was so boneless at times. "I thought I'd see how you were doing."

I lifted my glass in a mock salute. "Getting there. Come on in. Where's Toad?"

I looked around behind him, as though I might see the dog. I wasn't the only one. Remy would have dashed out the door had I not grabbed his collar.

"Didn't want to presume you wanted company." This time his smile held volumes of rue instead of his usual blatant sex appeal.

"What I want is closure," I said.

His face underwent an interesting array of emotions. Frowning dismay gave way to resigned understanding as he continued to allow the door jamb to prop him up. Finally, he nodded and said, "I can help you tie up loose ends."

"Go get your dog, then." I waited by the door until he returned with Toad, who greeted Remy with hysterical glee.

The two dogs raced into the living room and began to wrestle, their play punctuated by fierce growls.

I headed back toward the kitchen.

"Have you eaten?" I called back over my shoulder. "I picked up a rotisserie chicken."

"Sounds great." His voice was close enough that I jumped a little.

Annoyed with my reaction, I entered the kitchen and began pulling open cabinets until I found a steam basket. Setting down my glass on the counter, I filled a pot with water and dropped the basket down into it. "How does kale sound?"

"Ridiculously healthy, but I'm not picky."

I snorted at that and dumped a good portion of chopped kale into the steamer. "Help yourself to the wine."

He poured himself a glass and watched as I sliced the chicken into thick slabs. After a few minutes, the pot on the stove began to produce steam.

"Dinner will be ready in a bit." I picked up my glass and a bag of pretzels, indicating we should retire to the kitchen table. "So what happened after I left?"

He sat down across from me with a little groan of relief. I could sympathize. I held out my glass. "To the end of long, brutal days."

"Hear, hear." Joe clinked his glass against mine, and then watched me over the brim as he took a sip. "Let's see. Doc called in a lawyer from Clearwater who is pushing for second-degree murder, calling the impulse to shoot Rachel an unplanned act that occurred out of a moment of anger."

I rubbed my forehead wearily. I could feel the beginnings of a headache there. "Good luck with that. He wore gloves and tried to make it look like a suicide."

"So says our district attorney." Joe nodded once in agreement. "We found out Hazel had taken Doc's truck out past Goose Creek for repairs. Some hole-in-the wall garage. Told them she'd struck a deer."

For the briefest of moments, I could picture Montanaro lying in the spill of light from the car blocking the road, and I winced in remembrance.

"I can't believe they killed Montanaro just to cover up their tracks." The warmth of the wine began to seep into my bones and flush my cheeks. If I wasn't careful, I'd doze off any minute now. It had been a hard couple of days. I took a handful of pretzels in an effort to stay awake.

"And would have killed you, too." Joe reached across the table to take my hand in his. "By all rights, you should be dead."

"Sorry," I murmured, withdrawing my hand with a light laugh. "Maybe they'll succeed next time."

"There'd better not be a next time," Joe growled. He looked as sulky as a twelve-year-old boy, and I stifled a snort at his expression. "I'm serious, Ginge."

There it was. Somehow, his use of a nickname got through my defenses when nothing else had. Tears pricked at my eyes, and I wiped my face with the heel of my hand, pretending I was merely tired. "It's not like I put my life in jeopardy on purpose."

"No, not on purpose." Joe took another sip of wine with narrowed eyes. "But when bad stuff comes your way, you don't back down from it, either."

"Like backing down from a fight helps when your life is in danger."

"Maybe if you weren't so stubborn and independent, your life wouldn't be in danger so often."

My eyebrows shot into my hairline. "You're not seriously saying you'd rather me wring my hands and say 'woe is me' when someone is trying to kill me?"

"No, of course not." Joe set down his glass to rub his temple. My guess was he had a headache too. Propping his chin on his hands, he said, "You can ask for help, you know. You don't have to fight all your battles alone."

"I did ask for help, by the way. It's not my fault you didn't understand the text." I crunched on one of the pretzels. "Anyway, so says the man who is so forthcoming about his own fears and issues."

A little half-smile made an appearance. "What do you want to know?"

Momentarily stunned by the unexpected offer, it took me a second to come up with a response. "What happened when you got shot?"

He made a face. Seeming to recognize that he'd opened this door, he rotated his glass in his hand, as if fascinated by the play of light in its ruby depths. "We were investigating a homicide. The suspect got squirrely on us and took his neighbor as a hostage. He was as high as a kite and impossible to reason with. We'd almost persuaded him to release the hostage when she lost her cool and began screaming. He killed her before we got in the door, and I took a bullet in the leg for trying."

"And then?" I pushed, sensing this was the only time I'd get any answers.

"And then?" He repeated my words. A smile took hold of him and spread slowly across his features. "I decided to come home."

"But Greenbrier really isn't home for you anymore, is it?" I asked, confused. He'd been so adamant about getting out of this "Podunk redneck town" on graduating from high school. So much so that he'd made plans that hadn't included me. When I'd challenged him on that point, he'd looked surprised, and then calmly told me that no one expected high school romances to last. I recognized now that my mother had used almost the exact same wording when she'd spoken to me the other night.

At the time, his decision had been a bitter pill to swallow, but I'd made my own plans to leave after that. Plans that were perfect for an independent woman who didn't need anyone to hold her hand.

"I mean, your parents have sold the farm and moved away. What could have possibly brought you back?"

"Nostalgia, perhaps. Or maybe there was someone here I wanted to see again." An eyebrow twitched upward, daring me to ask who that might have been.

Me. He had to mean me.

I'd been in the act of taking a sip of wine, but my hand froze partway to my mouth, and my breath caught as I stared at him. There was so much I wanted to ask him, but my tongue seemed to be tied in knots.

The hiss of steam from the pot on the stove made my leap to my feet. "Dinner's ready."

I served up carved chicken and steamed kale, wishing for rice or potatoes to offer with it. Instead, I sliced several pieces of crusty French bread, slathered them with butter and brought everything to the table.

We ate quickly and quietly, as hungry and tired people do. When we were done, I cleared the plates and brought the bottle of wine back to the table to top off our glasses. He put his hand over the brim when I would have poured him some more.

"No more for me, thanks." He stifled a yawn. "I really should be going."

I glanced at my watch. It was nearly ten. If Joe left this very minute, he wouldn't get back to his place before eleven. That meant another night on the couch at the station.

"It's late. Why don't you stay?" I nudged his hand away from his glass with the bottle and refilled it when he moved. "Your stuff's already here."

"When you say stay, what exactly do you mean?" His eyebrows twisted comically as he tried to figure out my intent.

"I mean, it's a big house and we're both tired. It's been a brutal week, and tonight I found out the man I loved like a father is a murderer." I added wine to my own glass and took my seat. "This is my first night sleeping here in this house, and knowing you were just down the hall would make me feel better."

He seemed to be weighing his words carefully before he spoke. Finally, he said, "If word gets out, people will talk."

"Let them." I met his gaze calmly. "We're both adults here."

"One of those people would be your mother."

I took a deep breath and released it slowly. "You're right. But it's none of her business. This is me, asking you for a little help here. One friend to another."

He lifted his glass. "To friends ... for now."

I clinked my glass against his, hoping he would assume the sudden flush of my cheeks was caused by the wine.

We took the bottle with us into the living room, where the dogs were crashed out on the floor, sound asleep. Toad lifted her head and wagged her little tail when we came into the room, but Remy never moved.

"Poor dog. He's exhausted." I tucked my feet underneath me on the couch and pulled a soft blanket down over my legs. The air conditioning, which had felt like heaven when I walked through the door, seemed too chilly now.

"Don't I get any?" Joe complained, and then grinned when I flipped a corner back to let him slide beneath it. "So, Remy was the hero again today, was he?"

"How do you mean?" The warmth of the blanket combined with my full stomach and the wine had me yawning. Even warmer was the heat coming off Joe's thigh as it rested near mine under the blanket. Tempting as the idea of resting my head against Joe's shoulder might be, I fought to stay awake.

"He defended you from Hazel. You said he jumped on her, like he did with Montanaro."

"Er, he jumped on her yes." I scrunched up my face as I tried to figure out the best way to tell the truth. "But it wasn't like when he got between Montanaro and me."

"I don't understand." Joe squinted at me doubtfully. "According to your statement, she came at you—or maybe Doc—with a tire iron. The dog jumped on her, knocking her down. She hit her head on the floor, losing consciousness. What am I missing?"

"The reason for his jumping on her in the first place." I squirmed with embarrassment, all the worse when Joe fixed a piercing gaze on me.

"And that would be?" he asked.

Sighing, I smoothed the blanket over my legs before murmuring my answer. I flinched and pulled my hand back when my fingers brushed Joe's leg by mistake.

"I'm sorry." Joe cupped a hand around one ear and leaned closer. "I didn't catch that."

"I said, he thought the tire iron was a stick." I frowned at Joe's incredulous expression and explained. "When she raised her arm, he thought she was going to throw a stick."

The laughter came over him slowly at first, bubbling beneath the surface until it boiled over into a loud guffaw.

"He thought ... he thought—" Joe wheezed as he tried to get the words out.

I swatted him with a throw pillow. "It's not that funny."

"That big tough Shepherd." Joe laughed until he snorted. "He just wanted to play fetch."

"Stop it. You sound like a little pig." I punched him in the shoulder. His laughter was contagious, however, and he had me laughing as well, particularly when he began braying like a donkey.

I'd nearly forgotten the donkey-laugh. It was the only uncool thing about Joe I could recall; the fact he had such a dorky laugh when he really let go. The louder he brayed, the more I laughed in return, until I whooped for air.

"He's such a bad dog." I wiped away tears of mirth. Remy lifted his head at the commotion, only to go back to sleep again.

"He's so bad, he's good," Joe said with a grin. "Like his owner. Promise me you won't get involved in any more murders, Ginny. I'm not sure my heart can handle it."

"Don't be silly," I said as I sipped my wine. "If we have any more murders around here, they'll have to build a TV show around us."

"That is not an answer." Joe shot a particularly sour glance in my direction. "I know evasion when I hear it. I'm a trained investigator."

He tapped his chest with an obvious wink, but I could hear something else behind the humor. Definite concern. Perhaps even a touch of fear?

"It was the worst feeling," he said quietly, all amusement wiped away. "Hearing that hostage scream and knowing I wasn't going to get to her in time. It would be ten times worse if it was someone I knew. A thousand times worse if it was you."

I stared at him a long moment, conscious of every inch of him only a breath away.

Remy chose that moment to get up, stretch, and come over to me with a yawn. When he shoved his nose into my lap, I bent over him to give him a hug.

"Ginge," Joe said warningly, reminding me I still hadn't answered him to his satisfaction.

It's not like I went around seeking out unnatural deaths. They just sort of fell into my path. As for sticking my nose in where it didn't belong, to date, my investigations had been purely ones of self-defense, either for me or my mother. That wasn't likely to happen again, now was it?

"I promise not to interfere in any more murder investigations," I said. But the hand buried in Remy's ruff had its fingers crossed.

The end

M.K. Dean lives with her family on a small farm in North Carolina, along with assorted dogs, cats, and various livestock.

She likes putting her characters in hot water to see how strong they are. Like teabags, only sexier.

Under the name McKenna Dean, she has penned several award-winning stories in the Redclaw Origins and Redclaw Security series. If you like your mysteries with a paranormal flair, check out McKenna Dean's books!

If you enjoyed this story, please consider leaving a review on the platform of your choice. Reviews help with visibility, and therefore, sales. Likewise, be sure to recommend it to your friends. Every recommendation means more than you could know.

If you want to follow M.K. Dean on social media, be sure to check out her linktree account: https://linktr.ee/McKenna_Dean. All important links are there, including how to sign up for her newsletter, follow her blog, or find out when the next Ginny Reese book is coming out!

M.K. Dean

The Ginny Reese Mysteries

An Embarrassment of
Itches
The Dog Days of Murder
A Corpse in the Condo

Made in the USA
Monee, IL
17 October 2024

68214101R20125